Cruising
for Bad Boys

An Erotic Anthology
Edited By
Mickey Erlach

STAR books
PRESS

Herndon, VA

D1527234

Published in the United States STARbooks Press PO Box 711612 Herndon VA 20171 Printed in the United States

Many thanks to graphic artist John Nail for the cover design. Mr. Nail may be reached at: tojonail@bellsouth.net.

Herndon, VA

Other titles by Mickey Erlach

Boys Will Be Boys – Their First Time

Boys Caught in the Act

Pretty Boys and Roughnecks

Contents

SILENT AS A SCREAM
By Christopher Pierce

Some nights I just want to get used and abused by a tough son-of-a-bitch. When my little apartment seems even tinier than usual, when my body aches with need, when nothing can distract me from my holes that crave filling, when I've tried and failed to go to sleep too many times, it's time to head down to the docks.

That's what we call the waterfront, deep down deepest downtown in this city of the damned that's plunging toward oblivion, where a maze of warehouses butts up against the sea, where the cargo ships load and unload endlessly every day – the most dangerous part of town – that's the docks.

If you're careful and lucky, you can get thrown a good fuck down there. If you're careless and stupid, you can get yourself killed.

But, I'm not stupid.

Crazy and blind with lust, sure, but not stupid.

It was after 1:00 a.m.

I dressed quickly – white tank to show off my chest and shoulders, cut-off denim shorts to show off my ass (no underwear; it just wastes time), hiking boots with white socks stuffed in them. I adjusted my cock through the denim (ouch, tight) and dragged my hands through my short spiky hair. I ran my fingers over the metal in my ears and eyebrows, then down over my chest with its nipple rings.

I was ready.

I could walk from my crappy neighborhood to the docks, so I didn't have to drive. It was easier that way anyway – it was a bitch trying to find parking down there, and your car was likely to get broken into anyway. As I walked down the long streets toward the docks, the baleful white light of the dingy streetlamps blended with the moon's. I ignored the attention I received, ignored the eyes of the young punks looking to trade sex for drug money, the married men out hoping for a thrill, the rich johns in their expensive cars – none of them had what I wanted.

I kept my eyes down and let my feet carry me to the place they knew so well, where they had taken me many times before.

I slipped through the shadows as if I was one with them, moving silently between the buildings, the stink of the ocean like a wall I walked through. I had been cautious getting ready – I had nothing worth stealing on me, no wallet, even my door key was in the dirt of a potted plant inside my apartment complex.

My every sense was heightened – the smell of smoke, the taste of salt, the different shades of shadow, the feel of my dick – raw in my shorts, and the sounds of water and the dull roar of the city.

Around the next corner, standing in the dead-end of a trash-lined alley, there he was. I put my back to the wall, trying to disappear. I didn't want him to see me yet. There was no way I could've known it then, but he was already well aware of me, waiting like a spider in the middle of its web.

Peering into the dark, I willed my eyes to penetrate the murk and make out the details of him.

He was taller than my five-ten, over six feet, and was wearing a biker cap and a black leather jacket. He was built, but in a slender long-muscled way, not overly bulky like a bodybuilder. His wrists were encircled with black leather bands. His powerful arms were crossed, except when one hand brought a fire-tipped cigar to his mouth every few minutes. The smoke he blew clouded his face, but it almost looked as if his eyes were lit with the same fire as his cigar. A spiked leather collar was around his neck, and he wore black leather chaps over dirty jeans with shit-kicking knee-high boots.

My eyes traveled up from his feet to his crotch to his abs to his chest to his arms to his collar to his face – was looking right at me! Playing the part of sighted prey, I stepped into a patch of moonlight, so he could get a good look at me.

His eyes roved over me, but if he was impressed, he didn't show it.

"Hey …" I said.

He threw his cigar away and made a gesture that said *Fuck off.*

I raised my hands and made the signs that said *I was hoping you'd rough me up first.*

Now he looked impressed.

You know A.S.L.? he signed.

What can I say? I responded, *There's so many hot deaf guys.*

You a little faggot? he asked.

Yeah, I answered, *I just want your cock up my ass.*

No limits?

I shook my head. *And, no safe-words.*

He smiled at me, but it wasn't pleasant. It was more like the salivating grin of a wolf who's found a tender young lamb to feast upon. He gestured me over, and a minute later, I was standing in front of him.

Get on your knees and let's see what you can do, he signed to me. My knees hit the hard pavement. I ignored the pain. This was part of the deal; you cruise the docks, you're gonna feel pain.

All different kinds of pain.

The deaf stud looked down at me scornfully. *You're just a little cocksucker, aren't you?*

Yes, Sir, I signed back to him.

3

He loosened the big buckle on his belt and pushed his pants and chaps down enough for his cock to flop out. My mouth watered at the sight of it. Big, thick, long, uncut, just hanging there between his legs like a baby elephant's trunk. I lunged for it, and he smacked my face away, hard.

Beg for it, he signed. It was interesting how the hands he so expressively communicated with were the same ones that he hit with. I could feel the red mark appearing on my cheek without having to see it.

Please, I signed. *Please let me suck your dick, Sir. I need to suck your cock Sir, please.*

He laughed silently and grinned down at me darkly.

I see you're no stranger to begging.

No, Sir.

A cocksucker? he signed, *a whore is more like it.*

Yes, I answered, drooling for a chance at his meat but wary of being hit again. *I'll be anything you need me to be.*

He hit me again, this time with his other hand, knocking my head the other way.

Don't patronize me, you little asshole, he signed, real anger in his eyes. *You're not an actor on a stage; you're no star of a movie; you're just a cocksucking faggot whore that'll do anything to get fucked up by a stud like me. And, I'm not even going to pay you.*

Yes, I signed, *Yes, Sir, you're right.*

Then open your mouth, motherfucker!

I did what he said, and he shoved himself into me, all at once. Instantly, I was choking, coughing, gagging, my air channel completely filled with his intruding dick. I glanced up at him, and he was laughing at me again, silently laughing at my discomfort and pain as he prevented life-giving oxygen from getting into my mouth. I tried to inhale through my nose, but he grabbed it with one hand, smashing my nostrils closed and holding them tight. I tried to pull off of him, but his other hand grabbed the back of my head and held me in place. I struggled, but it was useless.

I don't know how long he held me this way.

Seconds, minutes. I know my vision was clouding when he finally pulled back a bit and let go of me. I just sat there for a second, getting used to the fact that I could breathe.

He hit me again.

I snarled in pain and anger and looked up at him defiantly.

His lip was curled in a sneer.

Suck me, you stupid fuck, he signed, *and keep your hands behind your back.*

I obeyed, and took his cock, which was now dripping with pre-cum, back into my mouth. Its length was amazing, veined and sweaty, pulsing at my attention. I licked up and down his shaft, trying to give maximum sensation. I wondered at myself as the pavement dug into my knees and my cheeks throbbed where he had hit me. Is this what I want? I asked myself. Is this how I want to be treated?

My own cock, raging and drooling in my shorts, seemed to be the answer.

I turned my attention to the head of his monster dick. I slid my tongue under the hood of skin and was rewarded with a disgusting mouthful of stinking, funky cheese. I ate it gladly, slurping it up, happy, somehow feeling that this is what I deserved. Now free of the obstruction of the cheese, my tongue and mouth could properly attend to the head of his cock. I swirled my tongue around it, playing with it, teasing it, loving it, worshipping it.

Unable to help myself, my hands came out from behind my back, reaching up to him, desperate to touch him, desperate to feel him. I wanted more of him – I could see him; I could feel him in my mouth and where he hit me, but more I wanted more! My hands groped him, feeling his abdomen and chest, feeling the hard flesh and muscle beneath the fabric of his shirt. He grunted and swatted my hands away like they were annoying insects. When that didn't stop me from clutching at him like a crazy person, he smashed his fist against the side of my head, perhaps realizing that was the only way I seemed to obey.

I dropped my hands, pain exploding through my brain, but kept sucking. Suddenly, I felt his cock tense, like a coiling spring. The deaf stud grabbed my head with both hands to make sure I wouldn't try to pull away. He made no noise as he came, shooting his load down my throat. I felt the jets of his hot sperm hitting the back of my mouth and sliding down. I gulped and swallowed until all of it was gone, until I'd licked every last drop from him.

Only then did he release me.

Tired and hurting, I sat back on my ass and pulled my legs up. My knees were bleeding from where they'd been rubbed against the rough asphalt. I sat there and tried to catch my breath.

The man stepped forward.

I assumed he was done with me and was going to walk on.

I was wrong.

He turned sharply, so he was directly behind me. There was the quick squeak of leather as he grabbed something out of his inside jacket pocket. Then he was pulling my arms behind my back and metal bit into my wrists. He was cuffing me!

"Wait …" I started to say, but realized that of course he could not hear me.

And wouldn't care, even if he could.

The handcuffs snapped in place, and my hands were bound painfully behind me.

He was in front of me then, grinning down at me with a smile that could kill. I wouldn't have been surprised if his teeth were sharp. He put one booted foot on my chest and pushed

6

down, hard. My cuffed hands and arms were trapped between my back and the ground, and I cried out in pain, uselessly.

This was the docks.

No one was going to come and save me.

I was among the damned, and I was one of them.

He pressed his boot harder and harder against my chest, putting more and more of his weight on me. It felt as if the bones in my arms were bending to the breaking point. I cried out again.

"Please, stop!" I screamed at him.

Sorry can't hear you, he signed back to me.

Just when I thought my bones were going to break, he took his boot off my chest, leaving mud and gravel and a deep footprint on my shirt, and probably my chest, too. I struggled, trying to get up, but I was like a turtle on its back.

He laughed at me – silently.

He lunged down suddenly, like a bird of prey swooping to sink its talons into doomed prey. He sat on me, with one leg on either side of my head, his soft but still huge cock hanging into the hollow of my throat. Even though his full weight wasn't on me, it was just as painful to have him like this. He took his dick in his hand and fisted it repeatedly, returning it to full hardness, even so soon after shooting off.

Once it was hard, he started to hit me with it.

He used the stiff tube of muscle to smack me on the mouth, on the cheeks, on the nose. Tears streamed from my eyes, and I moaned with pain and fear. The cock-whipping continued for several minutes. When he finally tired of it, he stood up, grinning sadistically down at me. The darkness and the moonlight made him look like a demon standing above me. His erect cock cast obscene shadows on the alley walls.

Then he took his pants off.

His legs were just as lean and muscled as his arms. After his chaps and pants and briefs had been removed, he put his boots back on.

I was hoping he was going to let me get up – my wrists felt as if they were bleeding from the cuffs, and my arms were still trapped and twisted painfully between my back and the ground – but I was not so lucky. He straddled my face, and I stared up at his stiff dick and his big balls, swinging pendulously above me. Suddenly, they filled my vision.

He sat on my face.

Darkness covered me. He was my whole world. His sweat and musk filled my nostrils. I opened my mouth and stuck out my tongue. He had aimed well – my tongue went up his asshole. I wiggled it around, feeling inside him, invading him with my tongue as he had invaded me with his cock. Little tremors made his hips shake, so I assumed I was pleasing him. He pistoned his legs up and down, and I gasped for air when it was available, as all the while he fucked himself on my tongue. His big balls slammed up and down on my chin. When my tongue was dry and spent, I pulled it back in and used my whole mouth on him.

I kissed his asshole, running my lips up and down his asscrack, trying to give him as much pleasure as possible. The sooner he came again, the sooner he would (hopefully) have no further use for me and let me go.

His body shivered above me, more urgently than before.

He was on the borderline of something.

But, I didn't know what.

Suddenly, he rose off me, and the light of the moon and the streetlights returned, bright and harsh. I almost missed his butt on my face – even though I had been trapped by him, it felt somehow safe, as if there were only a small number of ways he could hurt me that way.

Standing up over me again, looking down at me as if I were the lowest maggot who crawled on the earth, he had a world

8

of possibilities open to him. But, he didn't take long to choose. His cock was still hard and dripping, so he hadn't come again.

Shit!

That meant this wasn't over.

He reached down and grabbed me by the shoulder. With surprising strength he flipped me over onto my stomach. Free of their crushing prison, but still aching and bound together, my arms were flushed with relief. But, now my ass was available to him, just sitting there with my hands twisting and bleeding above it.

Now unable to see him, I feared him even more, and I moaned in pain and terror.

His hands were on my shorts then, ripping them down and away. The night air touched my ass cheeks and my butthole clenched tightly closed. I felt him sit down on me again, this time his legs straddling mine, holding me in place. He smacked my ass a few times, the blows stinging cruelly. Then I heard him spit into his hand and the unmistakable sound of him slicking up his dick.

With my cuffed hands, I tried to push him away, prevent what he was about to do, but I was powerless against him. One of his strong hands pushed my arms away and held them, preventing me from moving them further. I was terribly aware of what I knew he must be using the other hand for – aiming his cock.

Without any preparation, he forced himself into me, his dick skewering me as if I were fresh meat about to be roasted. I cried out, unable to help it; knowing he didn't hear me, knowing that no rescuer would come, I cried because I had to. He fell on top of me then, finally putting his whole weight onto me, crushing me beneath him. My arms were once again trapped and my torso unable to budge under him. He lay on top of me and fucked me.

He fucked me for a long time.

I just tried to hold on to my sanity as he rammed inside me over and over again, just breathing through the pain and telling myself, it'll be over soon. It'll be over soon. It'll be over soon.

But, it wasn't.

Maybe because he'd shot so recently, it took him a lot longer to climax this time.

My whole body was aching, my chest pressed against the unforgiving pavement, my cock grinding painfully under the force of his attack, my arms crying for release, and my asshole screaming helplessly against intrusion and violation.

Then he let go of my hands, letting the weight of his chest keep them in place against my back. With his cock so deeply inserted in my ass, he must've figured his own hands were free for the moment. He used them to cover my mouth and hold my nose closed. He would hold them so long I would begin to lose consciousness before he released me, then did it again.

And, all the while he fucked me.

Just when I had resigned myself to this fate, when I realized that this was why I had come here, why I had ignored the punks and the johns and tricks and the married men – this was what I wanted. This is why I came to the docks.

Suddenly, the man was stuffing something in my mouth. It smelled and tasted of sweat and piss, and I guessed it was his underwear. He stuffed it in so deep and far that I was lucky I could breathe through my nose. I prayed he wasn't going to plug up my nose in the same way, or I was a goner. He used some other piece of cloth, a sock or a handkerchief maybe, to tie his shorts in place inside my mouth. He had gagged me most effectively. His thrusts were becoming more ragged, more savage, more desperate. He was finally getting close to coming again. My eyes were clenched closed, and I was breathing rapidly through my nose.

He knocked me on the side of the head again. I didn't know what he wanted – what more submission could I give him;

what more debasement could I lower myself to; what more could he want?

I suddenly realized he wanted me to open my eyes, and I did.

He was signing in front of my face, his hand feverishly forming the shape of one word in front of me, one word over and over and over again.

Scream

Scream

Scream

SCREAM

I did and was horrified to discover that I made no noise at all. I screamed again at the top of my voice and heard nothing. My mouth was so firmly gagged that no sound of any kind could escape.

I had been silenced.

In panic and terror, I screamed once more, with every ounce of my being, with every remaining shred of strength in my body, with all that was left of me, I screamed …

… and heard nothing.

And, the man that was fucking me came, shooting his load deep inside of me. I collapsed under him as he writhed and contorted on top of me. I wanted to sink into the ground, to become one with the asphalt and never rise from it again. My brain was reeling as my body's violation reached its climax. I started shivering uncontrollably, but the man on top of me didn't seem to care. He lay on top of me until his orgasm was completely spent, until every last bit of him was inside me.

When he finally pulled himself out of me and rose to his feet, I could hardly tell the difference. I was floating between nightmare and reality, trying to figure out which was worse.

But, reality was definitely worse when he used his booted foot to kick me in the groin.

White filled my vision, and I was lost in a void.

I woke up, and it was nearly daylight.

I was still lying on the hard street, so it had not been a nightmare.

But my wrists had been uncuffed, the gag removed from my mouth, and my shorts pulled up to cover my cock, balls and ass. I was aching and sore all over, bleeding from several places no doubt, but it was better than before.

Almost anything would've been better than before.

I heard the man near me, so I closed my eyes and didn't move. It sounded as if he was putting his pants and chaps back on, then his boots back on. I kept my eyes closed as he stepped closer, gravel crunching under his boots. I didn't move or struggle when he grabbed me by the arm and yanked me off the ground. Leaning under me, he picked me up and slung me over one shoulder. Then he carried me a little ways, probably about half a city block or so.

There was a sound of metal creaking, and the man threw me off his shoulder into something soft, dark and stinking. The metal lid slammed shut above me, and I realized he'd tossed me into a dumpster.

I waited until the sound of his footsteps faded away.

Only then did I raise the lid and carefully crawl out of the dumpster.

It was very early. There wasn't anyone up around the docks, so I walked home without been seen by anyone.

When I got home, I did three things.

The first was triple-lock my front door.

The second was get my first-aid kit out of the bathroom and attend to myself.

The third was jerk off.

COUCH WITH A VIEW
By Derrick Della Giorgia

The bond the performer and the spectator share is often of the highest nature. Regulated by clear rules, yet utterly manipulated by invisible glances, unspoken words, implicit agreements, and a profound desire of watching and being watched at the same time. Seeing and not noticing, staring but ignoring.

You wouldn't have thought that reflection came to me as I was waiting in line for one of the five urinals in the black tiled bathroom of Boy Shop, but that's because you were not there. Outside, Manhattan was strangely dormant under a thick fluffy layer of snow. The fresh flakes falling through the holes between the buildings, slowed down the city noises and movements, and only the by now sporadic, yellow cars blackened that white carpet. It hadn't stopped snowing since I had landed, day and night, and the city still preserved its humming. I was amazed and constantly trying to dissect what made the Big Apple so different from my Zagreb. I had left snow there, too, yet nothing compared. I had spent my whole life in Croatia, with only one remarkable event to tell, substituting the precise and rigid love that my mother had given me with the cautious and anti-exploratory sex that my boyfriend had forced me into. My trip to New York was meant to be a second big mark in my life. From the safe past to the daring future. From strictly private to generously public. During that week, I took my erections out of the bedroom and made sure there was always a public for my orgasms.

Inside Boy Shop, the meteorological conditions were quite different. The pumping dance floor squeezed sweat out of every single shirtless body, and the dim colored lights produced warmth and safety in every corner and every corridor of the club. I was torn whether to take off my tank top or not, and I looked in the mirror at my right to decide. My shoulders looked wide, and the damp grey fabric wrapped my torso and my waist perfectly, sweetening the candid whiteness of my skin. I liked the way my collarbones were highlighted. I kept it on.

The restroom was packed. Restless bodies of different sizes and shapes stood one in front of the other, eyeing the urinals or exchanging quick words by the sink, desperate for something. Among the heavy breathing of those who took the opportunity to cool down, the metallic unlatching of belts, the swishing of denim over thighs and asses, the water constantly flushing. When I finally reached one of the five white pieces of ceramics, I was completely comfortable and ready to play the game; I figured that hardly half of the guys in the room actually needed to piss; the majority were there to admire cock. I unbuttoned my fly and freed my Croatian device out of the white and red silk briefs. Instants after, I could feel the heat of my neighbors propagating to my skin and their stare knocking to get in. They pressured to conquer that intimate space between me and the urinal. The guy on my left sported a full hard-on and pushed against my sneaker to invite me to his feast, while the twink at my right played with his belly button piercing, careless of the direction of his urine, his blond trimmed pubic hair gratuitously exposed. The door opened again, letting more guests in, and for a couple of seconds, the music vibrated more violently against our chests. I wasn't into any of the guys who were provoking me, but the whole situation was a charming tease.

Back in Europe, we were more dark room people. The space where everything that was prohibited in public was welcome, the time when nobody cared about the music, the clothes they were wearing, the things to say. You walked in, you grabbed and you enjoyed. No complications, no explanations. But, that wasn't quite the same. The hard-on guy pushed down his inviting cock and let it spring up against his abs, then looked at mine and banged it against his shaved pubes, making that noise of flesh being slapped that everybody behind me recognized. His head was shaven, too, and both his nipples pierced. He had a nice body, and my meat started to awaken in my hands, drawing the twink's attention, who nonchalantly whispered, "That's nice."

The smell of cock got to my head, and I wondered how hard he was or how heavy his balls would feel in my hand. And, as I was still debating about how far we were actually allowed to go, he landed his palm on my helmet and slowly pulled back my foreskin, spreading his saliva all over my cock and giving me the hot pleasure shiver that caused more blood to be pumped into his hand.

"Love your huge balls," the twink joined in, inserting his hand in between my thighs. My only desire was to step back and let them work on me, but the voices of the hungry guys behind me distracted me. I quickly looked over my shoulders and suddenly felt that everybody knew what was going on and instead of getting irritated for the wait, looked anxious to approach the urinals and participate to the event. As in a silent agreement among men. I had to go. The excitement was so overwhelming that I got scared I wouldn't have been able to thoroughly control my body.

I pushed my erection back in and walked to the sink to splash some cold water on my face. I fixed my hair, and after checking how my successor in the urinal was doing, I left the room.

The electricity running along my body was unbearable, and I was tempted to go back in the bathroom and attempt another urinal, but eventually decided to sit and have a drink. I couldn't get out of my mind the image of that cock market where everybody was busy shopping. I needed some more alcohol in me, so I ordered my Long Island iced tea and dropped myself on the white couch in front of the bar area. It had the best view. Screwing was the only thought on my mind. The guys in front of me kept moving back and forth as in a procession, and the flow from the dance floor to the bar perfectly equaled the one in the opposite direction. The DJ played a Madonna remix, and the crowd roared in approval. I wasn't a fan (actually, I couldn't stand her at all because my ex loved her), but I recognized the beat because it was the same remix she played at the concert in Zagreb, to which I had been dragged against my will.

I spread my legs and rested my right foot on the hot pink metal table full of glasses containing only melted ice cubes. As my left hand distractedly rubbed my crotch, I enjoyed the show. The dance floor was at its best. It looked like an overcrowded gym where all the machines were taken away. They all moved together, like in a group dance, feeling one another, kissing, licking their heated muscles, fixing every now and then the shirt hanging from the back of their pants. Instead, the few people that were fully dressed, like me, danced more toward the DJ area, responsive to the play list more than to the hotness of their neighbors.

It was three in the morning when I pushed my empty glass among the others on the table and checked the map I carried with me everywhere. I was only five blocks away from the sauna I had visited the previous day, and the idea of having a towel wrapped around my hard-on until some volunteer offered to take care of it, sounded so good. I folded Manhattan back into my back pocket, and I paused for a second, remembering my first adventure in the United States.

I had literally devoured that hot dog. Not the greasy fat dogs from Bana Jelacica square in Zagreb, where the old lady wouldn't take Euros because she thought it was fake money – we still have *kunas* – but the fit New York dog from the corner on Eighth Avenue and Eighteenth Street, where I was free to eye and get as many guys as I could bear. What would she have thought? For some reason, I couldn't get the image of her holding the enormous, smooth and lubricated chunk of meat out of my mind. Those were my thoughts in front of Duane Reade before entering the sauna.

When I stepped into the Swedish sauna, I felt all the horny eyes of the men sitting on the benches landing on me at the same time. Making their way through my towel, up and down my naked body. Eager to find out what I demanded. Leaving Croatia, I had sworn I would try everything and take advantage of my young body before it rotted. My ex-boyfriend had kept me leashed to his narrow-mindedness for more than five years and had never wanted to get beyond it. I was only twenty-six, and I desperately perceived the need to bite more off of life, to taste, to grab before it was too late – as if I had already missed a lot. I hadn't had sex with anybody else but him; I hadn't had sex outside my house; I hadn't invented sex but just replicated it; and I wanted to fuck with New Yorkers.

The hot dry vapor that assailed me as soon as I'd pushed the door open immediately neutralized the change of temperature that my emotions were causing: the cold in my hands and the red heat on my face. The sultry wind swept it all away and sucked me in, voraciously. Men were sprawled next to each other, and you could almost cut with a knife the desire of carnal contact. Some were more visible, others camouflaged in the mist. They all seemed ready to attack, peaceful and at the same time on alert. There were two levels of benches. I sat in the right corner of the higher circle, leaned against the wooden walls and explored the room with eyes of enlightenment. Most of the white towels had lazily fallen off the waist – in some cases they hung around the neck – and unraveled sinewy erections that pointed toward the ceilings like flowers looking for sun light. My body got adjusted to the environment in a matter of seconds, and after the initial discomfort, my muscles started to relax, and my lust became more acceptable. A big hairy muscular guy in front of me enthralled me particularly and lit my fantasies when he shut his eyes and gave permission to the two men in their forties sitting below him to suck him and feel him the way they most liked. It was a no-stress exchange, everybody offered and grabbed selflessly. Everybody contributed to everybody's pleasure, with the rapid movement of hands, with the sharp dance of the mouth or simply with a thick and supportive stare. The white towel I had been given at the entrance with the key to the locker, started to part under the pressure of my hard on, and Arthur didn't wait any longer to help me.

"Where are you from?" he asked as soon as my cock appeared in between my legs. I guess my face and foreskin together suggested foreignness.

"Croatia," I answered as I forced myself not to care about my erection growing in front of everybody.

"Can I suck you?" he gently questioned as his hand was already holding my balls first and my shaft right after. The intimacy that is usually shared by two people only, there, was made communal. The desire of being watched in your most secret pleasure triumphed.

"Yeah," I heard myself saying. I hosted him in between my legs and let myself go. He slowly approached my sack with his lips and teased me with the tip of his tongue then pulled down my foreskin and massaged with his thumb my slit, wetting it every now and then with his lower lip. Two men got closer and watched the show inches away from my knees. They seemed to get inspiration from my pleasure. A wave of complicity commenced to circulate in the room and avoiding it to concentrate on my blow job but enjoying the multitude of sex acts going on in the little space, I navigated every single sensation in my crotch. I put my hand on my mate's hair and pushed him on me, rubbing hard his drenched shoulders. He didn't refuse to open his mouth to me and let me enter his throat, allowing me to crash his face into my groin. As I was about to come, I leaned on the guy next to me and grabbed his cock. It was thick, and it slightly veered to the left. Its root was trapped in my hand, and I shook it in my face. Deciphering my spasms, Arthur stopped blowing me and started jerking me off with my dick pointed to the center of the room. I felt somebody pinching my nipple, and I shot two hot loads toward the entrance door.

"Yeah ..."

"Nice ..."

All the eyes met on my stomach contracting and their sighing mouths looked as if they wanted to comment the quantity of white cream secreted. They supported me, whispering but with vehemence, and accompanied me through my orgasm.

"Can I sit here?" Love Aid squeezed his ass in the half space left between me and the arm of the couch and brought me back to the reality of Boy Shop. I scooted over and ended up with my elbow in the couple next to me. But, they didn't seem to care, too busy Frenching each other.

I fixed my buttocks, rubbing against his leg and reconsidered my decision to go back to the sauna. He was very sexy, and by the pressure of his bicep against my arm, hard and fit. In fact, the Love Aid white writing across his chest illuminated his black shirt and moved only when he brought the drink to his mouth or contracted his pectorals. I wasn't about to leave. If my only recently dumped other half could have seen me, he would have probably had a heart attack.

I launched my obvious double entendre and waited to see if he would take the bait. Meanwhile, he ruffled his hair in the middle, refreshing his hairdo and looked at me from the corner of his eye. My arm slid in between our legs and slowly made its way onto his thigh. As I expected, it was firm and solid. He didn't even blink and kept sipping his vodka red bull – I could smell the funny sweet flavor of the red bull. I squeezed my cock through my jeans – as if I needed to scratch – and obscenely lingered on the head, drawing his attention to my hard-on. The alcohol, the music, the view, made it difficult to resist the temptation of grabbing his crotch and stroking his pouch without waiting for the right time. He scratched his right temple and slightly turned to me, stealing a look at my puffed out jeans. His movements were slower now, somehow awkward and sort of fake: all signs he was receiving the message and playing indifferent.

When I was just about ready to caress his leg, the logical next step, the saliva swapping couple next to me decided to bring their show somewhere else and suddenly stood up, leaving a hole at my left and putting me in the position where I could easily move a bit and grant my man some more room. I thought about it for a second, and then I simply reset my weight, without increasing the distance between us. He didn't mind.

I wanted to ride him, in that precise position. His shoulders rested on the couch, which allowed me to have a better view of his fat crotch. He buried his glass in the cemetery of died drinks and pushed his leg against me, without looking. The last three fingers of my right hand were completely on his thigh. And then, finally breaking the distance, he dropped his palm half an inch away from where my hard cock was hiding. He checked with me for approval and went on to feel my erection.

"Good," he smiled and looked into my eyes, massaging my cock. Then, he unbuttoned my fly and stuck his hand inside, avoiding my briefs and reaching my skin. A short blond guy walking in front of us saw and smirked at us, almost showing envy. A second later, my fingers wrapped his fat cut cock, spreading the thick precum drops that blossomed from his slit. It was so unusual, I could have come right there.

"Take your tank top off," he whispered in my ear as he did the same. He peeled the black T-shirt and unveiled a much hotter torso than I had imagined. His black tattoo was the only imperfection and his stomach a smooth board marked by the beginning and the end of every muscle. "Put it like this …" He covered his crotch with his shirt and unbuttoned his pants, letting me take a look at his pubes before directing my hand in there.

"Here?" I naively asked. He only blinked at me, making a face as if who's gonna care? I smiled and thought my ex-boyfriend would care! You know, he throws a dark foulard over his night stand lamp to obscure the details when the face is too close to the groin. "Some things are to be kept in the dark!" – his favorite quote while naked in bed.

20

It was like a dream, the perfect balance between the sweet anxiety in my stomach that somebody could see us and the warm desire burning in my groin. His hand was excitingly lazy on me, and the slower he touched me, the faster I got close to the orgasm. Luckily, we were often interrupted, and the pleasure started all over again. One, two, three, four times. My cock felt so comfortable in his hand, completely abandoned to his big palm and expert thumb. It was painful to abruptly stop again when the waiter bent almost on us to recollect the glasses. We waited immobile, our hands in each other's pants. In silence, anticipating the next touch.

As soon as he left, I wet my hand in my mouth and reached his stick again, giving him the pace he requested. At the same time, he controlled the throbbing of my cock with his left hand under my grey tank top. We took it slow, alternating fast strokes and softer ones, according to the crowd around us and trying to limit the shaking of our shirts under the jerking off. I occasionally wandered on his warm smooth thighs and his petrified stomach, and he often stopped giving me pleasure to pull my sack and squeeze my balls to the point it hurt. Our chests moved in synch, and our respiration accelerated with every new move. We realized some people noticed and some others watched for a while, but that only made everything sexier. Even the fear we might be kicked out of the place faded as we got deeper into our pleasure.

When he closed his eyes I knew his balls were pushing cum into his cock and that he was about to explode. I looked at his face, and he gaped as my hand got wet, and the sticky hot fluid covered my fingers. He didn't stop his hand, and breathing on my neck brought me to the orgasm. From across the room, the twink I had met in the bathroom earlier called his friend and pointed at me. And, that's exactly when I felt my cum hit the fabric and drop back on my balls and his hand.

"Can I sit here?" Our hands still hidden and wet with cum, when Derrick asked to use the couch.

COCK ROCK
By Rob Rosen

I was on my way to see Debbie Harry perform at an out of the way club. It had been a long while since I'd been there, but figuring that Debbie had few touring years left in her, I better not have missed the opportunity. Pushing fifty – and the slippery slope of it at that – I assumed her vocal chords were reaching their limits, so I braved a Sunday evening on the wrong side of the tracks, choosing to walk rather than catch a cab. Why not? It was a warm night. Well, warm enough. And, I'd certainly walked through that part of town before; many times and to many bars, in fact. Or, should that be "too" many bars? Yes, I was reaching my limit as well, though fifty was still a good ways off. Thank goodness.

It was, of course, a tad unsafe to make the walk in the mostly run down, mostly warehouse, and nearly deserted part of town. It was dark, and there were just a few too many alleyways for my liking. But again, this was for Debbie Harry. *The* Debbie Harry. It had been my dream since I was a teenager to see her perform live, ever since I saw her in *Creem* magazine with that peroxided hair of hers and that skin tight ripped outfit and a fuck-you look spread across her angelic face. Now, that was a woman I could relate to. So, I made the trek through the neighborhood – alone, as not many of my friends shared my predilection for the diva of rock and roll.

I sang a little of "Call Me" under my breath as I walked. It relaxed me. And, I'd made it nearly all the way there, passing the darkened side of several warehouses, without incident – almost. Just as I was about to make my way across the street, a beat-up, ancient, brown Chevy Impala pulled up alongside me. The windows were rolled down, and I could smell the vestiges of an aromatic doobie and could clearly make out the music blaring from the car's rear speakers: *Domo arigato, Mr. Roboto, domo*. It wasn't Debbie, but it would do in a pinch.

"Hey," shouted the stranger in the strange car.

"Hey," I answered, bending down to see whom I was talking to.

"Um, where am I?" he asked, which wasn't as odd as it sounded considering we were practically out in the middle of nowhere.

"Seventh and Peach," I responded, smiling all the while. From my vantage point, I could see that he was about my age and cute; cute enough for me to remain friendly, despite the bad-ish neighborhood, that is.

"No, I mean what part of town am I in?" he asked.

"Ah, you're in the warehouse district," I said, moving in closer to the car. The song had changed to "Jukebox Hero." The stranger must've had a compilation on. Still, not an awful selection.

"Huh?" he asked, leaning in closer to the passenger side window in order to get a better earful. Now, I could see him better, as well. He was blond, with long hair down to the middle of his back, and he had an equally blond goatee, which hung a couple of inches down his chin. He was nice looking, symmetrically speaking. Even in the dim light I could see he had crystal clear blue eyes. Oh, and yes, like the song said, he had stars in them. But, that might have been the pot. And no, he wasn't my type, not by a long shot, but it was late, I was alone and, well, did I mention that he was cute? Naturally, there was some instantaneous lumpage in my jeans.

"Warehouse," I said to him again, slower and louder, trying my best to pierce his pot-induced fog.

"Ah," he said, and nodded. "My bad. Guess I got turned around. I was looking for Park Drive, by the marina."

"No, you're a ways off, sorry," I told him, bending further down and almost leaning into the car, so he'd be able to hear me clearly. (Okay, so, really, I was flirting.)

He pondered what I had said and then looked back up to me for advice. "Could you point me in the right direction?"

"Sure, just stay on this street, and when you start seeing seagulls, you're probably pretty close."

"Thanks," he said, turning back to face the road. He was off with a wave and a smile. I watched his car as it drove down the street, trailing a dusty cloud in its wake.

Oh well, I thought, *no harm no foul*. Now, back to Debbie.

Staying along my route, I crossed the street and once again made my way toward the club. I sang "Heart of Glass." My mood turned from apprehension to glee. In just a couple of short minutes, I'd be standing in the same building as Debbie Harry. Hallelujah.

I started to cross the last street to the Promised Land, but something out of the corner of my eye made me stop. The brown Impala was headed back my way, this time in the opposite direction. It had circled the block and, for the second time that night, it stopped dead at my feet.

"You get lost again?" I asked, secretly glad to see him.

"Nope, not exactly."

"You need directions again?"

He paused and thought. "Nope, not exactly?"

"Well, what exactly then?" I stood there, shifting my weight from my left foot to my right. I was eager to hear what the exactly was.

"Where were you headed?" he asked. "I thought I'd offer you a ride, since you were kind enough to help me out."

Hmm, nice, if a bit unexpected. My cock went boiiing, yet again.

"Oh, actually, I'm headed right down there," I said, pointing to the club, which I could easily see a few hundred feet ahead. He followed my finger with his eyes and nodded before he spoke again.

"Oh, okay," he said, without emotion; but still he sat there with the engine running. The "Kid is Hot Tonight" was now blaring from the speakers. Appropriate, I thought, and a better selection than the previous two. I looked at the stranger, waiting for him to say something else, anything else, and I sang in my head, "but where will he be tomorrow?"

After a brief moment, and with no further repartee, I announced, "Well, I better get going to my concert then."

That perked him up. "Oh, you're going to a concert?"

"Yep. Debbie Harry. Live and in person."

"Debbie Harry? No kidding? She still singing? She must be pushing fifty now," he said, grinning and nodding his head back and forth in disbelief. I was amazed he even knew who she was. His musical tastes didn't seem to point toward her. Then he upped the ante. "Mind if I join you?" he asked, grinning up at me. "I'm a Blondie fan from way, way back."

That was a toughie. Yes, he was cute, but he was also a stranger I had just met on the street. Just barely met, I should say. Still, I wasn't totally thrilled at seeing the concert alone, and so … "Sure, why not. I mean, it's not every day you get to see Debbie Harry perform live."

"Hell no," he agreed, and opened the door for me to get in; which was kind of silly considering all he had to do was turn his car up one more street and then park; but I got in and rode with him for the minute or two that it took.

"Names Jeff," he said, pulling the car into a parking space nearly across from the club. I figured that the parking Gods must like him; therefore, I must've made a good decision.

26

"Steve," I introduced myself, shaking his hand once he was done parking. Flesh on flesh. His skin was soft and warm. My heart skipped a beat.

"Nice to meet you, Steve," he said, grinning at me. "This should be fun."

"Won't your friends in the marina be worried?" I asked, curious that he was suddenly so available.

"I wasn't meeting anyone there. I was just looking for it. This is my first time in the city, and I have a room at a hotel there, but that can wait," he explained, getting out of the car.

Okay by me, I thought.

Thankfully, there was someone scalping a ticket as we walked up to the club. As I suspected, the concert was sold out. This was, after all, a big deal to a lot of people; a lot of people dressed twenty years beyond how they should've been dressed. Jeff and I clearly stood out in our jeans and tee shirts. Though Jeff's rather hippy-like appearance made him stand out even more than most.

We walked in and quickly got our bearings. Bar to the right, dance floor to the left, stage to the far end of the dance floor, upstairs for coat check or to view the festivities below. Not much had changed. I was glad; this would be the perfect way to get close to Debbie. And Jeff. But first ...

"Drink?" I asked, already bellying up to the bar.

"Gin and tonic," he responded.

"Two gin and tonics," I informed the bartender, a tall man in pigtails and bright red lipstick.

"To Debbie," I said, clinking our plastic cups together.

"To Debbie," he echoed, his blue eyes twinkling magically beneath the dance floor lighting, locking laser intense onto my own.

We stood there like that, drinking our drinks, our feet bouncing up and down to the eclectic mix of pre-show music, until the crowd started to swell, and we were pushed closer and closer together. My leg quickly ran up against his leg, my arm brushing his, the hairs tingling at the contact. He turned to me and smiled. I did the same. The loud music, thankfully, muffled the sound of my increasingly quickening breath.

And then …

"Ladies and gentleman, please welcome to the stage …Miss … Debbie Harry."

And, there she was. My God, she looked exactly as she had way back in the early eighties, give or take ten pounds and a heck of a load of makeup. Her skin was still the same shimmering white, though, and she still looked just as beautiful, just as blonde and dark-rooted as ever. The effect was dazzling. She was dazzling. Yes, I was dazzled. And, looking over at Jeff, I could tell I wasn't alone. It's as if she had been cryogenically frozen for the last twenty years, popping out of an MTV time machine, to perform for us at that very club in the very next century.

Oh, and when she sang, man, it was magic. I had goose bumps.

Actually, the biggest bump I felt was coming from behind me. I could swear I felt Jeff's crotch pressing up against my ass. Of course, the crowd was pushing forward in an effort to get as close as possible to her, and with Jeff behind me and to my right a bit, he had little choice but to push in tight. Still, I took it as a good sign.

Two or three songs into the concert, and with the gin amply taking effect, and with Jeff's crotch still poking me from behind, I decided to be brave, and made a strategic move. I swung my right arm around my back and placed the back of my invitingly open hand against my hip. Well, sure as shootin', he took the bait. He shifted over a couple of inches, and now his crotch was pressed firmly against my hand. I gently gave a squeeze to his denim-sheathed cock to see what reaction I'd get, just in case I was tactically off base.

Thankfully, I wasn't; he moved in even closer to me, until I could feel his hot breathe on the back of my neck. Now, normally I wasn't so brazen. But, normally I wasn't at a music hall on a Sunday night by myself with a perfect stranger. How many times would I get this chance? Judging from my previous ten years experiences, I'd say none. So, I played on. The fourth song, "French Kissin' in the USA," bolstered my bravado.

I could feel he had on 501s, which, fortuitously, have those lovely gaps in between the buttons. I deftly jimmied my index finger through one of the holes and let my finger do some walking. Woohoo, no underwear! Even better, Jeff was already semi-hard. By the end of the song, my hand was practically stuck in his now swollen jeans. It was all I could do to concentrate on the show.

Song number five was "One Way or Another," Blondie's big, big hit. I took the lyrics as an omen and continued my exploring. I added another finger to the fray and effortlessly flipped open one button, then two. My entire hand easily slid into his jeans. A soft moan erupted from Jeff and into my ear. He put both of his hands on my shoulders and moved in even tighter. The only chance anyone could have seen what we were up to was if they were crouching on the ground along side of us; an impossible stunt given the size and depth of the crowd.

Jeff was just the right size in my hand, but still, I was cramped; so I slowly worked him outside his jeans until his cock and balls were brazenly hanging against my pants. It was an unusual sensation to be standing there, surrounded by a throng of people, mostly straight, unaware that a partially naked man was being stroked right in front of them. I ached to turn around and see the expression on his face, but knew it might call attention to the scene below. Instead, I stood there, dancing to the music, singing along with Debbie, and stroking his swollen rod.

Like a blind man, I read his prick like a Braille card. It was long, a good seven inches that arched up and to the left, with a fat, precum-slicked head that I squeezed in between jacks on his vein-lined shaft.

"Yeah, man," he rasped into my ear, clearly eager for the attention, his hands working their way over my shoulders and down my shirt, tweaking my nipples and sending me into rapturous heaven.

A good forty minutes into the show, both Debbie's and our own, I added fuel to the fire by inconspicuously spitting into my hand so as not to rub him raw. He responded with another moan and an even harder cock in my hand, plus a soft kiss to my ear and a nibble on my lobe. That was all I needed, and I started pounding his prick even harder and in time with the music. When he tightened his grip of my chest, I knew there was no turning back. After a quick frenzy of rapid strokes and with his hard-on now pointed down to the ground, he shot his hefty load straight onto the dance floor. Luckily, by that time, there was so much shit down there that I seriously doubted that anyone would ever notice. Jeff's softening prick found its way back into its home, and then it was my turn for a go.

We switched positions, him in front and me in back. Quick as a wink, my straining cock was in his upturned hand. I wrapped my arms around him and felt the familiar warm eddy of adrenalin shoot from my cock as it made its way through my body. All the while I stared ahead, as if Debbie was only singing to the both of us.

"Close," I whispered into his ear, my head pressed up tight to his. He pointed my cock downwards, as I had down to him. The music reached its crescendo just as I had, my cock spewing forth ounce after creamy white ounce of molten hot cum. I stifled my groans as best I could, waiting for my prick to soften, and then quickly stuffed it back in. "Thanks, dude," I purred in his ear, once again returning to his side.

With almost an hour left of the show, I returned my concentration back to the stage, almost forgetting that Jeff was even there. And, when she was finished and the house lights were turned back up, I turned to him and said, "Wow, that was amazing." But, he was nowhere in sight. I waited around for a while, but he never returned. When I left the club, his car was no longer there.

Oh well, I thought, *it was still an amazing night*. But when I started walking back the way I originally came, I noticed something in the street where Jeff's beat-up Impala had once been parked. There was a cassette lying there, which I bent down to pick up. Printed across the tape was, "Best of a Decade."

Yep, I thought, *the eighties were a great time, but hey, the next century was looking a hell of a lot brighter by the moment*. And, with a grin on my face and Debbie's voice still singing to me in my head, I headed on home.

SCRUBBING UP
By Mickey Erlach

I had just come home from a business trip and was still wound up from days of meetings and travel. Normally, I would have had a martini then crashed for the night, but I hadn't worked out in a few days, so I decided to hit the gym. It was after 10:30, but they were open until midnight on Friday nights, so I had plenty of time.

After changing into my non-descript workout gear as I never really went for the Spandex/Lycra look, I walked upstairs to the free weight area, and to my surprise, no one else was working out. Usually this would bother me as seeing hot guys pumping up is inspirational, but I just wanted to get a good sweat going.

After an hour of working my chest until I swore my nipples would pop off from the pressure, I did some crunches and decided to call it a night and go downstairs to the locker room and shower. Interestingly, no one else came in to work out while I was there, and from what I could tell, only the night manager remained on duty.

As I undressed at my locker, the manager walked by and smiled. I am usually a talkative guy, but I noticed a while back, that although he was friendly and smiled a lot, this particular manager wasn't much of a talker. He was also the kind that never went for me – buzz cut, tattoos from neck to ankles, earrings, and from what I could tell through his tight shirt, nipple rings. He was also the bodybuilder type with big, thick muscles that were obviously enhanced through chemistry (and I'll leave it at that). He did have those dark features I find enormously attractive, but his look told me that I was not his type.

I bent down to slip off my jock, and I stood up to find him standing in front of me and checking me out.

"Pretty slow tonight," he said.

"Yeah, made my workout that much easier." I didn't bother covering myself up with a towel, as by then he had a full view and what was the point. I am also very well built with a naturally smooth physique and slabs of lean, hard muscle from years of working out, so I like the attention. My dick hangs nicely, too, with a pair of round full balls to support it. This would have been a good time to put on the moves, but as I said, this type never goes for me. My being blond doesn't help either.

"I still have time to shower before you lock up I hope."

"You have plenty of time," he said as he walked away then shouted over his shoulder, "I'm going to lock up early, but take your time."

We have open showers, which I like because there is nothing better than having a hot view of pumped up muscle-heads after a workout, and I had picked up my share of tricks after a shower in this gym as well.

I stepped up to the second shower head that I knew had the best pressure, turned it on and let the water cascade down my back as I faced the wall. I then shampooed my hair and turned around to rinse out the suds. I almost jumped when I felt a hand on my balls. I opened my eyes to see the night manager, naked and feeling me up while grinning at me.

"Mind if I soap you up?"

I just shrugged as if to say what the hell. He then squeezed some soap from the dispenser and proceeded to rub the soap on my chest, down my abs, back up my sides and indicated I should raise my arms as he scrubbed my pits. We didn't say a word as he continued to soap me up from head to toe while I drank in every tattooed inch of muscle on his beautiful body. Not only were his nipples pierced, but his belly button and big, thick cock were as well. I was intrigued by his body art, turned on by his beauty, and getting horny from his touch. My cock was standing straight up, thick and long, and the head was more swollen than usual.

He turned me around and worked my back, paying special attention to my hard, round glutes before he worked his hand between them and stuck a finger in my hole while he reached around with the other hand and stroked my now aching cock.

Then he licked the back of my neck. That did it. About a quart of precum oozed from my cock, but the water and soap disguised it, although my moan was loud and clear.

I then felt his hard cock sliding up and down my crack and the smooth metal of the ring tracing its path. What a feeling and I didn't want it to end.

I hardly ever bottom, but he was doing things with his hands on my body that had me almost begging out loud. I know he sensed my desire because he then let the head of his cock slide between my cheeks and without stumbling, fumbling or mumbling, he found the hole.

Yes, he was an expert top – a rare breed and a fantastic find. The few times I ever bottomed, I got annoyed when they would struggle to find the hole and get to work, always thinking, "Find it already, fuck me and leave."

He penetrated me ever so gently but with a steady movement, and before I knew it, that hard, thick pierced tool was all the way in, and I oozed another quart of precum. The metal ring just added to my pleasure as doing me from behind allowed it to rub my prostate just right. He continued to lick my neck and stroke my cock while he fucked me slowly never increasing nor decreasing his pace. I was in heaven. And, I was getting close.

Within a minute, I shot with a loud growl and painted the tiles with my thick load while he continued his steady fuck. Once he was sure I was drained, he withdrew his cock, and I ached for its return. It was over, and I wanted it to go on all night. I was embarrassed at my quick orgasm, but he seemed not to mind.

He turned me around and proceeded to soap me up again as he did before, but this time he leaned in and planted his full lips on mine. Not only was he a great fuck, but also the best kisser I have ever known. My cock, which I thought was through for the night, got hard again (his stroking it did help).

This time instead of turning me around, he turned around and rubbed his big hard muscular ass on my cock. I got the message. I found the hole with no problem and penetrated him with the same gentle but firm steady stroke he had shown me. I ran my tongue up his back and all over his neck, while I reached around and stroked his cock. He moaned with pleasure as I fucked him steadily, figuring he liked it as he gave it, slow, steady, firm and sensual. I have learned from years of casual encounters that if someone does something to you, they usually like it done to them.

He liked it.

Within a minute, he growled out his own thick load and painted the tile floor.

Strangely, we had only been at it for no more than ten minutes, yet we had both come and fucked each other. I could have come again, but I withdrew. I also decided to return the favor and scrub him up.

His body felt fantastic; the more I felt of it, the more I wanted to go at it again.

"Come home with me," he said.

Those were the first words either of us had spoken since he entered the shower.

"OK."

We rinsed off, and as I walked toward his car, I wondered what a guy like him wanted with a guy like me.

That was more than twenty years ago, but I no longer wonder what he sees in me as long as he fucks me slow and steady and lets me return the favor every night.

MY FIRST JESUS – A JERUSALEM STORY
By David C. Muller

One time up in Jerusalem, I found myself finishing off a fifth of Scotch at the bar in the world famous King David Hotel at two o'clock on a Wednesday afternoon and asking myself: "What the hell am I doing here?"

The next thing you know I was banging on some door minutes later, interrupting a curiously unheated game of *shaysh-baysh* being played by my two friends, Grofit from Kfar Saba and Joel from Ohio.

Joel asked me, "What are you doing here?"

"I had to come here for some reason," I said. "School related, I think, but I wasn't really paying attention … you know … and I need a place to stay tonight."

"You can stay here," Joel said.

"Cool man, thanks." I liked their place; it was clean and usually filled with an exotic buffet of foreign-born homos hailing from nearly every random corner of the globe.

Joel asked me, "What's up?"

I had my reasons, "Where are the gay clubs?"

"Oh," Joel nodded; his eyes never rose off the backgammon board, "that's why you're here."

Joel said, "Shushan was the last gay place in town, but now even that shithole is closed."

"You're kidding," I said. "They closed Shushan?"

"Months ago," said Grofit. "Now we have to go to Tel Aviv for all that stuff."

"Well fuck!" I dropped years of proverbial luggage in disappointment on to their foyer floor, "What are the good homos of J-town supposed to do when they're horny?"

"Go online."

"How ... suburban," I said. "Isn't there like a ... sauna or a bathhouse or a yeshiva or something I can just go to?"

Grofit said, "There's always the park."

"The park?" It had been years since I went cruising in a municipality-controlled public space. "People still go to the park?"

"Yeah," said Grofit.

Joel nodded without taking his eyes of the backgammon board, "We do it all the time."

I gave the idea about eight seconds of thought and said, "I'll need a taxi."

I waited until nighttime before saying goodbye to Grofit and Joel, still busy with their *shaysh-baysh* game, and walked out to their curb to hail a *monit*.

A taxi pulled up, and I eagerly hopped in, "*Kach oti legan!*" I told the driver, "Take me to the park!"

The taxi driver drove up toward the center of town, passing by the lesser-known King Solomon Hotel, right-turning at the corner with the Conservative Yeshiva of America, coasting between the Rehavia taxi stand on one side, and a large Scottish church on the other. Turning left sharply through opposing traffic, the taxi darted onto a narrow road slicing through a dark grassy knoll set against a sloping hill beneath and behind the looming tower of the old and decrepit Sheraton hotel. In that instant, I saw a fit-looking man with a shaved head and tight, generic-looking jeans disappear between the trees.

That's when I said, "*Vehegahnu, ahh*? And here we are. This is Independence Park?"

The driver nodded his head, "*Cein.*"

"I'll get out here," I took out my wallet to retrieve some shekels for the taxi and practically jumped out of the car.

Present-day Jerusalem, still the holiest of holies for Jews, Christians and Muslims the world over and not to mention the most fought-over city in the history of humanity, had, in its center a park called Independence Park dedicated to the establishment of modern democracy. Due to its close proximity to the city center, *Gan Haatzmaut*, as it is known in Hebrew, serves as a crisscrossing point for all sorts of people, from housewives to wannabe bohemians, religious students, the elderly, the bewildered and, of course, tourists. The park itself was split in half by a street bookended on one side by a pedestrian mall and, on the other, the American consulate. During the day, young couples picnicked romantically while children flew kites, but once the sun set at night, the park, just like so many other parks around the world, became an altogether different kind of meeting place.

And, as I climbed up the dew-dripped, sloping expanse of the park, I saw the shadow of legs moving about in the darkness between the trees and bushes. I knew there were men wandering around the park. I could almost smell their cologne, and of course, we all knew we were in the park looking for the exact same thing. I walked quickly up the hill and past the trees and came to a low-level decorative wall lining the top northwestern edge of the park. From this strategic standpoint, I could sit and watch virtually the whole area and, more importantly, the men wandering around it that night.

A few minutes passed and so did a man; about forty years old with a scraggly unkempt beard. He came out from somewhere behind me, saw me and smiled. I quickly looked away disinterestedly, but I don't think he really got the hint. He came around to stand about two meters away from me off to the right, just standing there like an expectant statue, obviously waiting for one of us to start the "procedure."

Cruising for Bad Boys

I also watched a pair of yeshiva boys, both wearing black leather kippot on their heads and dressed in their little orthodox uniforms of white shirt and black wool trousers. They came in from the left and walked in front of me. These yeshivas boys were young and clearly inexperienced with the social niceties of nighttime gay park cruising; they tried to be discreet as they passed through my line of vision, glancing at me and making eye contact. Moments later, that same pair of yeshiva boys came back out, this time going off to the right. Walking in front of me a second time, the pair whispered quietly and passed furtive and indiscreet glances in my direction and then disappeared into the darkness beyond the light.

That forty-year-old was still there, and by this point, he'd moved in closer to where I was sitting on the wall and stood there looking at me, waiting expectantly for me to say something, but I continued to ignore him. A few seconds later, those two yeshivas boys returned to my periphery to sit on a side bench nearby. This time, however, they stared straight at me, both of them. Every now and then, one would lean over to the other to whisper something without ever lifting their eyes off me. After a while, one of them nodded, and they rose up from the bench and came to stand about two meters off to my left. These two also started straight at me, whispering and shuffling all the more closer to me slowly and systematically.

I lit a joint and ignored all of them and looked further out into the park and saw, in the distance, what I believed to be a better-looking man wearing a blue shirt with the words "Fucking Angel" written in yellow letters across his chest. That's really all it took for me. I looked at the three homosexuals standing around, moving closer toward me slowly like chess pieces pursuing checkmate; two yeshiva boys; probably aged eighteen and nineteen, respectively; and that forty-year-old man with a beard. In this orbit of testosterone and in the dark light of this particular night; I could easily see that none of them tickled my fancy.

I got up from the wall and took my joint and marched away, through the two yeshiva boys and that bearded forty-year-old, taking off like a lone-plane flying off into the night sky to find a better man to screw.

And, find him I did. He stepped out of nowhere really, and he stopped me dead in my tracks.

I stared at him, and he stared at me; he fidgeted a bit and glanced at his wrist.

He asked me, "*Yesh lecha et hazman?*"

I didn't understand what he said, he spoke Hebrew poorly. I squinted my eyes and shook my head.

I looked at his wrist and saw the watch. I said, "It's seven thirty."

He looked at me and cocked his head. He smiled nervously, "It's not seven thirty. It's much later than that."

"How would I know what time it is?" I held up my hands to show I was without a watch. "What's wrong with your clock? Is it broken or something?"

He looked down at his sleeve and pulled it back to reveal a wristwatch. He laughed, "Oh yeah … well … how else am I supposed to start up a conversation out here?"

I nodded, "Are you an American?"

"I'm from El Salvador."

"El Salvador?" I hadn't been expecting that. "How did you end up here?"

He laughed and asked me, "Are you American?"

"Israeli."

"Oh," he nodded and scratched his jaw. "But you speak English perfectly."

"Yeah, it's nice isn't it? So," I asked, "What's your name? What do they call you?"

He said, "Jesus." He pronounced it like "Hay-Zeus."

"Jesus? Your name is Jesus?" I pronounced it like "Jesus."

Jesus smiled, "Yeah."

"You mean, like, the Christian guy? That Jesus?"

"Yeah," Jesus nodded, "but we say Hay-Zeus because the J makes a Y sound in Spanish."

"Well, Jesus," I shifted my weight to one leg and sighed, knowing the drill; I'd done this countless times before, "What are you doing here in Israel?"

Jesus said, "I'm a Christian, and I study at a seminary."

"Oh really, I'm a Jew," I said.

"Really?"

"Uh huh."

"Are you from Jerusalem?"

I said, "I come from a *moshav* in the north of Israel."

"What's it called?"

"Metzitzah."

"Oh," he nodded and scratched his jaw, "I don't know it."

"No one does." I looked Jesus up and down; he was wearing khaki pleats, a green cotton polo shirt with the two top buttons unbuttoned, and a brown suede leather jacket, and standard American-style loafer shoes. "You sure are cute ... for a seminary student." I winked shamelessly, "You have a place we can go?"

"Why?" Jesus smiled, "Where exactly would you want to go with me?"

"That depends."

"What do you want to do?"

I smiled but cut the bullshit, "I heard you seminary boys are uncut. Is that true?"

Jesus laughed.

I said, "We're all cut over here, you know … Jews … It's a real treat to find a guy with a big, fat, juicy uncut cock." I waited for Jesus to say something, but he just scratched his jaw. "So…" I asked him, "are you cut or uncut?"

He started rubbing his jaw, shook his head and smiled, "I'm not circumcised."

"Well," I raised an eyebrow, "you Latino *goyim* usually aren't. Is it thick and juicy? I want to see it. Is it big?"

Jesus laughed. "Do you think it's big?"

"Yeah," I nodded, "and I really want to see your uncut cock."

"Do you have a place we can go to?"

"What does it matter? Just take it out right now and show it to me. Is it hard?"

"No," Jesus laughed and gently rubbed his pants-crotch. "What do you want to do?"

"We can do whatever we want."

Jesus asked me, "Are you a top or a bottom?"

"Oh I'm a top," I replied quickly. "For a guy called Jesus …" I cocked my head, "I like to fuck."

"Okay," Jesus nodded and looked around at the trees, "do you want to go somewhere?"

"Do you have a place?"

"No," Jesus shook his head, "I live in a seminary."

"Right, I remember now. There's that whole '*no posada*' thing or whatever it is. Let's start walking." I pointed off somewhere, and we started moving,

"You're very cute." Jesus moved up close, next to me, "You don't have a place to go?" Jesus asked, "Where are you staying in Jerusalem?"

"I'm staying with friends."

"Do they know you're gay? Can we go to their place?"

"We can't go to their place."

"Oh," Jesus looked back out at the park. "We can go over there, in the trees."

I watched him for a second and then looked out into the green darkness. "How often do you come here?"

Jesus said, "Only sometimes. Not too often."

We walked for a few moments silently before I said, "Fine," and shook my stoned head. I asked Jesus, "Do you know where we are going? I'm thinking there's a place over up or around down over here … or something."

Jesus said, "I know of a better place."

I said, "Fine," and followed Jesus down the sloping hill of the park, over rocks, across paths and through the trees, finally crossing the narrow street I'd come in on. The lower end of the park was a collection ground, it appeared, for temporary fencing and construction materials, haphazardly strewn all around the place, intermingled with neglected olive trees and piles of stones and concrete slabs left over from the era of the Ottomans. I realized, in that moment that we crossed over to the lower end of the park, that although I'd been to the park before, I'd never been to this particular section of the park.

Jesus and I walked past all of this and came to a large, deep abandoned pool. Later on, I would come to know this place as Mammilla's Pool, a luxury pool built centuries earlier by the Turks, but now dried up and hollowed out, about four meters deep and nearly as long as a small football field and overrun with weeds. Jesus started down the stairs that lead into the empty structure.

I said, "We're going to do it down here?" and followed hurriedly after Jesus.

"No one is here," Jesus assured me, "don't worry."

"Do you think someone might see us?"

"No one is here; don't worry."

We walked down the stairs and wandered into a dark corner lit only by distant street lights and stood face to face at the bottom of an empty pool. Jesus pulled me close to him, and we started to kiss. He was a very soft kisser and very good at it, and I practically melted in his big strong arms as I felt my dick harden like a rocket ready for launch. I rubbed my crotch up against him, feeling for that tell-tale pole in his pants before I pulled away to look around. Jesus and I were completely alone in this huge wide open space.

I wanted him naked, "I will take off all of my clothes if you will take off all of your clothes."

"Here?"

"Yes," I grinned, "right here, right now."

Jesus looked up at the top of the pool and at the lights in the distance. "Okay," he pulled his shirt off.

I unbuckled my belt and stepped out of my pants. Jesus undressed quickly, and I took a step back to get a good look at his big El Salvadoreño uncut Latino cock. Jesus was hung, and I was impressed; his penis was long and thick and lightly brown, wrapped up in foreskin yet rising; ready for pleasure; like an expectant rod of throbbing coital beef. Two giant, man-healthy meatball testicles; perched perfectly and located succulently at the base of this manhood; were clearly held up by two, thick and rapturously muscular thighs. Naked, Jesus was a god; he certainly was endowed like one.

Jesus came over to me naked, and we started to kiss again. We wrapped each other in our arms and held ourselves naked against the breeze of the Holy Land. Jesus moved his lips down my neck and chest, he suckled on my nipples and headed further south, kissing my stomach and belly button. Bending over, he came to my hard erection and looked at my member with wonder.

Jesus said, "This is a nice penis."

"I'm glad you like it." I grabbed the base of my cock, "Now get down on your knees and suck it, Hay-Zeus."

Jesus nodded his head in deference and got down on his knees to suck on my throbbing crankshaft. He went to grasp my penis, but I pushed his hands away. I swirled my cock around in his mouth, fighting him with it. At one point, I yanked my staff from his lips to whack him across the face a couple of times.

"Do you like that cock? Yeah," I said, "suck that cock, Jesus." I slapped him upside the head with my phallus and shoved my guy wire back into his mouth. "Yeah that's right, you suck that cock!"

Jesus clutched my ass and pressed my groin into his face, and my cock filled his mouth. Jesus dabbled his tongue across my hot, hard horn, and when I felt him getting too comfortable with my main brain in his mouth, I'd jerk my penis from between his lips and slap him across the face with it before shoving it back into his mouth again. I latched on to his curly brown hair and forced him to lick the length of my meaty tower and the bulbous-lip of my mushroom head. I pushed his head back on his neck and moved my hips over his face, dropping my nads into his eye sockets and taking a commanding lead as I left him no choice but to lick and swallow my balls. It was hot, and I enjoyed it, but then I pulled off him and turned around suddenly.

"I want Jesus to French kiss my rectum," I held my ass crack open for him and pushed his face into my hole. "Get in there and lick my hole."

Jesus dove right in to my juicy dark penny with licking tongue and kissing lips. He tossed my salad. I pressed my hands against the wall and pushed myself toward him causing his face to go deeper into my ripened derriere.

"You like eating my asshole, don't you Jesus? You like my holy asshole, huh? Does Jesus like my hole, huh? Do you like it, bitch?" I growled in pleasure and groaned, "Yeah ... it feels like Jesus likes licking my hole."

Jesus pulled away for a second, his face dripping with my anal perspiration, "I like it. I love it. I love eating your hole."

"Good," I grabbed his head, pushing his face back into my dark secret. "Gots to give it up to Jesus, he'll eat anything! Jesus Christ, that feels good!" I let him gently tongue-fuck my hole before I turned back around, causing my erection to whack Jesus inadvertently across the face yet again. "Now suck my dick, bitch."

Jesus took my cut cock into his mouth as I leaned against the wall and looked up at the stars in the sky above us. Jesus swathed my pole for twenty minutes; I was barely able to hold back the floodgates of my ejaculation while he twisted his jaw and took painstaking effort to bring me closer to oral-induced climax. I closed my eyes and imagined buttfucking this Latino hard in the ass. I thought I heard something move in the distance, and I opened my eyes quickly. Jesus remained down at heel, with my skin dagger firmly planted in his gaping mouth. I looked up along the top edge of the pool but could see nothing but lights through the trees. I looked around the pool, and standing less than ten feet away, I saw that forty-year-old bearded man from before, staring with wide eyes at us; at this naked Jesus; down on his knees, sucking my cock. I ignored the old man as he took off his shirt, and instead I looked down upon Jesus as he licked my dick.

I clutched at his jaw, stopping Jesus but not pulling my manhood from his throat and I looked into his eyes. "We have to get out of here." I nodded my head toward the old man, who had stripped naked except for shoes and socks, "We have an audience."

My cock popped out of Jesus' mouth, and Jesus said, "I know where we can go."

In quick succession, Jesus and I grabbed all of our clothes and climbed, quickly, out of Mammilla's Pool, leaving behind that forty-year-old man, now masturbating fully. I followed Jesus up and out of the old pool and chased him around construction materials, passing piles of stones, finally coming to the post-midnight shades of an olive tree. Jesus put my clothes next to his on top of a concrete table and smiled at me.

I laughed, "It's been years since I've climbed out of an abandoned land mark and gone running naked through the night!"

Jesus leaned against the concrete slab and started playing with his nuts invitingly. Jesus asked, "Do you want to fuck me? Right here," Jesus slapped the concrete slab beneath him, "right now?"

"You know, I've never fucked a guy named Jesus before. Can we fuck out here without viewer interruption?"

He didn't answer; Jesus just flipped over and brought out a condom and a bottle of lubricant.

"My goodness," I said, "where did all that come from?"

Jesus said, "Be gentle with me. It's been a while since I was on the bottom." Jesus pulled his ass apart, allowing me to see the edge of his dark hole and said, "Just put it on and lube up my hole and fuck me ... hard."

"Ok then," I said as I popped the bottle open, "so much for not wanting an audience." I poured a liberal amount of the cool clear gel onto his ass crack and pushed apart the twin hams of his butt, letting the lube fall directly onto his wanting hole. I massaged his opening only on the surface before I pushed deeper inside him with my index finger.

Jesus groaned and arched his back. "Yes," he cried softly, "I want you to fuck me."

"Patience, Jesus," I said, "Patience, my child."

As I played with his rectal ring, I opened Jesus wider. I opened the condom and unrolled the blue rubber down my shaft. I held his ass open as I pushed my way inside him; his hole welcomed me in and, despite his whimpering groans, I was only encouraged to pump deeper into my Jesus. Once I was all the way in there, I went to town. I pumped his ass full of my hot cock and fucked Jesus wildly. I built up a sweat quickly, and I held the small of his back down with my hands. I bucked and I fucked, and soon Jesus and I developed an organic in-and-out rhythm. His hole fluctuated between tight and loose, depending on the way my pulsating penis stretched away at him.

It took me a good while to cum, my breaths came quicker before I felt the space between my legs warm up with the heat of premature cum.

Jesus, in tandem, started to pant, "Oh yes, oh yes. Oh God yes, fuck me, fuck my hot ass!"

I only had a few lines during all of this, "Yeah? You like my cock shoved up your ass? Does Jesus like my Jew cock up in his ass? Huh, Jesus," I latched on to his torso as I fucked him. I grunted, "Does … Jesus … like … it?"

"God yes!" Jesus squealed, "I love it; I love how you fuck me! Fuck me harder, harder!" As if for dear life, Jesus clutched on to the corners of that concrete slab, holding on to the edges with tension as I fucked him from behind.

I pounded at Jesus with all my might; my thighs slapped his ass violently as I entered him harder and deeper.

"Oh God," he said, "I've never been fucked like this before. Fuck me, fuck me harder! Oh God. Oh God!"

In the reflection of lights coming in through the branches of the olive tree, I saw a bead of sweat rise up out of Jesus' skin and felt the burning spasms of release sprint through every vein of my body.

"Fuck!" I groaned slowly and loudly, perhaps others in the park heard me. "Oh … Jesus … Fuck!"

"Yeah, you like fucking me? You like fucking my ass!"

I could only grunt. "Yeah, I'm gonna' fuckin' come!"

"Come in my ass, yeah!" Jesus said, "Fuck me hard and come with your dick still in my ass!"

I could not hold back my boiling hot seed any longer. I shot my load and felt the condom fill with my jism.

Jesus curved his back and brought his head up to wail at the moonlight. "Ah," he cried out, "I'm gonna' come; I'm gonna' come." Jesus spewed out the cream of his sex, his sperm squirted all over the place, all over the concrete slab. His juice wasn't as thick as mine; it looked more like water; and aside from some initial bursts of ejaculation, in the end only a minimal amount of jizz poured from the slit of the Jesus penis.

I pulled my cock out of Jesus and yanked the spunk-filled condom off my shaft. A tiny white spot of my semen dripped from the condom and landed on the toe of Jesus's shoe, but I said nothing to him about it.

Afterward, we both had to sit side by side, on that concrete slab, to catch our breath. I lit another joint and offered some to Jesus, but Jesus didn't inhale. In the afterglow of having just buttfucked my first Jesus, I smelled a mixture of sweat, condoms and lubricant as the sticky humid stench of Palestine's finest hashish burned together with the smell of cheap Israeli tobacco.

"That," Jesus told me, "was the best fuck I've ever had."

"Ha!" I laughed, "I bet Jesus says that to everyone."

"Where did you learn to fuck like that?"

"Jesus," I exhaled dramatically, "They tell me practice makes perfect."

"Why do you call me 'Jesus'?" Jesus started putting his clothes on, "I told you, my name is Hay-Zeus, not Jesus."

"Well, Jesus," I pulled a shirt over my head and noticed some semen on my fingers; "I just don't know what to say."

Jesus retied a shoe and said, "We should go. They give tickets if they see us here at night like this."

"Where? Here?" I buckled my belt, "Why would they give us a ticket? We can't be in the park at night or something?"

50

"We're not in the park." Jesus said, "Over there, on the other side of the street is the park. This part down here, this isn't the park."

"This isn't the park?" I looked around and saw many concrete slabs, hidden under or behind things, each one covered with weeds. "What the hell is it, then?"

"Don't you know?" Jesus smirked, "This is a cemetery."

I looked around and shook my head slowly, "You're kidding!"

Jesus laughed as he adjusted his brown shirt, "I hope you realize what you've just done."

"You're telling me," I shook my head and sighed. "Do you mean to tell me that I, a nameless Jew from the north, just buttfucked you, a Christian Jesus, on top of this, a dead Muslim's grave, right here in O'Holy Jerusalem?"

"Wild, ain't it?" Jesus zipped up his fly and flashed a devilish grin, "Makes you wonder if my angels are down there telling corpses to roll in their graves."

"Well now Hay-Zeus," I put the joint, which had sparked out by this point, between my lips, "what would you do?" I relit the joint and inhaled

Jesus looked at me suddenly and asked, "What do you mean?"

I rolled my eyes and looked at Jesus.

Jesus was cute.

I smiled at Jesus, "You want a drink before you head back to the seminary?"

RIGHT UP MY ALLEY
By Barry Lowe

He was standing under a street light. That was unusual enough because the street light offered no illumination. It had been repeatedly vandalized, and the glass shattered. This particular street light was at the top of a very short set of cement steps leading to a laneway between two houses and served as a shortcut to the front of a string of inner-city terraces.

I usually cut across the small graffiti-ridden park reclaimed from a number of burnt out homes and down the steps to my front door about half way along the street. It was a shorter walk from the bus stop, and most of us in the street used it for that reason.

Glancing at him, I saw he was dressed in a dark shirt and jeans that blended into the muddy darkness that was spreading over the last rays of dusk. I wouldn't have seen him at all except that he drew on his cigarette as I passed. It illuminated his face. A little younger than my thirty-odd years. Olive skinned. His abbreviated greeting "Nin" just before he puffed his cigarette was undoubtedly to attract my attention. I smiled and responded non-committedly and walked on.

Half-way along the lane, I realized something was not quite right. I turned, and he was still lounging against the wooden telegraph pole. But, the most unusual aspect of the scene was that he had his jeans unzipped, and he was nonchalantly stroking his cock, hard as the pole on which he leaned. It poked invitingly from the fly of his jeans.

Although he didn't glance in my direction, he must have heard that the crunch of my shoes on gravel had ceased. If not that, he must have heard my gasp of surprise. His behavior was not an everyday occurrence even in rampantly gay Surry Hills –

the increasingly gentrified suburb of choice for the upwardly mobile homosexual male. In the early years, I'd found it difficult to persuade sex partners to come to my home, the area was such a slum and had such a rough reputation.

Not anymore. Gay public sex had obviously replaced the razor gangs on the streets. And, I could only applaud the courage of the men who were pioneering the move.

The moment was rife with possibilities, but for a second or two, I cursed that I didn't smoke. I moved as silently as I could to the mouth of the laneway where reflected street light would at least silhouette me. He'd know that I was watching.

But, he gave no indication that he was concerned by my obvious voyeurism or that he had any intention of following me. He also gave no indication that he cared if anyone else should happen upon him, something that was very likely given the circumstances. He would be able to make his escape easily if he was discovered by anyone less inclined to indulge him in his masturbatory exhibitionism.

It was frustrating that he made no attempt to follow, and as I was about six or seven body lengths from him, my view was less than satisfactory. Eventually, I realized that if he had the courage to display his bona fides then the least I could do was meet him half way. I strolled back as if it were the most natural thing in the world to do when confronted by an erect penis on your way home from a hard day at the office.

He flicked the cigarette in my direction, and the sparks skidded along the asphalt coming to a halt near my shoes. I ground the lighted red tip under my heel, and I heard him suck in his breath as he leaned his head back against the pole and closed his eyes. He played with the glistening tip of his cock, as I moved forward. We had observed the niceties of the ritual mating dance, and it had been a hell of a lot more seductive than the usual. "Got a light, mate?" Now it was time to get down to it.

54

He didn't open his eyes as I wrapped my hand round his jutting prick and took over the stroke from him, nor did he when I smeared my thumb and his leaking precum across the sensitive head of his dick. He did, however, when I fell to my knees and engulfed his rod down to his balls. I gagged a little because I'd misjudged the length in the dark.

He dragged me to my feet and whispered, "Not here," as he tucked his cock back in his jeans although he didn't bother to zip up. That was a good sign. I guess he liked me.

"You want to come back to my place?" I said quietly although there was absolutely no need.

He answered in a more normal tone. "You live in that brown terrace just down the street, don't you?"

"Yes," I said wondering if I had a stalker. No matter, for a stalker he was remarkably cute. And endowed. "You want to come back with me?"

"Nah," he said and my visions of sexual gratification began to fade. My alarm must have shown even in the near darkness because he added, "You write that sex column in the local bar rag, don't you?"

"Yeah," I hesitated slightly.

"I've been waiting for you," he said.

I waited.

"I read it every week," he admitted. "It gets me hard. Last week you wrote about living in the area and mentioned that your terrace overlooks a school."

"Yeah, I did. I remember."

"I live in the street on one side of the only school around here, and I knew you didn't live there, so you had to live on this side."

I couldn't fault his skills at deduction, but it sure was killing the mood.

"And?"

55

"I wanted meet you," he said. "We have a lot in common."

"Like what?" I asked.

"Well, your boyfriend for one."

I laughed. It all made sense now. "You've been waiting here every night since the paper came out?"

"Yep," he admitted.

"And you picked up my boyfriend some time over the last couple of nights and went home with him? That's how you know where I live."

"That won't cause a problem will it?"

"Oh, I think I might get some mileage out of it," I smiled.

"I thought you have an open relationship."

"We can go back to my place and have a threesome," I said by way of reply.

"Nah. I want you to myself tonight."

"Where do you want to do it?" I asked.

"So you don't mind it in the open air?" he said.

"You're talking to the man who spent forty minutes sucking a guy off in the middle of the cricket pitch in the park last New Year's Eve."

"That's only exciting if the lights were on," he smiled.

"They were," I said.

"Great. In that case I know just the place."

He took off down the laneway and along my street.

"That's your place, isn't it?" he said as we passed it.

"Uh huh."

He walked to the paved area blocking access to the adjoining freeway constructed by a local council intent of greening the area by installing bricks and a rotting timber frame, which barely supported gnarled leafless vines like outsized varicose veins. In the shadows were a number of splintery benches that I thought he intended using. But no, he detoured down a short laneway that led to the garages at the back of half a dozen houses. Roughly nailed sheets of corrugated iron piggy backed fence posts.

The laneway itself was asphalt pimpled with weeds, oil smears and broken glass. He stood with his back to a sturdy looking post and lit a cigarette. He unbuckled his belt as a sign for me to drop to my knees. I pulled his jeans down to his ankles, and his cock was already hard.

I looked up at him, "The fact we'll probably be caught excites you, does it?"

We were locked in a dead-end should anyone appear at the mouth of the street. More importantly, cars would pick us out in their headlights. There'd be no scaling these fences without the likelihood of slicing off fingers or other extremities on the sharp edges of the iron.

At least here in the open air there were stars between the camphor laurel leaves on the tree jutting out from the school playground. Too high, however, to serve as an escape route. And, the air was fresh not the odiferous combination of stale piss and shit mingling with the disinfectant of urinal cakes in which I'd spent my formative years of public toilet sex. The setting was romantic as well as provocatively dangerous.

I played with his balls as I ran my tongue round his greasy slit sucking up any escaping juice. My tongue was a slimy pillow track as he slid his cock into my mouth. I gagged when it hit the back of my throat.

"Good boy," he said. "Take all of it!"

He smoked and offered the occasional groan of encouragement, sometimes grabbing the back of my head and fucking savagely for a moment until I choked, and my mouth filled with gag.

He flicked his cigarette away and told me to stand up and take off my trousers.

"Right off!"

He pushed me against the fence and spread my legs. His cock was slick from my gag juices, and he augmented it with his spit. His finger at my ass entrance slipped in easily although his cock was considerably bigger, and it took a few more gobs of spit for lubrication before it slid in comfortably.

He picked up the pace, shoving his cock harder, slamming his balls against mine, and each time he slammed into me, he pushed my head against the corrugated iron, which squeaked and creaked in opposition. In the quiet evening, the sound was like a call to arms.

I heard a window fly open, and light shone from a second floor window.

"What's going on out there?" someone yelled.

He didn't pause in his stroke into or out of my asshole. He grasped my drooling cock and began to jerk me in time to his thrusts. The sounds of our fucking carried and set dogs barking in the neighboring street. Backyard security lights clicked on like truss lighting on a stage.

His excitement increased with each new sound of activity around us as if he sought an audience to validate his performance. The realization that I was abetting him and on the receiving end of that performance did nothing to lessen its erotic impact. It heightened it.

Someone threw an old boot at us from an upstairs window. "You faggots are worse than alley cats!"

"It's all right, Jim. I've called the cops," a woman's voice said.

And, there was the annoying mosquito-like screech of a siren off in the distance. He picked up the pace. I was close now, and my sphincter was pincering his cock every time it rammed its way in. His breath was shorter and sharper, and my head was slamming into the iron fence with such force, I thought it would give way. He gave a howl of triumph, and I felt the contractions of his cock as he shot up my ass triggering my own ejaculation.

He slapped me on the ass. "That was great, thanks," he said and was gone.

I grabbed my trousers and bolted down the street and in the front door as I heard a siren now only a few streets away.

Wally, my boyfriend, came to investigate and found me standing in the hallway puffing holding my pants while my now limp dick oozed the cum I hadn't had time to clean off.

"Oh, so you met Paul then?" Wally said.

"We didn't get round to introducing ourselves," I gasped as I grabbed a handful of tissues.

"Why didn't you bring him home?"

"Because you'd already had him," I said. "And, in the comfort of your own home."

"Yeah," Wally said. "He didn't like it much. He prefers it in the open."

"So I discovered."

"He leaves the door of his terrace open and sits just inside naked playing with himself."

"Does it work?" I asked as Wally began to remove his clothes.

"Seems it does. Most of the guys in this street have had him. You must have been the last."

Wally inserted two fingers into my butt.

"Hold on a second," I said as I took off my shirt and tie.

59

AFTER SUNSET
By Amanda Young

Toby sauntered into the park and headed for the wooded area toward the back. Nervous sweat matted a white tank top to his back and sides, making the thin material stick to his skin like a lover's greedy hands. The full moon peeked from between gauzy clouds, staring down at him like a randy voyeur. It was going to be a damn good night. He could feel it in his bones.

Following along the paved trail, he ignored the deserted swing sets and slides and continued on, keeping an eye out for all the things that went bump in the night. He wasn't above a little vicarious voyeurism himself.

Up ahead and a little to his right loomed a white cement building that housed the public restrooms; a picturesque reminder of all the fucks and sucks he'd swindled during days gone by. Although he knew he could score some easy ass within those four walls, a sloppy blow at the very least, he'd grown a little choosier about his partners these days.

"Psst. Hey, mister. Over here, mister."

A grin spread across Toby's face as he slowed to a stop and looked around. He knew that voice. It was the one he'd been waiting for. Anticipation sped his pulse and fed a steady supply of blood to the cock rapidly hardening against the inside of his fly. He sped up his pace as he reached down and adjust himself to keep his zipper from biting into his dick. Free-balling could be a pain when he was trapped inside the snug denim, but it saved crucial seconds when time was of the essence. There wasn't time to dill-dally with underwear when you were fucking around in public.

Toby kept to the path, though it grew dimmer with every step. The voice had sounded as if it were coming from up ahead, instead of in the bordering trees. He rounded a bend in the walkway, traveling beyond the reach of the illumination behind him.

A hand shot out of the murky darkness. Rough fingers latched onto Toby's forearm and clamped down around his flesh. He jumped, but quickly masked his surprise behind a casual mien of indifference, allowing himself be tugged off the path and into the wooded area beyond. With every step, adrenaline spiked his blood and made his heart race in both excitement and a touch of apprehension. The same rush of mixed emotions always bombarded him when he came out on night's like this – which was probably why he kept doing it. There was nothing like those first few seconds of uncertain possibilities to get his dick hard and his pulse thundering. He fucking loved it.

A stray beam of moonlight revealed a quick peek at the man in front of him. Loose golden curls topped the head of a man several inches shorter than Toby's own six feet, three inches. Although the guy appeared slim in the black T-shirt and jeans he wore, his forearms were corded with sinew and hinted at the muscle beneath the clothing. The brief glimpse of a bulge beneath the man's fly made Toby's mouth water for a taste. He wasn't too proud to drop to his knees in the dirt and blow the man's mind right out of the top of his head, if given the chance. It wasn't as if it would be the first time.

He wasn't offered an option as he was dragged behind a tall oak tree and shoved back against the rough bark. The man crowded up against Toby, using his weight to pin Toby between a firm, hard body and the immovable tree.

"Jesus …" Toby said, wiggling against the stiff bark. "You would have scared the piss out of me if I hadn't gotten your message to meet you here after sunset."

The distance between them closed as the shorter man stretched upward, his mouth centimeters away from Toby's. "It's about damn time you got here, lover. I was starting to think you would chicken out."

"Who me?" Toby grinned in the darkness. "I'm sorry I'm late, baby, traffic was hell."

"You can make it up to me." The scent of peppermint floated on Billy's breath as he pressed his lips to Toby's in a quick, smacking kiss and then pulled away. "Now show me your cock."

"Yes, Sir," Toby said, unfastening his pants. He separated the denim flaps and pulled his cock out, the night air caressing his sultry flesh.

Billy stepped between the tree and Toby, braced his back against the trunk and kneeled. He gripped Toby's hips, his fingers digging into Toby's flesh, and leaned forward to rub his cheek against Toby's cock. Prickly stubble abraded Toby's shaft, up one side and down the other.

Toby shivered and palmed Billy's scalp, carding his fingers through the silk of his lover's hair. "Come on, Billy. Quit teasing. Suck me before someone comes through here."

"Calm down. Everything's going to be all right. Besides, I have a surprise for you."

"Oh, yeah? Well, let's see it."

Billy nuzzled Toby's crotch, and flicked his tongue over the fat, leaking crown of Toby's cock. Warm, wet heat bathed the tip and then the slick edge of a tongue prodded the slit and the tender depression beneath. Billy's fist wrapped around the base of Toby's cock and squeezed as he worked his mouth down the thick shaft.

"Oh, hell yeah. That's it, baby ... swallow it all." Toby's eye fell closed, a riot of pleasurable sensations coursing through his body. Unaided and forgotten, his jeans slid down his ass and puddled around his ankles. Billy's free hand snuck between

Toby's thighs and cupped his balls, rolling them in the palm of his hand. After years of being together, Billy knew just the right places to apply pressure, the most sensitive spots to lick.

Toby dragged air infused with earth and pine needles into his lungs and tried not to come right away. It was damn hard when just being outside, where anyone could catch Billy sucking him off, turned him on like nothing else. After five years together, they'd only recently begun exploring their shared kink of exhibitionism. Since they were both geared toward being more turned on by the risk of being viewed, rather than the act of being watched itself, their trysts were both varied and perpetually hurried.

They were also hot enough to keep them both fucking like bunnies between encounters.

The sounds of leaves crunching warned Toby of someone approaching long before he felt the presence of another behind him. A glance over his shoulder revealed the bulky outline of a man standing a few feet away. He tightened his hands on Billy's head, trying to gain his lover's attention without calling awareness to his actions. Whoever the man was, he obviously wasn't the law or he would have said something by now. However, that didn't mean he wasn't some freak who was going to roll them for being gay and fornicating in the woods.

"Psst ... Billy ... there's a guy behind us ..."

If anything, Billy sucked harder in response to Toby's warning. What the hell? Was this what Billy was talking about when he'd said he had a surprise in store for Toby? They'd talked about having a three-way but hadn't decided anything concrete about it.

If Billy had taken it upon himself to arrange a threesome, he sure as hell wasn't going to complain. He loved the idea of being spit-roasted between Billy's sucking mouth and a long, fat cock in his ass. Being outside when it went down made the whole thing feel more sordid and pushed his kinks into the stratosphere.

Although he wondered who the man was and hoped Billy hadn't chosen someone they were close friends with, Toby decided to just roll with the flow. Far be it from him to turn down a once in a lifetime opportunity.

The third man approached from behind and sidled up close against Toby's back. A shiver raced down Toby's spine in spite of the heat at his backside. He pushed his ass back toward the man as hard hands gripped his hips. The crinkle of a foil wrapper being torn open broke the silence. The man behind him cleared his throat and spit. Cool liquid splattered Toby's ass and slid down his crease.

Toby resisted turning to glance back over his shoulder. Part of the fun lay in the suspense of not knowing what was happening – or with whom.

A blunt object ran through his crack. "Tell me you want it …" a deep voice whispered into Toby's ear "… and I'll give you every hard, fat inch."

Billy looked up, his mouth stretched wide around Toby's dick. He blinked twice – their signal for yes, when either of their mouths were occupied by phallus or gag – and bowed his head to resume sucking on Toby's dick.

What the hell, Toby thought, *I'm only going to live once.* "Do it. Fuck me."

Billy groaned around Toby's cock, his mouth vibrating around Toby's shaft. He then sucked faster, bobbing his head up and down in rhythm with the tight fist pumping Toby's shaft.

The meaty fingers biting into Toby's hips tightened almost to the point of pain, and the blunt pressure against Toby's hole increased. He gritted his teeth, knowing the initial sting of penetration was going to burn like hell. It'd been ages since he was on the receiving end of a cock, since Billy wasn't interested in topping.

One thick inch after another infiltrated his ass, stretching the taut ring of muscle guarding his entrance until it burned. He inhaled, one deep breath after another, as more and more cock filled his ass. Pubes brushed against his tender hole, and Toby let out breath of relief. He'd begun to wonder just how big the other man's cock was; the damn thing felt huge.

A heartbeat past, his body slowly accommodating to the monster lodged in his ass. Before he could get completely adjusted, the man behind him began to withdraw. He only pulled out partway before shoving home with more force than earlier, rocking Toby forward into Billy.

Billy let go of Toby's balls and gripped his thigh for balance, never stalling in his attention to Toby's cock. He kept moving, licking and sucking, his hand pumping up and down Toby's shaft.

The man fucking Toby's ass picked up his pace, lunging in and out with long, deep strokes that pinged Toby's sweet spot and made him grit his teeth against the tingling in his balls. Every stroke propelled Toby forward, his dick sliding through Billy's sweet lips time and again.

They'd barely gotten started, but Toby was already hanging right on the edge of release, so close he could almost feel the lightning racing up and down his spine. His taint tingled; his sac pulled taut against his groin preparation for lift off. "Oh, fuck … gonna come … can't hold it."

The contractions hit him strong and fast, each one coming on the tail of the one below, making him shiver and shake. Billy's lips gentled, took every drop Toby had to give and then searched for more. His ass clenched around the dick buried inside him, holding on tight as he finished unloading.

The man fucking Toby cursed and shoved in deep, grinding himself against Toby's ass. "Fuck, yes. Coming right up your ass, slut."

Toby's back stiffened at the slur. Below him, Billy moaned and released Toby's cock. Toby bent forward, dislodging the cock from his ass, and cupped his lover's cheeks. He kissed

Billy, while the younger man jacked himself to completion all over the leave-strewn ground. Billy whimpered into Toby's mouth, his tongue lazily dueling with Toby's as he finished shooting.

Toby dragged himself away from Billy's mouth and straightened. He turned to thank the man who'd fucked him, and found only trees behind him. He glanced at Billy as his lover struggled to his feet. "Who was that guy?"

Bill burst out laughing. "Christ, Toby, I don't know who he was. I thought you set that up."

"No, I …" Toby snapped his mouth shut and stared at his lover, at a loss for words.

"Fuck." Billy grabbed Toby's hand and gave it a tug. "Come on. Let's get the hell out of here."

Hand in hand, they hurried out of the woods and back down the path to safety. They didn't stop until they were inside Toby's car.

By the time he had the car started and the heater running, Toby had time to find the humor in the situation. He couldn't believe he'd just let some stranger fuck him, but he had to admit it was hot. He'd come like gangbusters. He glanced at Billy across the console; his lover's face tinged green from the light shining on him from the dash. "I cannot believe we just did that."

Billy shook his head and grinned. "Just wait until you find out what I have planned for next Saturday."

RAUNCHY SURPRISE IN THE REST ROOM
By Jay Starre

Why did we hook up like we did? Why didn't we take it further, exchanging phone numbers, actually going back to each other's places? I'm not sure what his reasons were. Or even my own. But that's the way it was. And, since I got what I wanted, I really can't complain. Not really.

A new high rise was being built next to my office building that winter, and every day as I went to work I'd check out the hot construction workers. I wasted hours on the job fantasizing about their big arms and chests – and their hard cocks. One rainy evening, I found myself working very late, mostly due to my constant daydreaming. That's why I ended up in the underground rest room of my building at nine o'clock at night.

I didn't expect to see anyone that late. I'd just finished taking a leak and turned around when I literally bumped into him.

"Sorry, dude. I hope I didn't get your suit dirty."

I was face to face with one of the objects of my desire. His lemon-yellow hard hat was askew over blond hair above a square-jawed face. A grizzled blond fuzz coated his cheeks while soft blue eyes stared out at me from equally blond brows. His face was sweaty and grimed. He wore a T-shirt and work vest that stretched over taut pecs.

He practically exuded sweaty, sexual power. He looked only about twenty-two, five or so years younger than I then. The boiling combination of raw sexuality and youthfulness I found very exciting. Very exciting.

Our eyes met for a breathless moment while I inhaled his work reek, and he inhaled my cologne. I didn't move away, not an inch. I'm sure that must have told him all he needed to know.

Suddenly, he smiled. A big hand thrust forward to clutch at my crotch, squeezing my cock and balls right through my slacks. "Interested in a little action? My name's Joey, if it matters." He grinned in my face, his hot breath in my nostrils.

His hand massaged my cock, which began stiffening the moment he'd bumped into me. That rising boner was a dead give-away.

"I'm Jay. Why don't you suck my cock before you fuck me up the ass," I blurted out in a trembling voice.

For a terrifying moment, I regretted blabbing my desires so blatantly. Joey, the muscular construction worker who was a total stranger, was in fact smiling. But, he could have been a roughneck intent on robbing me after he fucked me. I had no idea. Yet, my stiff cock lurched under my slacks with his fingers around it. Fear turned to exhilaration.

Fuck it! I wanted Joey.

Whatever Joey thought, his grin remained in place until his mouth drove forward to smother mine with a sloppy kiss. Fat tongue slid between my gaping lips while his hand stroked my hard-on through my slacks.

I groaned deep in my throat as my own hands groped the hard-hat's substantial body. He was solid! A broad back led down to an ass that was rounded and rock-hard. I pulled him close by those firm mounds, grinding my crotch into his. His big shank pressed into my stomach. I fantasized that throbbing thing probing deep into my asshole.

He broke away. The blond construction worker leered in my face. "You're a hot fucker for an office worker! Your body is as tight as a drum. Is your asshole that tight?"

I glanced around quickly before answering. No one was in sight, but I wanted at least a little more privacy. "Why don't you find out?" I hissed as I dragged him by the arm into one of the stalls.

He chuckled behind me, one beefy palm cupping my butt-cheek. I shivered at the touch, my cock lurching and my stomach churning. I was as horny as hell from weeks of hard-hat watching and definitely ready for action. Besides, Joey wasn't only beefy and sexy, he was actually cute, too. My momentary fear seemed stupid as I heard his light laughter behind me. He was twice as broad as me, sweaty and dirty. But that didn't make him a criminal. Just sexy as hell, and god, how I wanted him.

"I wanna suck your cock first. I've got condoms. Why don't you get it out," Joey suggested gruffly.

We crowded into the stall with the reek of public washroom all around us. Joey was on his knees in front of me and ripping at my fly before I knew it. He was really going to suck my cock, right then and there! What an awesome turn-on. This was the first time I'd dared anything so public, even though I'd thought of it whenever I ran into a hottie in a public rest room.

I stared down at him, his broad shoulders practically filling the stall. His hard-hat had been turned backwards so the rim wasn't in the way, a splash of vivid yellow in the drab washroom. Then my pants were down around my ankles and the stubble of his unshaven face pressed against my thighs.

I gasped loudly at the feel of that rough flesh, but then groaned even more loudly as he began to play with my cock. I thrust it in his face as he grinned up at me and winked.

"Don't be so pushy. I'm wrapping the fucker first. Then I'll swallow it down to the balls," he chuckled.

Although he was grinning, the look in his eyes was absolutely intense. I shivered as he rolled the rubber over my boner, his fingers sending a rush of sensation up into my stomach and chest. I was already panting.

His lips surrounded my cock-tip. "Fuck! Fuck yeah! Suck that big shank," I hissed. I didn't usually talk like that, but something about the setting, and the roughneck dirty from work on his knees with my cock in his mouth had uncorked my secret nastiness. What would I say or do next? I had no idea!

My hands went down to grasp his huge shoulders and steady myself, just as his hands went around my waist and grasped my naked ass-cheeks. He gripped my butt and shoved my hips forward, impaling his wet mouth with my cock. I shook all over as his tongue lapped my cock-head and his lips sucked all over it. He sucked me deep as he'd promised, his cheeks vacuuming my entire meat into his mouth. I stared at his incongruously pretty lips as they slurped wetly over my disappearing shaft.

What a steamy sight!

With that wet warmth surrounding my cock, I actually drooled as my mouth hung wide open. Relaxing into the sweet suck, I unconsciously spread my legs and squatted a little against Joey's beefy hands on my butt. That's when his fingers moved into the crack of my ass. I gasped as fingers probed up and down the hairless crevice until they were aggressively poking at my ass slot.

"Oh gawd! What are you doing to me?" I bleated.

Two big fingers rubbed my tender ass-lips while others stretched them apart. He was working on my hole with both hands! The itchy, ticklish stirring had me wriggling in confused circles. I wanted to shove my cock into Joey's sucking mouth, but I also wanted to shove my ass back over his rudely probing digits.

He had me so excited I would have done anything he wanted.

He spit my cock out of his mouth with a wet slurp. "Got any lube?" he asked as he looked up at me and winked.

Lube? Fuck! I wanted those fingers up my ass, and his cock, too. But I didn't have anything to grease the way. "No," I muttered forlornly.

"Don't worry. I got some of that, too. Enough to make a slippery ride for my bone up your butt," he laughed as he abandoned my ass to reach into his pocket and produce a small tube of butt lube.

He was prepared. Maybe he did this often. I flushed as I imagined him preying on other office workers, pushing them into filthy stalls and fucking them breathless. Perhaps, I was just one more of his conquests, a hungry slut to be used by the horny laborer. The thought lingered as I felt him squirting lube into my ass-crack and then immediately rubbing it all over my pouting butt-hole.

I gasped and bent over slightly, instinctively spreading my feet even farther apart. That opened up my hole, and Joey slid one finger into it. The stuffed thrill sent shivers up and down my spine. I squirmed as he twisted his finger around and then poked it deeper.

He crammed his face into my crotch and swallowed up my cock again, knocking his hard-hat to the floor as he did. I moaned like a bitch in heat as I felt pleasure overwhelm my body from both the front and back. He rammed his finger in and out of my greased asshole as he bobbed up and down over my cock.

Joey's sweat-plastered hair was almost as bright yellow as his hard-hat. I moved my hands from his shoulders to his head, twisting the short curls in my fingers as I fucked his mouth with frantic thrusts. I was on fire. My butt-hole expanded under Joey's finger-fuck as he twisted and probed relentlessly. My cock was so hard it seemed entirely possible it would explode.

The blond laborer abruptly changed course. Pulling his mouth off my stabbing boner, he reared back and rose to his feet all in one move. I stumbled backwards, but his hands were still on my ass, and he prevented me from falling. Face to face, his eyes shone, and his pink lips were wet with drool. He licked them lasciviously, half sneering, as he pulled me to him with his hands on my butt. He kissed me, wetly, as one of his fingers continued to probe deep into my greased asshole.

His big body pressed against mine. His fat tongue filled my mouth. His work stench filled my nostrils along with the rank odor of public washroom. I was limp in his arms, my feet as wide apart as possible with my pants around my ankles. My cock rubbed against his rough jeans.

Joey broke the kiss and whispered huskily in my face. "Time to fuck your sweet ass."

I was in total agreement. I was almost frantic as I tore at his jeans to open them up. He grinned as he released my butt with one hand while still probing my aching anus with the other. He dug in his back pocket and pulled out another condom just as I managed to get his pants open. I fished his big rocket out of his underwear, snorting greedily as I took in the enormous size of the fucker.

"Put a condom on it, Jay. And lube the big fucker so it doesn't hurt when it slides up your tight ass."

I appreciated his concern. "This thing is massive," I muttered as I followed his suggestion.

He handed me the condom and the tube of grease and held me close with one hand still buried up my ass-crack. While I wrapped his purple pole and then squirted clear lube over it, he dug a second finger up into my asshole, sending shudders up and down my body. I used both hands to rub the lube all over his cock. As his fingers worked around in my ass pit, I stroked and massaged his tool. It only seemed to get bigger, if that was possible. Huge, erect and swollen with blood, it was stiff as steel.

I groaned. "Fuck me with this fat monster!"

"Turn around and bend over."

I released the giant meat reluctantly as he turned me with his fingers still planted way up my butt. I shivered again as I bent over, feeling those fingers thrust deeper, banging my prostate with aching force.

"What an ass! White, tight and smooth ... ummmmmm yeah ... my cock is gonna look damned good buried between these sweet mounds."

He wiggled his fingers around before yanking them out. I grunted, my butt-lips pouting outwards as they followed those digits on their exit. I shook like crazy, my own cock bobbing and drooling into the condom that still wrapped it. I felt Joey's hands grip my butt-cheeks and pull them apart.

My crack was wide open.

"Here it comes ... fuck yeah ... nice and slippery for your greased hole," he muttered.

I felt the blunt head rub up and down my crack. My head swam. His calloused hands gripped my ass, and that thick pole rubbed all over my vulnerable butt crevice.

It was coming! He was going to fuck me with that huge thing!

"Ready, Jay?"

I groaned loudly. "Stuff it up there! I want your fucking cock!"

Hopefully we were still alone! I hadn't heard anyone enter, which was unlikely this late at night anyway, but I hadn't really been paying attention to anything but Joey and his steamy cock and big hands and nasty grin. For a moment, I strained to listen for sounds of anyone else in the rest room, but couldn't hold the thought as cock-head suddenly centered on my throbbing slot.

It seemed as big as a ripe plum! But it was well-lubed and so was my asshole. I willed my sphincter to relax, just as Joey pressed forward. I gasped at the moment of truth. My butt-lips stretched, wider and wider. The monster cock-head pushed steadily. I felt him filling me with it.

"Oh god ... oh god ... oh god ..." I hissed like a broken record.

It was suddenly inside, my asshole swallowing the entire head and more. I sighed and licked my lips as Joey pushed deeper, and the tension in my stretched butt entrance released. Cock was filling me! I shuddered and shoved backwards, impaling myself on a good three inches of steamy shank.

"That's hot ... yeah man ... fuck yourself up the ass ... with my big ... goddamned meat!"

I imagined what I looked like. Dangling over the toilet, my slacks and boxers around my ankles, my coat and dress shirt pulled up past my waist and my ass bare. A big cock was sliding past my puckered butt-lips. And, I was taking it, half stuffed with the gigantic thing already!

That nasty image served to open me up. He thrust as I bucked backwards. We both cried out as another four inches of cock slid into my guts. Then he took over. His hands came up to my back, and he shoved my clothing toward my shoulders. His hands groped me all over, sliding around to explore my torso, from my aching cock to my tight nipples. He fucked my ass with his steel pipe-dick while he groped me with his rough hands.

Deep thrusts tortured my aching butt-hole. The pleasurable pain was constant as he buried his pole to the hilt, his hairy ball-sack banging against my hairless ass-cheeks. Thrust and withdraw, shove and pull out, harder and faster. My steady groans were echoed by his.

His hands were as relentless as his cock. He pumped my stiff tool and tweaked my nipples. I could hardly breathe with my clothes around my shoulders and head. I could only think of my asshole and that giant salami massaging and reaming it.

He began pumping my cock in time to his steady ass-fucking. The ache in my prostate intensified. My entire body flamed into a pre-orgasmic heat. I blubbered incoherently, riding his driving shank faster and faster.

"I'm blowing," I finally blurted out.

It was a sudden torrent. Jizz sprayed into the condom over my cock, filling it with sticky juice. My asshole clamped and convulsed over his ramming boner. Every thrust teased another squirt of jizz from my churning balls. I rode that hard fuck to the very end.

"Sweet ... you are one hot and raunchy fuck ... dude," Joey whispered huskily through his gasps as he slid his cock from my battered butt.

I rose on shaky feet and turned to face him. He had the cutest grin.

He also had a very stiff dick. He rubbed the big pole with one clamping fist as he gazed into my eyes.

I understood. "Want that satisfied?"

"Sure. You can jerk me off while you stick a finger up my butt. I like my hole massaged, too," he suggested with a nasty smirk.

We both laughed, but knew he was serious. I'd copped a feel of his solid butt earlier, and I definitely wanted more. With my pants around my ankles I stepped forward, pushing him against the door of the stall. I reached around behind him. He grinned in my face as he helped me pull his jeans and underwear down to his knees. My breathing had barely returned to normal as I slid my hands over the naked expanse of his hefty butt. I began to breath quicker again as I got a good feel of all that ass under my fingers. Big, solid, blond fuzz on the cheeks. So nice!

"Lube a finger and stick it up my ass," he huffed in my ear.

He was getting pretty steamed up again with my hands on his ass. He thrust his hips and crotch against mine as he leaned his shoulders against the stall door, his ass grinding around in my palms. He managed to pull out the lube from his vest pocket with a shaky hand, and I managed to remove a hand from his beefy butt to offer it up for lubing.

He squirted it all over my fingers. I slid my hand back around to his butt and immediately crammed them up into his deep ass crevice. Heated flesh parted for my hand. I found his asshole, crinkled and hairless.

Joey moaned in my face. "Oh yeah ... uhh huh ... yank on my boner ... like that ... while you work a finger or two up there!"

Pinning him against the stall door, I used one hand to stroke his lengthy rod, lubing it as well. A pair of hairy nads hung down at the base of the big bone, swaying back and forth as he wriggled sexily between my hands. I explored his crack with my slick fingers while I pumped his cock. He shivered as my fingers grazed and tickled his tight ass-lips. He gasped out loud when I settled on the hole and began to tease it open.

"You like that? You like a finger tickling your tight little hole?" I said as I breathed heavily in his face. I surprised myself once more at how raunchy I'd become. And, how natural it felt.

Joey lunged forward, clamping his lips over mine and sucking my tongue into his mouth with a mewling sigh. I took that as the signal I needed. I crammed a finger deep into his snug asshole. Butt-lips quivered around my finger. Cock leaped and tightened under my flailing hand. He pressed his stocky body against mine, and his hands came down to cup my ass.

He squeezed my butt while I fingered his. Lube eased the way as I frigged in and out, and he wiggled his ass around my finger. My own asshole quivered in sympathy as I twisted that finger all around inside his throbbing pit. I pumped his cock up and down with swift strokes, feeling it turn to satin steel. I knew he was close.

One of his groping paws moved into my crack and two fingers suddenly drove deep into my asshole. I grunted and wiggled around the intrusion. My asshole was relaxed, but my prostate still ached from the recent fuck it had taken. Those blunt fingertips banging it had my cock rising up again. I wormed a second finger up Joey's tight hole.

"Oh fuck ... oh fuck! I'm shooting!" he cried out as his lips released mine.

I pulled the condom off his cock just as he began to detonate. A geyser of warm goo splattered out onto my coat and dress shirt. My fingers probed far up his ass as his fuck tunnel convulsed. My own asshole was on fire as he thrust into it with his fingers.

A sudden heat rocketed out from my prostate. My balls churned and my cock spurted its second load, taking me totally by surprise.

We were both coming simultaneously.

Joey planted his unusually pretty lips on mine again and wrapped his arms around me in a fierce embrace. Our fingers remained up each other's asses as our cocks drained. I melted into his bulk, feeling totally satiated.

When our passion finally burned itself out, we broke away and grinned at each other. I was surprised when he proposed we meet again in the same spot the next night. I happily agreed, and it became a regular occurrence that winter. He fucked my ass good, and I fingered his. It was actually sad when the building was shiny and completed.

"Catch you later, dude," were his final words to me as he walked out of that rest room for the final time as winter turned to spring, and we both knew it was over.

I could have asked him for his number. I could have set up a date, or asked him to call me. But I didn't. It was best that way, I thought. A no-strings, casual, fuck-fest. No annoying phone calls, no unanswered messages, no waiting for a call that never came.

He'd never stood me up, always satisfied me, and we'd never been caught. All in all, what could I complain about?

I did miss that sweet smile though. A lot.

NAKED ON THE BEACH
By Jay Starre

I hadn't been to Wreck Beach yet this season. An unusually cold spring delayed my first foray to the nude beach until nearly the end of May. A glorious morning unfolded below as I jaunted down steep stairs. Forest-clad cliffs protected the isolated beach from the prying eyes of the public above.

Blue sky sparkled over gentle waves and an expanse of sandy beach. Hundreds of naked men and women dotted the sands, from all walks of life and in all shapes and sizes. A gay section occupied the northern end of the strand, but I was headed that day for the wooded trails and quieter beaches even farther north.

As I reached the sands, I found a convenient log and stripped off right away. This was the erotic foreplay to the day, getting naked in the open sunshine with a big smile on my face. Then, bare butt exposed, balls and dick bouncing, I slung my pack over one shoulder and headed off into the trails.

Almost everyone who braved the narrow wooded paths was gay. And, most were as naked as I. The anticipation mounted as I hiked along the forested trail with my naked ass bare to anyone following, my dick swaying for anyone approaching. Of course, we eyed each other as we passed, every dude checking out my lengthy dick and plump balls, and almost always staring at my muscular chest and taut nipples.

I was half-hard as I traipsed my way toward one of the secluded openings ahead, recalling their locations from previous seasons of beach bumming. The vigorous growth of the forest altered everything from year to year, though, so it was like exploring a new place all over again.

Some landmarks led me on, an enormous fir rearing high above, a copper-bright birch leaning precariously over the path, and the hidden side trails that sprouted off toward the water. I passed a few hot guys as I searched, turning around once to check out a hefty white butt and seeing the same dude turning to check me out. We both grinned as I continued on. Maybe we would meet up later, the possibilities sending a tingle through my swinging cock and a throb of excitement into my bared butt-hole.

Veering off on a narrow path that opened up into a clearing on the edge of the water, I was lucky enough to find one of my favorite spots free. A huge drift log, which had found its way to the clearing years ago and lay stranded, offered me the perfect sunbathing perch.

After draping a towel over the log, I draped myself over that, naked and spread-eagled. I sighed with pleasure, the warm sun heating up my back and butt and thighs while a pleasant sea breeze wafted over me.

This was my preferred position; bare white butt exposed, crack wide open with my thighs dangling down on either side of the log. I could feel both the sunshine and the breeze on my puckered asshole.

Now the wait.

There were basically two paths that led men to my lounging spot. There was the side trail I'd followed, where others might meander down to check out whatever lay in wait, and the wooded shore line with a rougher track the adventurous sorts took advantage of.

My naked position sprawled over that log was comfy and relaxing. The exposed, and nasty, vulnerability I offered got my dick hard under my belly against the towel and log, while my asshole throbbed with anticipation.

I had no idea who would show up, or what would happen – adding another dimension to the morning's thrill.

The bay itself was actually a huge logging boom with decks of floating logs awaiting their journey to the saw mills upstream. Rarely did any boat come along, so there was privacy in that direction. The woods hid me from passersby. It was only those who dared to venture off the beaten path who would discover me, naked, draped over a log, and horny as hell.

After a few pleasant minutes of merely soaking up the sun, I prepared myself for visitors.

I got out my small tub of grease and scooped out a few fingers-full. Reaching back, I found my hole and slowly shoved a pair of fingers deep. That felt awesome, my hole opening up and ready for action. Relaxed from the golden sun, my sphincter bloomed apart for two probing digits. I anticipated plenty of action back there before the day was through!

I left the grease coating the pink ass-lips and smeared some along my crack, a blatant invitation not to be missed by anyone bold enough to take a look.

Barely had I pulled out my greased fingers before my first caller arrived. I spied him approaching from the south, naked and carrying his pack, picking his way through the jumble of logs along the shore. Coming right toward me.

I closed my eyes and lay there, sighing with pleasure. Let him take a look! I could hear him coming as his boots tramped over the logs and a few tree branches rustled nearby.

I knew he was there, sensing it as the woods grew very quiet. This was the moment of suspense – and extreme anticipation. I lazily rolled my hips and raised my husky white ass slightly off the log, humping the air suggestively.

There was an intake of breath very close by. I heard boots stepping up to the log behind me. He was right there, obviously staring down at my naked ass – and greased hole and crack.

I rolled my hips again, pulling up my knees a bit so that my crack was even wider apart. I willed my asshole to pout outwards, a dribble of grease oozing out.

Cruising for Bad Boys

If that didn't turn him on, what could I do? I held my breath as I heard the tell-tale hawk of spit, and then some wet rubbing going on just behind me.

The dude was standing over my bared ass and jerking off! Hot!

I'd checked out his dick earlier when he first approached, a thick tool hanging down between firm thighs. I recalled he was tall and lean and had a baseball cap turned backwards above bright blue eyes. He'd been naked as me, wearing only muddy boots.

I kept my eyes closed and slowly writhed over the log, showing off my smooth white butt as it grew pink from the morning sunshine. My greased hole twitched and oozed.

He breathed heavily, gasping every time I raised my butt and wriggled it. I could hear the slap of his fingers up and down his cock. I imagined the fat tool stiff and throbbing. I imagined his blue eyes riveted to the sight of my spread ass.

He groaned loudly, and then I felt a rain of cum splatter my thighs. He was coming on me! I found that so hot I almost blew a load myself, but held back in anticipation of more steamy action to come during the long day ahead.

His boots moved away. I grinned and relaxed into my sprawled position, soaking up the sun and feeling my ass grow nicely pink. I was already tan everywhere else from afternoons in the park, but that smooth, hairless butt of mine had been lily-white, until now.

It wasn't long at all before my second guest approached, this time from the opposite direction. Facing north, I couldn't see who came from the south along the shore. I could have turned and checked out the rustle of shrubbery and the light tread of boots. Instead, this time I chose to lie still and stare quietly at the lapping waves and sparkling lights playing over the bay.

The boots stepped up to the massive log I sprawled over, coming closer and then halting. My breathing grew quicker, and I lifted my ass just slightly, a subtle invitation.

A light caress traipsed along one of my naked butt-cheeks! Fingers!

They trailed slowly over the muscled mound, making their way toward my parted crack. I let out a big sigh, obvious encouragement, and pulled my knees forward to offer a wide-open ass-crack.

The fingers moved down the hill of my ass-globe, descending toward the parted valley, slithering into the greased crack. I shuddered and lifted my ass slightly off the log, more invitation, along with an intense craving for those tantalizing fingers to find my pulsating hole!

A husky whisper broke the silence. "Oh yeah. Sweet ass."

The fingers trailed along my crack, barely grazing my pouting hole. I gasped and lifted my butt as those digits tickled my butt-lips. They moved up and down slowly, halting only briefly at the hole to stroke and then slide away.

I was on fire! The heat of the sun felt suddenly intense. Those teasing fingers had me craving more. The heavy breathing and sighs from behind increased as I felt a pair of hairy, muscular thighs press into mine.

The dude straddled the log right behind me. I imagined his cock, big and swollen in one hand as I thought I heard fingers pumping it. The fingers in my crack settled on my hole, tickling the pouting entrance.

I writhed over the log, shoving upwards against those fingertips. I wanted them in me!

He chose to tease me, stroking the puckered lips and just barely pushing into the distended hole. I groaned and rolled my naked butt, rising up in an attempt to impale myself on those maddening digits.

My anonymous partner leaned into me from behind, his heavy thighs and knees pushing my ass forward and thighs even farther apart. Something thick, hot and slippery pressed into one of my ass-cheeks.

Cock!

Leaking pre-cum, the knob slowly rubbed along my left ass-cheek as those fingertips tickled my pouting asshole. I groaned and writhed, sweat dribbling down into my armpits and along my back.

He drove those fingers up my ass, two of them knuckle-deep!

I grunted and shoved backwards, driving them even deeper. His cock-head on my butt-cheek rubbed back and forth. His fingers twisted and probed.

My own cock leaked onto the towel under my belly. My asshole throbbed. Those fingers, so gentle before, now became rough and demanding. They drove deep, yanked out, slammed back in, twisted and stretched.

I gasped, heaving up into the cock fucking my ass-cheek, the big thighs pinning me from behind, and those fingers probing my poor butt-hole.

He expelled a loud grunt, slammed his fingers as deep as they could go and held them there as his slippery knob suddenly released a gusher of nut-cream all over my butt.

The fingers came out, the dripping cock slapped against my butt a few times, then the thighs moved away, and he rose behind me. I didn't even look, choosing to preserve his anonymous memory as he turned and picked his way back the way he'd come.

My asshole felt nicely stretched and aching. I hadn't come, but had been so close! My cock remained hard as I rose up to stretch and survey my quiet surroundings. I felt around in my own asshole, sighing at the warm gully I found back there. Ready for more!

The seagulls soared and dipped over the water. Bird song twittered in the dense shrubbery. Otherwise, there was no sound of civilization. The forested cliffs muffled all but nature's own music.

I was hornier than ever. I drank some water, nibbled on a few tidbits from my pack, and returned to my sprawled position over the log I'd claimed. The wait for my next accomplice began.

I dozed a little as a dappling of shade from an overhanging oak moved across my naked body. It was so pleasant, the breeze, the bird song, the occasional dragonfly, the lapping waves, and my own nakedness.

Footsteps disturbed my reverie. I opened my eyes to see a nude dude approaching. Husky, hairy, pink from exposure to the May sunshine, entirely naked. Bright green eyes poured over my sprawled nudity. A mop of auburn hair capped a broad, handsome face. He looked like an ex-rugby player of sorts, solid body, determined stride.

And, he had a cock that swayed between those hairy thighs with potent promise!

As I watched him come closer, he looked right into my eyes and grabbed hold of that swaying weapon, stroking it into a growing hard-on!

A bold one! Perfect!

I shuddered with expectation, my ass-cheeks clenching and my cock twitching. He moved toward me, stepping over logs and beach debris effortlessly. His big hand pumped a hard-on.

He came over so quickly I barely had time to catch my breath before he stepped onto my log and strode right at me. His big thighs and calves suddenly hovered over my face, his muddy boots rising and then stepping over me.

"I'm gonna fuck that hot ass. I see it's already greased. Awesome."

The growl sent a stabbing shudder up and down my spine and directly into my throbbing asshole. He gave me practically no time to respond, dropping down behind me. Both his big paws seized my butt globes and began to knead them possessively.

"Big cock up that hot hole. That's what you need. I can tell."

His deep voice matched the powerful build. His brazenness had me shaking all over. He scooted up against me, hairy legs pressing into my smooth ones. One hand reached up and grabbed a condom I'd placed beside the tub of grease on top of my pack beside the log.

I said nothing, mewling instead and pushing back into that kneading hand on my ass. From a pleasant doze into a heated frenzy had occurred in moments, and I was eager for the cock he'd just promised/threatened.

The hand relinquished my butt momentarily as he rolled a condom over his tool, but the hairy thighs hadn't relented, shoving against mine and splaying me wide open so that my crack was totally exposed, and my hole pouted into a gaping tunnel, greased and waiting.

He reached back up to scoop out some more grease from the open tub on my pack. I let out another moaning mewl, biting my lip as I awaited whatever he planned.

I heard the slick pumping of a hand as he coated his fat cock with the grease, then felt both those giant paws grip my sun-flushed butt mounds and spread them.

"Here it comes. Greased bone!"

His warning was quickly followed by the stab of a blunt knob directly against my puckered sphincter. I let out a yelp as that slippery weapon drove into me. My asshole swallowed cock like a sump pump, totally hungry for it.

Cock drove far up into my guts. I lay there and took it, split in two by his massive thighs and big hands. He gored me, thrusting balls-deep as he rode forward with his body and practically sat on me.

"Take it! Take all that cock! I know you need it!"

I did! It felt absolutely amazing. He rode my ass, rising up to straddle me like I straddled the log under us. He fucked in and out relentlessly while crowing his steady song.

"Take that cock. Take it! You love it!"

Not only was the powerful fuck amazing in itself, but the thrill of being out in the open, with the possibility of being caught, added an extra dimension to the steamy moment.

And, we were caught!

I spotted the newcomer approaching as cock slammed into my hungry ass from behind. The on-comer halted in his tracks when he spied us rutting over a log like pigs in a muddy farmyard, but then he resumed his approach when his eyes caught mine, and I didn't look away.

That was hot. Here he came, dark eyes drinking in the nasty scene. He was very tall, with a buzzed crown of dark hair over a narrow face, athletically slim, naked except for sneakers and a light tank top. He was nicely bronzed and obviously had spent much time in the spring sunshine already. Probably on these trails, searching out hole to fuck or dick to suck.

He stopped along the edge of the clearing, half-hidden by branches, dark eyes practically devouring the nasty scene unfolding on the log ahead. I grunted loudly, letting him know how much I appreciated all that meat ramming home up my greased butt-hole.

He stared, but came no closer. His cock, rising up to jerk stiffly at his belly, glistened in the sunshine with dribbling pre-cum. I stared back, gazing boldly at his twitching bone, then up into his eyes. He remained where he was, watching.

I loved that, spread and fucked, taking it and loving it out in the open, while someone spied on us from the bushes, getting a good look at the big stud riding my ass from behind, my smooth, muscular body splayed and porked.

But I wanted more. I was all-out greedy for it that morning.

I stared at the tall dude with my blue eyes boring into his. Then, I opened my mouth wider, stuck out my tongue and wagged it.

The message was clear, I imagined. Come forward and fuck my gaping gullet!

I rocked on the log, cock steadily thrusting into me as I offered the tall dude my mouth. He moved forward out from behind the shrubbery, then hesitated for just a moment.

"Come on over and join us. Fuck his mouth while I fuck his ass! He wants it bad."

The growled offer from behind encouraged the dark-eyed watcher enough so that he nodded slightly, then began to pick his way forward.

I opened wider, offering my mouth and grunting as my ass got pounded even harder from behind. The approaching stranger had galvanized my fuck-buddy! He rode up higher on top of my butt, sitting on me as he slam-fucked my hole with his thick tool.

The dark-haired one stepped over to our log and came forward. I was drooling, and moaning. His lean, bronzed legs were less hesitant now as he came up to us and then dropped down to stand with boots on either side of the log. I looked up into his dark orbs as he reached down and grabbed my blond hair and held my head in place. His cock, which looked like it was a foot long, stabbed down into my face.

I began to lick it all over as he pumped it against my gaping lips. He sighed, writhing his hips forward as my tongue lapped all over the lengthy shaft and bulbed head.

"Fuck yeah. Lick it. Use your mouth on me!"

His voice quavered. His lean body twitched in front of me. His cock tasted like salty sweat and then sweet nut-cream as I licked off the dribbling crown. My hands came up and under his spread thighs in an attempt to grab onto something as cock pounded my butt more furiously than ever from behind.

Under his parted legs, I found his ass. Clenched, solid, perky butt-cheeks rolled in my hands as he probed my lips and tongue with his long boner. I was rocked forward on the log by the eager fucker behind me, and my hands slipped down into the dark-haired dude's crack. I found a quivering hole, smooth as satin.

"Oh yeah," he hissed, his hips jerking as my fingertips ran over his asshole. Then, he surprised me with his next words. "Eat my ass while you get fucked!"

"My pleasure ... unnhhhhgggg ... turn around ... and gimme your hole!" I managed to grunt out between licks up and down his stiff bone.

He lifted one lean thigh and whirled around, and just like that, he straddled the log in front of me, bent over, bronzed butt facing me.

He shoved ass into my face, reaching back to grab my neck and press me into his crack. The heated butt divide was absolutely hairless and the cheeks were firm as marble. He gripped my neck fiercely, forcing my face into that spread crack.

I clamped my mouth over his pouting hole and began to suck and lick noisily.

"Fuck! So fucking hot! Eat out that ass while you get cock up the butt! What a greedy hole!"

If I'd imagined my rugby stud had been rough-fucking me before, now he really gave it to me. Right on top of me, his heavy thighs pinned me, his knees splayed me, and his thick cock rammed down into my greased anal channel.

I suckled on hole. I teased it open, then stroked the exposed inner flesh with my tongue. The dark-haired stud in front of me appreciated my efforts with moans and wild wriggling. He held my face in his ass with his strong hands, rubbing his butt up and down over my nose and chin as my tongue stroked and probed his tight little slot.

Out of the corner of my eyes, I spotted the pair of watchers on the trail. Wearing tank tops and little else, they stood there with fat boners and observed the action. I could only see their lower bodies with my face pressed into ass-crack, but there was plenty to look at. They began to jerk each other off as they stood and watched.

I was getting my ass drilled, eating a sweet tight hole, and being watched while doing it by two more studs! What a nasty thrill!

The heat of the sun had us all dripping sweat. Sweat ran down the firm crack in front of me, adding a salty tang to the stud's tasty asshole. My own asshole throbbed and ached. It was all too much. I began to shoot.

I jerked over the log, my jizz spraying the towel under me.

"He's coming with cock up the ass and his tongue up ass! I'm gonna shoot, too!" The rugby stud had been drilling furiously, knocking my butt all over the log, and it was no wonder he shot. The dude in front of me had been holding onto my head with both hands, and not even touching his own cock, but it didn't seem to matter. He gasped, wriggled his butt back into my face and tongue, and shot a load all over the log.

I was surrounded by hot flesh, writhing in the throes of orgasm. Out of the corner of my eyes, I saw the two watchers pull themselves to mutual orgasm. Spunk sprayed the trail.

They abandoned me there, the stench of cum and sweat lingering in the air to join the salty smell of the sea and the heated leaf stink of the woods.

I lay over my log and dozed again, holes satiated for the moment.

The day wasn't over. Not yet. What would come next?
I had no idea. But, it was sure to be wild and nasty!

IF YOU ONLY KNEW
By Martin Delacroix

At age thirteen a flame ignited within me, a desire for sex with other guys in public places.

My friend, Thomas, took me swimming at his country club. We changed in the men's locker room, and I saw Thomas naked for the first time. All these teenagers and grown men walked around in their birthday suits – a profusion of cocks and asses. And there I was, nude as well, my privates on display, a new experience for me. Two college boys showered and horsed about, snapping each other's butts with wet towels. Their dicks flipped here and there, and I thought, *Imagine if one guy touched the other's cock, right in front of everyone.* My penis tingled and I quickly donned my swimsuit to conceal my impending erection. I thought, *This place beats anything I've ever seen. How do I join?*

Later, when I asked my mom about a membership, she looked at me as if I was crazy. "We aren't the Rockefellers, you know."

Undeterred, I pursued my passion with gusto. One afternoon, while my mother bought groceries, I slouched in the front seat of her car in a supermarket parking lot. I pulled out my dick and jacked off, leering at a bag boy who gathered shopping carts. Another time, while walking our family dog, I ducked into a bank of shrubs in a city park. I stroked myself while watching sweaty men play soccer nearby, all the time thinking *what would they say if they knew?*

I became an adept Peeping Tom, skulking about my neighborhood in darkness. Several boys lived near me, and I knew the locations of their bedroom windows. I took note of their sleep schedules and shower times, learning which were careless with draperies and blinds. I became a maestro of voyeurism.

One boy, Nathan Crookes, an athletic high-school junior with blond hair and a big cock, routinely lay naked upon his bed with the lights on, reading girlie magazines and stroking his swollen penis. I'd scale his back yard fence then stand behind a gardenia shrub, touching myself while Nathan wanked. I'd squirt my seed in unison with him, and it was almost as if we were having sex together.

I continued my nocturnal wanderings for over a year, and I can't say which thrilled me more: my victims' unwitting participations or the risk associated with outdoor masturbation. I hit the alleys most every night, spying and wanking; my dance card was full.

Then I got caught.

A group of young men, community college students, shared a house a few blocks from mine. They must've rented the place unfurnished, as none of the windows had coverings of any sort. These guys often walked about in their undershorts or even naked. Their backyard was privacy-fenced and hedges grew out front, so I guess they thought no one saw them, but I sure did. I visited two or three times a week. These guys were hot, nineteen or twenty years old, with defined chests, flat bellies and fully-developed genitals. My favorite was a dark-haired boy, handsome, with a long cock and an ass like a pair of cantaloupes. He'd occasionally shave his balls in front of his bedroom mirror, taking his time, turning here and there, putting on a show of sorts.

One night I stood outside his window, watching him undress. A first-quarter moon hung low in the sky; it offered a bit of light, and I stood in the shadow of a laurel oak. Removing my cock from my jeans, I spat in my hand and commenced wanking, staring at the guy while he peeled off his undies. My fist pumped and my spine tingled, and I drew close to orgasm when, behind me, a twig snapped.

I froze, dick in hand. Who was it?

Two guys, residents of the house, grabbed me. One said, "Gotcha, pervert." They were both a head taller than I, and I didn't stand a chance. Their breath smelled of beer. One guy crooked his arm about my neck; he got me in a headlock while the other bent my arm behind my back. My cock bobbed before me in the moonlight, and one fellow flicked at it with his finger. He said, "Now that's a little jimmy."

They both laughed.

After hustling me into their garage, they switched on an overhead fixture, a bare bulb that made me squint. The room was empty, save for a tool bench and some shelving stacked with old paint cans and newspapers. The air smelled of mineral spirits and damp rot, and the cement slab was a leopard-skin of oil stains. One guy held me while his friend fetched the home's other occupants, including the dark-haired guy I had spied upon (he wore boxer shorts now). There were five in all, and they must've been drinking a lot because each seemed unsteady on his feet. They clutched beer cans, grinning at me like I was a Mardi Gras float, making insulting remarks about my rigid penis.

The boy who held me spoke to the guy I'd been watching. "Brian, is this the kid you've seen out back?"

Brian nodded, then someone said to him, "I think he likes you."

I thought, *Oh, shit. How could I have been so careless?*

Then I thought, *If he knew of my visits, how come he let them continue?*

The other guy who'd jumped me (a cruel bastard) suggested I suck Brian's cock and blood rushed to my cheeks. Surely they wouldn't make me?

Brian demurred. He asked for my name.

I said, "Robert." (It's actually Stewart.)

97

Brian swigged from his beer, swaying a bit. His voice was deep for a guy his age. He said, "You come here a lot. You jack off watching me, right?"

I dropped my gaze to the floor.

"Did you blow your load tonight?"

I shook my head.

"Then finish what you started. We won't let you go until you do."

Everyone but me laughed. The guy holding me yanked my pants and underwear down to my ankles, then he pulled my T-shirt up to my armpits. I had to stroke myself while these guys circled me and hooted, calling me a faggot. They slapped my ass and pinched my nipples. They tousled my hair, making kissing sounds with their lips. I trembled at their attentions and sweat drooled down my ribs. I was scared and felt like crying, but oddly, my cock remained stiff as PVC pipe.

Brian came to me, grinning. He placed a hand upon my shoulder, speaking in a mocking tone. "Here's something to remember me by, Robert."

Bringing his mouth to my neck, he sucked skin, nibbling, giving me a hickey. I smelled his hair and his body odor, too, – a musky scent that made me dizzy. I grew so excited by his touch, I lost control; my cock throbbed, and I shot my load – a series of healthy spurts. Some struck Brian on his upper thigh, and he jerked his lips from my neck, cursing.

"On your knees, punk," he cried. "Lick it off me, every drop."

Sinking to the concrete, I lapped my own jizz, shivering with pleasure as my tongue slid across Brian's flesh. When my nose got close to his crotch I smelled his genitals (a cheddar aroma) and nearly passed out.

After I swallowed, Brian pulled me to my feet and swatted my ass. "Get yourself dressed and scoot. Don't come back or we'll kick your butt. Understand?"

Later that night, I stood before my bathroom mirror, eyeing the purple bruise on my neck, fingering its edges, thinking of Brian. My cock swelled, and I took it in hand. I closed my eyes and pictured the garage, thinking of the college boys and their taunts, of my naked performance and Brian's mouth on my skin. I shot a fresh load into the sink.

As I studied my reflection, I thought, *Jesus, Stewie, I think you liked it.*

* * * * *

The incident with Brian and his friends (sexy as it was in certain respects) put an end to my skulking. I hadn't been as clever or careful as I'd previously thought, and I didn't want to get beat up or arrested, just for the sake of a jack-off.

My high school years were loveless and lonely. Gay sex was taboo in our town. One heard stories of local trysting zones, places frequented by homosexuals – a rest stop on the interstate highway, a municipal park – but I lacked the courage to visit them. I graduated a virgin, untouched, save for the hickey Brian had given me in his garage. I'd taken a Polaroid snapshot of myself before the bruise faded, and I kept it between the pages of my illustrated Bible. Occasionally, I'd take it out and wank to memories of that improbable evening. Sick, eh?

I dreaded my future, foreseeing a lifetime of solitude, and sometimes I wept in despair. My best years, I felt certain, were behind me.

* * * * *

I was eighteen, a freshman at our state university, when I met Grady McNeill in the men's room at the main library on campus. I sat on the pot, stall door closed, reading a *National Geographic*, when Grady entered and took the cubicle next to mine. I heard a belt buckle's tinkle, then a rustle of clothing and a toilet seat's squeak. Grady's feet came into view in the space between the linoleum floor and the privacy panel. His pants and undershorts sat bunched atop his sneakers.

I returned my gaze to my magazine, studying an article about Tanzania, when Grady cleared his throat and I looked up. A hole existed in the privacy panel, its diameter no greater than a snuff tin's. Through it, a long-lashed, cerulean eye stared at me. It winked when I met its gaze.

My cheeks burned with embarrassment, and I looked away, rustling the pages of my magazine. What was going on?

Grady made a noise. "Ps-s-s-t."

I looked at the hole in the panel, at the eye. We spoke in whispers.

I said, "What?"

"Let me suck your dick."

I made a face. "Where?"

"Here, dumb-ass."

"What if somebody comes in?"

"Don't worry. Just stick your wiener through this hole."

I glanced at my stall door. I considered pulling up my pants and leaving, but …

"Come on," he said, "be brave."

Grady was a fine cocksucker, adept with his tongue. In the middle of the blow job, a guy entered the room and pissed at a urinal and the presence of an unsuspecting stranger, together with Grady's oral gymnastics, got me very excited. Just after our intruder departed, I shot my load down Grady's throat. My hands and one side of my face were pressed against the metal partition, and my hips bucked against it. I felt so good I moaned.

Minutes later, I met Grady at the washbasins. I told him my name, and he told me his and we shook hands. He was half a head shorter than I, slender, with wavy black hair and a dazzling smile. His lips were full and crimson, still shiny with spit. His voice had a lilt to it, a musical quality, and he spoke as if we'd just passed an hour in a café.

I asked, "Have you done this before?"

He nodded. "I work part-time in the library, shelving books. I come here whenever I want."

"Aren't you afraid you'll get caught?"

He flickered his eyebrows. "That's half the fun – the danger."

I shivered at his remark.

He scribbled his number on a scrap of paper. "Call me if you'd like, and we'll stir up some trouble."

I nodded, pocketing the note, and before I could say goodbye, Grady was gone.

* * * * *

We rendezvoused, Grady and I, at Fraternity Row on a Friday evening. The sun had set a half-hour before, and light was draining from the sky. Stars appeared above us, but the moon wasn't up. This was early September, and the air felt warm and moist. We both wore T-shirts, khaki shorts and sandals. Grady carried a backpack on his shoulders. His hair was damp, and I smelled cologne when I drew close to him. We shook hands and he gave me his knockout smile, and I felt weak in the knees, thinking of our intimacy a few days before.

"Let's take a walk," he said.

The fraternity houses we passed varied in style: antebellum, brick colonial, cinder block and stucco, a couple of Mies van der Rohe knock-offs with plenty of glass. Each had a sign out front, bearing Greek letters. Windows offered views of brightly-lit rooms where boys gathered, playing cards and drinking beer. Others watched television or listened to music.

When I'd spoken by phone with Grady the previous night, he asked me, "Up for a bit of excitement?"

"What kind?"

"You'll see. Just don't wear undershorts."

"Huh?"

"You heard me. I won't wear any either."

Now, we strolled on the sidewalk, listening to crickets chirp while street lamps flickered on. It felt weird, having my cock and balls roll around inside my shorts, unimpeded, getting chafed by the khaki fabric. Knowing Grady was equally unrestrained made me feel horny. He was a good-looking guy, and I knew he planned on doing something wicked, but what? I stole a glance at him. He walked with his hands in his pockets, shoulders slumped, eyes on the sidewalk, as if he pondered something important. Glow from a street lamp reflected in his dark hair, in his eyes and their long lashes.

We came to an alley paved with crushed shell, one sheltered by live oaks, they formed a canopy overhead. The alley accessed backsides of certain fraternity houses, and its shoulders were lined with Dumpsters. The moon still had not risen, and I squinted just to see. We passed a few properties then came to a podocarpus hedge, one long as a transfer truck and taller than I. It blocked any view of the house beyond it.

Grady looked here and there, then he stepped to the hedge and parted branches. Glancing at me, he jerked his head. "Come on," he whispered.

We passed through dense foliage. Limbs lashed our arms and faces, and twice, I tripped over exposed roots. We came to a galvanized, hog-wire fence, six-feet high. Beyond it were a bank of camellias, several mature oaks, and the rear of a two-story fraternity house. I heard country-western music, the splashing of water, and much conversation and laughter. The aroma of chlorine hit my nostrils.

Someone hollered, "Deets, you faggot, fetch us more beers."

Light from the house filtered through the camellias, reaching us, allowing us to see. I looked at Grady and lifted my shoulders, making a face. He raised an index finger to his lips, flickering his eyebrows as he'd done in the men's room. Removing his backpack, he unzipped a pocket and produced a pair of chain cutters, heavy-duty, the kind you see in home improvement stores. He used these to create a hole in the fence, snipping here and there, making a passage wide enough to accommodate our shoulders and hips. The racket beyond the camellias drowned out whatever noise the device made when it broke through metal.

Grady set the cutters upon the ground. He got on his hands and knees and scooted through the opening, rustling oak leaves. He turned and whispered, "Follow me."

Moments later, we stood beside a live oak, among shrubs, hidden in shadows, staring at a dozen-or-so fraternity boys. Some occupied an in-ground swimming pool with an underwater fixture that cast a greenish glow. Others lounged on chaises and chairs. Most were naked, and my belly fluttered at the sight of their lean physiques and meaty cocks. They chattered away, wise-cracking and swilling beer while a portable music player blared.

Grady pressed his mouth to my ear. "They do this every Friday. No girls allowed."

"How'd you find out?"

Grady's eyebrows danced, and a smile crossed his lips. "I'm a brother." Raising the sleeve of his T-shirt, he showed me a tattoo – two Greek letters.

I grinned and shook my head before returning my gaze to the pool. One guy on a chaise drew my attention, a fellow with dark hair and a slim waist. His shoulders were broad, his biceps bulged, and I wondered if he might be a competition swimmer. His cock was uncut, and it rolled between his thighs when he shifted his weight. An upturned nose made his face look almost pretty.

"Ingraham," another boy called to him, "show us your back flip."

He rose and stepped onto the pool's diving board. Standing with his back to me and Grady, he extended his arms, raising them till they were level with his shoulders. His dimpled buttocks clenched a time or two, then he bent his knees and thrust himself skyward and the board jiggled, making a funny sound. Boing! Arching his back and neck, his face came into view, then the forefront of his body, and he struck the water with a subtle splash.

While his friends cheered, Ingraham swam to the pool's edge and hopped out. He seized a towel and commenced drying himself. His dive had rippled the pool's surface, and the underwater fixture cast slivers of light upon his flesh, making him look like a comic book hero in a striped, skin-tight outfit. My cock stiffened, and I gulped, staring. He seemed utterly at ease with his nakedness, conversing with his friends while his cock wagged before him. Water glistened on his shoulders and rump, it drizzled down his flanks. He turned and bent at the waist to dry his legs, and I studied a stripe of hair lining the cleft of his buttocks. I could see his ball sac dangling between his thighs.

Grady nudged my ribs. "I think you're in love."

In the shadows, I blushed like a schoolgirl. I whispered, "This is great. He's so sexy, plus he's got no idea we are watching."

Grady grinned at me like the Cheshire cat. He reached between my thighs and squeezed my boner. Sticking his tongue in my ear, he rolled it about, warm and moist. In turn, I seized his erection, a thick tube jutting down the leg of his shorts. I had never touched another boy this way; I was still a virgin, save for the blow job Grady'd given me days before, and my heart galloped in my chest.

Grady placed his free hand on the back of my neck, pulling me to him so our chests conjoined. Bringing his mouth to mine, he pried my lips open, and his tongue entered me, probing and twirling, rasping against my tongue. His breath steamed against my upper lip. His fingers found the tab of my zipper and lowered it. Then he opened the button at my waist, and my shorts plunged to my ankles. My cock bobbed before me.

I followed Grady's lead, dropping his shorts. His dick sprang forth (it was larger than mine by a couple of inches), pointing skyward. Grady joined our penises, enveloping both in his hand while we continued kissing. Our hips rubbed and our knees touched, and I sighed with pleasure.

While I traded spit with Grady, Ingraham discussed his car (an Italian convertible) with another boy. Ingraham's style of speaking – a syrupy drawl – charmed me. When his laughter erupted, it came from deep inside his throat.

Grady tore his mouth from mine. He whispered, "Let me suck your cock while you watch your boy."

I smiled at Grady and nodded. My pulse accelerated.

Grady turned me, so I faced the pool deck then he sank to his knees upon the oak-leaf carpet. Seizing the base of my cock, he slipped the head and shaft into his mouth. He tickled my ball sac, making me shiver. I rested my hands on top of his head, running them through his hair, teasing his ears while he commenced sucking and polishing the underside of my penis with his eager tongue. I moved my hips in unison with Grady's actions, finding a rhythm, enjoying the slurping sounds he produced with his lips.

My gaze fell upon Ingraham. I saw him in profile – his smooth chest and flat belly, his patch of pubic hair and uncut cock. His pert buttocks. Occasionally, while conversing with his friend, he'd reach down and scratch his testicles or pull at the foreskin of his dick, not caring if others saw him do so. My belly fluttered each time he did this, and I thought, *Oh, Ingraham, if you only knew.*

I glanced down at Grady. His hand stroked his erection, flying like a piston while he sucked me off. His eyes were closed, his breath huffed, and beads of sweat appeared upon his forehead. I stroked his sooty eyebrows with a thumb. Even with his mouth stuffed, he looked handsome, and I thought, *Lucky me.*

I looked back at Ingraham. He sat in a lawn chair now, facing me, knees spread wide, displaying his genitals, hands joined behind his neck, so his armpits were exposed. He wasn't talking any longer. Instead, he appeared to study the night sky, searching, perhaps, for a favorite constellation. His lips parted and light from the pool fixture reflected off his central incisors. He shifted his hips. His cock rolled against one thigh, and he reached between his legs to adjust the position of his nuts.

I envisioned him masturbating, working his foreskin back and forth. The picture in my head made my balls tingle and my heart race. My cock throbbed in Grady's mouth. I grabbed the back of his head and pulled his face to me, burying his nose in my pubic hair. My hips thrust, and I groaned, tossing creamy wads into Grady's throat, four or five spurts. "Oh, yes ..."

Grady made a whimpering sound while he swallowed my load. He kept his mouth wrapped about my dick, gazing up at me, continuing to pump his cock. I locked eyes with him and licked my lips while his breathing quickened. I combed his hair with my fingers. His chest heaved, then he moaned, and his cock splattered my shins with a series of sticky gobs, ones that oozed through my leg hairs and slimed my ankles before pooling inside my bunched-up shorts.

I studied tree limbs above us, thinking, *Jesus, this is nice.*

We kept still a minute or two, my cock in Grady's mouth, hands resting upon his shoulders. We listened to frat boy chatter, to more wisecracks and low-brow music, while our heartbeats slowed. Then, just before Grady released my dick, Ingraham turned his gaze from the sky. He shifted in his chair, looking into his lap and toying with his foreskin. Then he raised his chin and looked at me. His eyebrows arched, and a smile crept onto his lips. He gave me a conspiratory wink, and I gasped in disbelief.

In the darkness, I shook my head.

Grady, you minx.

HAPPY NEW YEAR, MAN
By Ryan Field

It's after midnight on New Year's Eve, the night is cold and still, and you just left a suburban banquet hall wearing a rented tuxedo. You take a deep breath and shake your head when you start the car, and then you look in the rearview mirror and vow that this is the last wedding party that will ever include your name. If Cousin Jeanie decides to get married next year, let her hire a trained monkey to smile while escorting Aunt Sally and her offensive mink cape down the aisle. If second cousin Maryanne with the orphan Annie haircut ever decides forty isn't too old to wear a bright, white wedding dress and toss a bouquet, she can hire a paid escort to dance with her pregnant college girlfriend in the lime green organza with puffy sleeves.

Though you should be exhausted from a long day of smiling and shaking hands, when you pull onto the interstate you realize that you are so horny you could spread your legs and ride the gear shift. You could have responded to the married guy in the cheap tan suit who kept following you all night during the wedding reception (there's always one). He would have done anything to ditch his wife for a few minutes to get into your pants, and he would have been so thankful in the end. It was extremely flattering when he said you reminded him of Brad Pitt; but younger. And, he wasn't that bad looking. It's just that his handshake had been so painfully weak and his round shoulders so eternally sunken you know you probably would prefer riding the gear shift to his tired dick.

So, you do what any young, blond gay man in the suburbs does when he's horny and desperate: You drive to the nearest rest stop on the interstate and hope for the best. You tell yourself: It's okay because you don't do this sort of thing very often. It's either the rest stop or the adult bookstore, and you don't want to cruise the glory holes in black tie. Though the rest stop might be a waste of time, and you realize the chances of meeting a decent looking guy there on New Year's Eve are probably rather slim, it beats going home to another solitary jerk off session with your computer.

But, the rest stop is slightly overwhelming. Holiday travelers in mini-vans and station wagons are pulling in and out of the parking spots nearest the rest rooms. Huge trucks are lined against the far side of a grassy section near porta potties and pay telephones, and you are not sure where to park or what to do at first. But, then you notice a gloomy, solitary parking section beside a long sidewalk that leads from the truck section to the restrooms; gay instinct kicks in, and you know that's where you are supposed to be. You slowly creep to the end of the rest stop and pull into a parking space where no one is directly next to you; there are other cars there, and you suspect those drivers are cruising for sex, too. But, you don't want to pull up beside the first car you see and give the wrong impression.

You were right, too. When you quickly glance to the left, you see that the guy sitting behind the steering wheel of a ten-year-old Lincoln Town Car two spaces over is about seventy-nine, and he's licking his lips. His salt and pepper hair is puffy and stiff; just lipstick and earrings, and he could pass for an old woman. The guy two parking spaces to the right in a dented Buick looks as if he's four hundred pounds, and he's pointing toward his crotch. His hands are small and chubby; they remind you of tiny plastic gloves filled with water. You don't, under any circumstances, ever make eye contact with these men unless you're interested in gum jobs or the heady, sour aroma of extremely aged provolone cheese between their legs. So you look straight ahead, without blinking, and hope they get the hint that you are not interested.

A half hour passes. The two guys on either side of you are still pointing and licking, and no one else with potential has pulled into the rest stop. The married guy from the wedding is starting to look good now. You sigh because this is typical from what you've heard about cruising rest stops. There are never any good looking guys, and everyone plays games because they are all afraid to make the first move. But, just when you're ready to start the car, planning ahead for that late night Web cam session with someone just as horny as you, a young guy steps out of a large truck cab and heads toward the rest rooms. He's a muscular, African American in his twenties, wearing an oversized black T-shirt and baggy jeans. Not bad at all; you suspect he's wearing those cute, baggy boxer shorts, too. He walks to the rest room, on the balls of his feet, staring straight ahead. But when he passes your car and looks through the windshield, his head jerks, and he looks back again. His brown eyes are wide; he puts his hands in his pockets and continues toward the rest rooms.

Now, you can sit in the car and wait for Mr. Baggy-pants to come back and play the cruising game, waiting to see if he will have the courage to make the first move (if he's the shy, straight-guy type that might not happen; if he's insecure it won't happen), or you can let him know, beyond all doubt, that you are seriously interested in him. You decide it's probably best to put a passive aggressive plan into action. You don't want to appear too dominant with his type, yet you want him to know, clearly, you are ready to submit to whatever he desires. But, you don't have much time; he probably went in to take a fast piss. So, you quickly remove all your clothes – shoes and socks, too. Of course, the guys who've been staring at you on either side open their mouths wide when they see you are stripping, and you know they are thinking it's for their benefit, but if you don't make eye contact, you won't have to deal with them. The worst that could happen is they jerk off while watching you undress; you smile and think of it as offering a kindly gesture to the less fortunate.

When you're completely nude, you put the black tuxedo jacket back on and wait for Mr. Baggy-pants to come out of the bathroom. You look around to make sure you haven't attracted a crowd, and then you scope the entire rest stop for cops that might be circling the parking lot. Your pupils are dilated, and your heart is racing with anticipation by then. A moment later, you see the hot trucker exit the rest rooms. You take a deep breath and get out of the car slowly and naturally. The pavement feels cold and hard against your bare feet as you walk around to the front of the car, toward the passenger side of the windshield. You know he's watching; you pretend to clean a smudge with the sleeve of your jacket. As you lean forward on your tip toes, you spread your legs a little, so Mr. Baggy-pants will have a nice clear view of your smooth, round ass when you reach out and the coat rides up to your waist. You have to do this quickly; just enough time for this guy to process the image of your soft naked ass for the rest of his life. When you stand up straight again and head back toward the driver's door of the car, all he can see are your bare legs. It's important to get into the car and lower the window all the way. If he's interested, he'll walk toward you with his tongue hanging out; if he's not, he'll literally run back to his truck and leave the rest stop.

His hands are in his pockets when he walks up to your open window and says, "I really need to come tonight, man." The hand in his right pocket moves up and down against his junk a few times, but he can't look you in the eye.

His blunt honesty makes you grip the steering wheel tightly. But, you smile and lower your eyes; you know he's staring into the car at your naked legs. "What do you want to do?" you ask. He reminds you of that hot rapper on TV. Your heart is racing now, and you can't stop staring at the bulge between his legs.

"Let's go to my truck; it's private there, with a bed in the cab," he says. He stares down again and runs his tongue slowly across his bottom lip.

You know you should probably put on your pants and shoes to cross over to where is truck is parked; anyone could see you walking around half naked. But, it's dark and deserted in that section of the rest stop; and you don't get too many chances to walk around half-naked in public with a really sexy guy like Mr. Baggy-pants. Besides, his truck isn't that far away; just across the grassy area. So, you pull up the window, step out of the car and follow him back to his truck. You know the guys in the parked cars are watching all of this; and that makes you smile. So, when Mr. Baggy-pants reaches back quickly to touch your ass, you lift the jacket up higher, so they can see his strong, dark hand squeeze your soft, watery flesh.

When you arrive at the passenger door of his truck, he opens it wide and hops up into the cab. He turns around as you are about to lift your bare foot onto the metal step and reaches down for your arm with his great, warm hand. With one quick tug, he pulls you up; his strength is outrageous. His thick arm brushes the side of your naked thigh when he reaches around to slam the door shut, then he places his palm on the middle of your smooth ass and whispers, "Day-ummm, that's just like candy." Then he backs up quickly, and while he opens a dark curtain behind the two front seats and climbs onto a mattress in the back of the cab, you remove the tuxedo jacket and follow him. He is flat on his back by then, with no shirt; his hands are behind his head, and his eyes are closed. You spread your legs as wide as they go, straddle his thighs and slowly unfasten his jeans. He's wearing loose yellow boxers, with blue and white checks.

While you are pulling down his zipper, he opens his eyes and says, "There's condoms in that tray next to the bed ... there's lube, too." His voice is deep and sturdy, with a slight southern accent. He's telling you that he wants to fuck.

You pull his dark, semi-erect dick out of the waistband of his underwear and smile. And, you know with prescient clarity you're never going to forget this New Year's Eve. When you open your mouth and lick the entire shaft of his dark brown penis, his head jerks, and his mouth falls open, as if he didn't expect you to suck him off. You can actually feel the soft flesh growing against your tongue; it jumps a few times and hits your upper lip. He hasn't showered all day, and you close your eyes and inhale deeply to take in the damp, tangy aroma of his unwashed cock.

He groans, very softly, and spreads his legs a little wider, so you can bury your head between them. When he places both large hands on top of your head, you lean forward and swallow the entire penis. It's rock hard now and so long you have to concentrate, so you won't gag when it hits the back of your throat. Before you start sucking, you keep it deep in your throat for a moment and breathe through your nose. You know he likes this because his eyes are closed, and he moans a few times. His public hair is rough against the soft skin on your nose; now he smells like raw meat and woody spices.

When he removes his hands from your head and folds them behind his neck, you know he wants you to start sucking him off. He doesn't want to do anything but remain still, while you do all the work, and enjoy your soft, warm mouth. So, you puff out your lips, indent your cheekbones and press you tongue against the shaft. Your head rises and falls slowly, from the hairy base of his long rod to the tip, with an even, passive rhythm. His cock is so thick your jaw starts to hurt. But, you don't stop because you know you have him near the edge when you start to taste his salty pre-cum. You close your eyes and suck with a faster pace until he leans forward, presses his palm against the back of your head, and says, "I'm getting close, man."

You look up at him with raised eyebrows and nod "yes" while his dick is still in your mouth. You want him to know that it's okay if he comes like this; that you don't mind at all.

But, he grabs a handful of hair and pulls your face away from his cock. "You've got a really hot ass, man," he says, "I'd like to get some of that."

Then he leans back, and you carefully grab his cock with your left hand. He closes his eyes again; you reach for the condom with your right hand. It doesn't take long to remove the condom from the package and cover his dick; it's a black one and it makes his dick look like a firmly packed, extra-large sausage. He moans and wiggles his powerful legs when you rub lube all over the condom. And, when you pull off his pants and underwear and climb on top of him so you can straddle his dick, he squeezes your ass a few times with both hands.

Then he slaps your ass hard a couple of times and says, "Sit on it, bitch."

You smile and say, "Yes, Sir." It occurs to you this guy probably has a girlfriend somewhere, and he's sneaking around on the down-low.

After you massage some lube around your hole, you spread your legs and slowly work his dick inside. It's so large there's a moment of pain, but you take a deep breath and let it slide all the way inside. Your own dick is so hard now it jumps a few times. When you press your hands against his chest and slowly start to ride, his hips begin to buck up and down, so he can pound it into your body as deeply as possible. He grabs your thin waist with both hands and presses down hard; your mouth falls open and your head begins to roll around in circles. You whisper, "Yes, deeper, man," and you start to ride his cock so fast the cab begins to rock.

He lets you ride like this for a long time, and then he grabs you by the waist and says, "Lay down on your back, bitch."

When you're on your back, he lifts your legs up high and rams the entire shaft inside until his pubic hair is pressed against your ass cheeks. He fucks with his pelvis, and his firm ass moves up and down so hard your head bangs into the side of the cab, and you gasp for breath. "Deeper," you whisper, "Man, fuck me deeper."

He bites his bottom lip and hammers your ass even harder. The more you beg for it, the more he responds. He knows you like dick; he knows you love his big dick fucking your tight hole. And, just when you think you won't be able to take one more bang, he pulls out and says, "Turn over now and get on your stomach, bitch."

You do what he says and press your face into his pillow. It smells like him: spice and meat and wood. Then he spreads your legs a little, climbs onto your back, and shoves his hammer back into your hole again. In this position, with your own cock rubbing against the white sheets beneath his heavy body, he fucks even harder and faster than before. His dark brown hands are now on either side of your face, and his stomach is pressed against your back. He pounds you into the mattress while your dick is rubbing against the sheets. His cock is so large you begin to feel your own climax from the lips of your hole all the way to the tip of your cock. You close your eyes and beg for more: "I'm close, man. Fuck me harder … don't stop."

He grunts a few times, and then says, "Here it comes, bitch … fucking hot, tight ass, bitch."

That's when his cock explodes and fills the condom buried inside you. And while he's still ramming, you explode all over the sheets. Then you whisper, "Yes, fuck me, man," while he sighs and falls on top of you with all his weight.

A minute later, while Mr. Baggy-pants still has you pinned face down to the mattress, you spread your legs and crawl out from beneath his strong arms. His breathing is less intense, and his eyes are fading, but there is a huge smile on his face.

You smile back at him. "That was really good." You feel hot and sexy now, sitting there naked in the cab of this young guy's truck, after he just fucked your brains out. You even silently wish he'd bend you over and do it all again – or that he had a buddy who could tag you, too.

He thanks you and says, "Man, I really needed to come tonight." Then he squeezes your ass one last time while you put on the tuxedo jacket and head for the door. You are thinking that you should probably be thanking him. But, you don't.

Then you turn back and stare at him for a moment. Your ass his still warm from his dick; you can still feel it inside. You lean forward and the jacket rides all the way up so your ass is exposed. You kiss him on the lips and say, "Happy New Year, man."

He laughs and slaps your ass again. "Happy New Year to you, too, bitch," he says. "You're a good fuck."

You shrug your shoulders and step into the cold January night.

When you're outside again, it seems lighter for some reason, and there's less activity now. The grass feels icy as you cross back toward your car on the tips of your toes. The other two cars that were parked on either side of you are long gone; there's only one car now, and it's parked next to yours. Your legs are a bit sore; Mr. Baggy-pants was more powerful (and needy) than you'd expected. There might be a few serious bruises on the backs of your thighs in the morning, and you smile again. It occurs to you that you should be ashamed of yourself, walking back to your car half naked after doing such unspeakable things with a total stranger. But, you're not.

The car parked next to yours is a red convertible; the top is down, and there's a young preppie guy with short brown hair staring at you. His green eyes are wide and his lips are puckered as though he's about to whistle when he sees that you're walking around almost naked. "You want to get in?" he says. He reaches over the passenger seat and opens the door. This is more like a polite order as though he's really saying, "Get in, bitch." He doesn't know where you've been or what you've just done with Mr. Baggy-pants.

"Isn't it a little cold for the top to be down?" you ask. But, you're smiling and licking your bottom lip.

"I can put it up," he says, "C'mon. Get inside." He taps the seat a few times.

"Ah, well," you say. But, then you smile, remove the jacket and slip into the black leather seat. You know you shouldn't be doing this, but just one more time certainly can't hurt. Besides, he's adorable, and you can't resist.

This guy isn't shy. The seat is reclined, and he's on top of you within seconds. "I didn't think I'd find anyone like you here tonight," he says. His hands are all over your naked body, and his jeans feel rough against your legs.

You put your arms around his wide shoulders and lick his neck. "I'm on my way home from a New Year's Eve wedding ... the longest fucking wedding in the history of the universe." His white cotton polo shirt is soft and clean. His arm pits smell like soap and powder, and his neck tastes sweet.

"I decided to stop here on my way home from the most boring New Year's Eve party I've ever been to," he tells you. His breath is heavy; it smells like beer. "And, now I'm really glad I stopped."

You spread your legs, lift them high, and wrap them around his waist. "So am I, buddy."

"I'm also glad you decided to walk around wearing nothing but that jacket," he says. He takes a deep breath and presses his erection into your thigh. His hands are all over your ass now, and he's practically panting.

You smile and curl your toes. "I wanted to ring in the New Year the right way."

HUNGRY CRAB IN THE LIBRARY
By David Holly

1

I am Zac, the hungry crab of the *bibliotèk*. I love books to read and to savor; the scent, sight, and touch of a rare *liv* awaken my feelings of lust. Then I find an attractive *blan* leafing through hoary volumes, and I seduce him with my mouth or my ass. I take him within me, and I devour the seed of his loins as the hungry crab eats the naughty child in the Haitian nursery rhyme.

My life has been devoted to sexual conquest, first in Jérémie, the city of the poets, where I was born, to a wealthy father who was a diplomat, a patron of artists, a novelist, and a social critic. In our private library, I read in four languages: *kreyol, franse, angle, e panyol*. And in that same library, my father's trusted *restavèk* took me for the first time, holding my ears as he drove his thick cock into my young ass. That servant called me his hungry crab as time after time, he fed my mouth or my bottom, and since then, libraries have provided rich food for my taste.

I once sucked a college professor's cock among the stacks in the central *bibliotèk*. He was standing in the Literary Criticism section, between Michel Foucault and Northrop Frye. He was about five-foot-nine, mid-thirties, *bèl*, with a creamy complexion, ruby lips, sparkling green eyes, and chestnut hair. He was wearing a pastel blue shirt and blue pinstriped slacks that showed provocative bulges front and rear. Reaching for *L'Usage des plaisirs*, I brushed his hand. When his eyes met mine, I held his gaze. We stood that way for a full minute before I dropped to my knees.

He was already hard before I pulled down his zipper. His cock popped free, thick and most succulent. He moaned, half in protest, half in lust. I touched my dark lips to his light-skinned cock. A tiny taste of his fluid, thin and rather salty, leaked onto my tongue. "*Krab la va manje ou,*" I whispered. I felt him turning from side-to-side, scanning the row to ascertain that no librarians would come cruising around the corner. I couldn't care less; or should I admit that the thrill of getting caught sucking cock in public made the task all the sweeter.

The professor must have been spending a goodly amount of time in a gym for his *bounda* were firm and round. Not quite as large or as round as mine, but I had the advantage of my racial characteristics in addition to a vigorous regimen of squats, lunges, and leg presses. I had both of my hands on his ass, caressing his mounds, kneading his buttocks firm as *lamveritab*, while my lips caressed the head of his cock.

I flicked his cock with my tongue as I worked its head with my lips. My tongue flickered over his pee hole, and the tiny opening leaked a thin stream that made me want more. "*L'acassan au sirop qui coule dans ma gargouane,*" I said, pulling my mouth back for a moment.

I hardly expected him to recognize the poem, so he shocked me with his reply: "*Ta fesse est un boumba chargée de victuailles.*"

Who would expect a *blan* professor to recognize Haitian poetry? Such erudition deserved the blowjob of a lifetime. I thrust my head downward, taking his cock along my tongue and into my throat. I swallowed repeatedly as his dick head passed over my choking reflex. I swallowed as though I were trying to swallow his dick, to take his rich, white food into my stomach. I was the *krab nan kalalou* preparing to devour the sleepless child, and I knew that his cum was the mush with syrup that would trickle down my throat.

Let them come and see, I thought. Let the library patrons, the librarians, the officials of the city come and see how I suck this professor's cock. Let them see the pleasure I offer. Of course, I knew that the professor must lecture at Reed College. Portland State would never be able to offer up such a specimen, and as for the University of Portland – the words fail me.

My lips were touching his pubic hairs, so soft, so forgiving. I turned my head so that the cap of his cock was twisting in my throat. Then I pulled back until his cock sprang free. I removed one hand from his generous *bounda* and masturbated him with his piss hole of bounty directed toward my mouth. I jerked his long cock, but the desire to take him into my mouth again overcame my hand's pleasure.

I tortured his dick's head with my tongue and with my lips. My purplish lips popped over his trimmed crown, time and again, and then I drove my head down to his soft hairs. His dick fucked my throat, which I opened for him with much swallowing. Just as he stiffened with impending orgasm, a woman of scholarly disposition rounded the corner. She was young and blonde, nothing that I would desire. She stopped in shock, which faded while she watched with growing curiosity. I cared nothing for her mounting interest, and the professor did not see her. He had forgotten where he was, so great was his need to deliver his juicy bounty to my appetite.

I held my head upon his cock, my lips tickling from his silky brown pubic hair, and my head turning back and forth so that his cock head gained the stimulation of my throat. I hoped that he would come then. I wanted him to shoot his fine professorial semen down my throat, to feed my impoverished Haitian stomach with his rich American bounty. He moaned, and I heard him whispering some words in a form of English I could not understand. The female continued to watch. I saw her out of the corner of my eye. Her eyes were wide with amazement, for she had never seen a cock taken so deeply before, but she did not comprehend my need for sustenance or Haiti's need for nourishment.

Stunningly, the professor's cock stiffened harder, turned on my tongue, then lost tension. Following the splintered second of relaxation, it tightened to the rigidity of iron and grew weighty. "Come in my mouth," I thought. "Feed me. Feed the *neg*, America. Feed the starving millions of my poverty-stricken island."

I twisted my neck upon his cock, but still he would not feed me. Still his cock refused to spread its bounty. I pulled back again, needing breath, and as I drew in the air, I jacked his cock, stroking the pale shaft with my black hand, fingering the finely trimmed cock head with my dark fingertips. I toyed with his dick, twisting his cock head with my fingers, as though I were twisting the cap from a bottle of Coca-Cola from Port-au-Prince.

Suddenly, his semen erupted from his cock, spurting a hot stream onto my lips and face. I buried my face on his cock, taking him deep into my mouth as he shot hot loads of his semen. I swallowed the rich nectar. I swallowed his cock into my throat again, and he could not help but shoot the remainder of his food down my throat. I took all he could offer. For Haiti, and for all Haitians, I took all he could deliver, and I swallowed the rich *sirop* down.

The female observer slunk away, awestruck at my need, and she never said a word to the library staff. I finished sucking every drop from the professor. When he had discharged his all, I pulled my mouth away from his delicious cock. Then, almost sadly, as if I were a nation receiving the last of its aid, taking loans from rich countries that it could never repay, I pulled up his zipper.

We exchanged names afterward, which is how I knew he was a professor. He said that he admired me. Who was to know what he meant? "Are you from Cap-Haïtien?" he asked, which made me suspect that he had visited Okap on a cruise ship.

"*Non*, Jérémie, birthplace of important writers such as Emile Roumer."

2

Over the course of a year, I met man after man at the library, and several times we were spotted, but no one ever reported me to the authorities (such as they are).

One day I was browsing through the West Indian literature, and there was my professor again. I had not spotted him for the past year, but he was glancing through a copy of Roger Mais' *Brother Man*, the original Jonathan Cape printing with the dust jacket featuring a painting by Mais. I slyly picked up *La bibliothèque Française's* printing of Jacques Roumain's *Gouverneurs de la rosée*, and pretended to read the first page of a novel I had nearly memorized in between taking the servant's dick.

"Have you read Roger Mais?"

The professor turned his head. I was not sure from his expression that he recognized me. "*Brother Man* is an important Jamaican novel," I added.

"I have not read Mais' novels or his plays," he admitted, emphasizing his pomposity. "I've just started studying Caribbean literature." He paused and studied me as though I was Caribbean literature. "You look familiar. I'm sorry if I've forgotten you."

"My ass is a basket full of all good things," I purred, turning my back upon him and rubbing my gay black *bounda* across his crotch. Through the whispery fabric of my flannel slacks, I could feel his white cock stirring.

I heard his breath in my ear as he gasped with recollection: "*Ta fesse est un boumba chargée de victuailles.*"

His cock stiffened; it rose so that it poked between my bounteous *bounda*. I flushed as if I was taking sick. "*Out ko mwen cho*," I said feverishly. The fever was a good one though; the heat ran through me. I would have the *blan* again.

Heedless of two young scholars seated around the corner, I unfastened my belt and allowed my trousers to fall. My underwear followed. I pulled an extra-strength condom from my shirt pocket and slid it over the professor's cock. He had already been so obliging as to open his zipper, so his erection popped free. I lubricated the outside of the condom before squirting lubricant into the professor's hand. He understood my intention at once.

I turned my back on him and bent slightly. His hand parted my big black *bounda*, and he slid his finger into my sweet *cul-de-sac*. The lubricant grew hot in my canal as the professor's finger probed. My lips suppressed the moan that I would have uttered. I wanted to let nothing out. All must come within. The American must give to me, I thought, and I will take all that he has. His finger probed and twisted, and a deep pleasure filled me. My cock was hard and leaking onto the well-trodden carpet. The smell of the books in front of me as my two hands gripped the edge of the metal shelf and the sight of the library's Dewy Decimal numbering system heightened my arousal.

He replaced his single finger with two thick digits and turned them in my ass so that he opened my sphincter for his thick cock. His fist separated my *bounda* as he twisted in my rectum. Soon I was open and lubricated. I wanted his cock inside of me, his hot cock, so *gwo*, so *blanc*. "Now, professor," I urged. "Now."

He hesitated a second, and I assumed that he was scanning the aisle for witnesses before he slid his dick into me. He made some adjustment to his cock, and then I felt the head of it sliding between my basket mounds. I pushed to let him in, pushed hard to give him easy entrance. His cock opened me readily, and delicious waves of pleasure radiated from my opening. My entire pelvis rippled with the bounding joy. My cock tingled as he pushed deeper up my ass.

"*Oui*," I urged. "*Oui. Oui.*"

"Yes," he moaned, more loudly than he intended.

"*Krab la va manje ou*," I said, driving my basket back upon him. I impaled my chute all the way, and I slammed my rear back again and again. My black *bounda* slapped against his slacks. I could feel the cool teeth of his zipper against my flesh.

He pulled back as I rocked my hips forward. Then we met, and bliss shot through me. My cock was tingling again, and I knew that if the blan professor could hold out, I would ejaculate as he did. However, it was not to be, for as we rocked rhythmically, the professor moaned, moaned way too loudly, because his groan brought a librarian scurrying around the corner. Her eyes widened at the sight, and she turned upon her heel.

The professor must have had his eyes closed. He did not alter his fucking rhythm except to thrust harder. He rocked vigorously for a minute. Then his rocking grew erratic, and he began thrusting faster. I sighed because I knew he would discharge his pleasure before I could. He was moaning in my ear, calling me his "black beauty," and telling me how he was filling me with his cum.

It was over all too soon, and he pulled his cock from me. I turned to ask him to thrust a bit longer. That's when I saw his white cock, still thick, though softening slightly, with a drip of semen hanging from the end. The condom lay upon the carpet, where he had dropped it before slipping his naked cock into my ass. That cruel trick gave rise to all my resentments against the *blan*, the oppressors, the exploiters, the colonizers. They had made us a colony, but we had thrown off their mastery. Then we faced the crueler mastery of the necessity of rice and beans.

The professor was laughing at my expression. "I don't have AIDS," he said. "You will catch nothing for me. I'm in greater danger from you, I think. But who cares."

My Haitian blood was running hot, but two security guards converged upon us. They ordered me to hoist my *pantalon*. Afterward, they led us to separate rooms. The library did not want the shocking publicity, so they did not involve the police. They stripped me of my library card and banned the hungry crab from the *bibliotèk* forever.

I agreed to abide by their conditions, but I lied when I did so. I knew that I would be back. The library changes its guards as I change my clothing. In a couple of weeks, I would come again, and I would take other men among their stacks. Beyond question, many would attempt to exploit me as the devious professor had done, but in the end, I am the hungry crab who will suck away the milk of this *blan* nation.

PICNIC
By Stephen Osborne

"What kind of sandwiches are these?" Brian asked, his upper lip curling as if the answer would be something repulsive.

Ed ignored the negativity in his tone and answered with a smile. "I made several kinds. Egg salad, ham, turkey. I'm sure you'll find something you like."

"I hate egg salad," Brian said, tossing the wrapped sandwich back into the basket.

"Then get something different," Mike told him, exasperation showing in his tone. "Ham and cheese. Whatever. Or go hungry for all I care."

I kept quiet. I was the newcomer to the group and was still figuring everyone out. Brian, a tall, athletic redneck type with shoulder-length blond hair and arms covered in homemade tattoos, was dating the guy sitting next to him. That much was obvious. What I couldn't understand was why Brian and Terry were together. Brian was kind of hot in a rough sort of way, but he didn't seem to match up with the thin, effeminate Terry. Terry performed drag on the weekends, and while I hadn't seen his act, I could only hope he made a prettier woman than he did a guy. Terry also thought it was funny to be bitchy, but to me he just came off as mean and petty.

Then there were the twins. Gay twins, everyone's wet dream. Mike and David weren't identical, but they were very hard to tell apart. Strangely, I had a crush on Mike. I don't know why I liked Mike more than David since they looked alike and were both extremely nice, but I did. Maybe it was because he was a bit more on the quiet side, like myself. A kindred soul.

David puzzled me. He seemed to be an item with the last member of our little group, an older guy named Robert, but I wasn't sure. I'd heard Mike kidding David about Robert being his sugar daddy and I knew that David lived with Robert, so I assumed this was the case. However, David had taken to flirting with me, often right in front of Robert, so I wasn't entirely sure. The flirting had escalated over the past several days to the point where now David would look at me and say things like, "God, I want to suck your dick so bad." If these statements bothered Robert, he didn't let it show. Maybe they had an open relationship, or maybe flirting was allowed and that's all it was.

I resolved not to worry about it and just enjoy the day. We'd decided to have a picnic out at Bricknell Park, not far from the townhouse that Robert and David shared. It was sunny and warm, a perfect day for eating outdoors. Everyone was wearing shorts expect me. I refused to let my knobby knees and too-white skin be seen by anyone. We hadn't been sitting there for more than a few minutes before Brian peeled off his wife-beater T-shirt to reveal sunburned skin. A few minutes later, Mike took his T-shirt off, and I had to force myself not to stare at his lovely smooth chest.

The park was fairly full, and I noticed that most of the occupants seemed to be gay. Everywhere you looked there were beautiful bodies tossing around Frisbees or enjoying picnics of their own. A few families with children were present, but these were the exception to the rule. I asked Robert if this was a gay park.

He smiled. "Technically, no. The city has really tried to make it a family park, setting up little league games, pee-wee football and whatever. Back in the day, though, this was where all the queers hung out."

Terry snorted. "Old dudes hanging around the bushes. How sexy."

128

"You have to remember that this was in the days before PCs and the Internet. Some guys didn't like to go to the gay bars, so where else was there? Guys used to hang out here. In fact, there are lots of trails down in the woods over there," Robert said, indicating the direction with a nod, "Where guys used to hook up all the time. The police used to raid this park a lot."

"You mean," David asked, amazed, "that guys used to do it out there in the woods?"

Robert laughed. "They still do, although not the extent they used to. I remember going out there, and the woods would be full of fags. It seemed like everywhere you looked guys were sucking or fucking each other."

Terry gave an exaggerated shudder. "Ugh. I can only imagine. Bugs, dirt. No thank you!"

Shrugging, Robert continued. "Well, it was a place for guys to hook up. I have to admit I spent a few nights out here when I didn't feel like heading downtown to the bars. Met some great guys out here."

"Wasn't it kind of dangerous?" Mike asked. "I mean, you didn't know if the guy would be a serial killer or anything."

"It was probably safer than today and meeting someone over the Internet. At least out here, there were hundreds of fags within shouting distance. If anything happened, all you had to do was yell." Robert reached into the basket to get a second sandwich.

The conversation turned to movies, television, and other things. Mike and I finished our meals and began to rate the guys around us on a scale of one to ten. We usually agreed, which made me even more convinced of our compatibility.

The afternoon stretched on, and a slight breeze began to cool the effects of the July sun. Mike, Brian and Terry went off to find a relatively uninhabited patch of ground where they could toss a Frisbee around. Robert had spotted some old friends nearby, and he went over to chat with them, leaving David and me alone on the big red and white checkered blanket we'd thrown down for our picnic.

"We should check out some of those trails," David said. There was a glint in his eye.

"Maybe later," I said noncommittally.

David was not to be put off. "We could find a nice bush to hide behind, and I could suck that dick of yours."

I frowned. "What about Robert? Aren't you guys together?"

David shrugged. "So? He doesn't care if I fool around as long as I end up back with him at the end of the night."

The arrangement may have worked for Robert and David, but I liked them both, and I had no intention of getting in between them in any way. Besides, there was Mike. David seemed to read my thoughts.

"You've got a thing for my brother, don't you?"

"I didn't think it was that obvious."

David chuckled. "It's pretty clear. I mean, the way you look at him and all."

"Does he know?" I asked, suddenly apprehensive.

Nodding, David said, "We've talked about it. He likes you and all, but ..."

My heart sank. "But ..."

"You're not really his type. He usually goes for the bigger, burlier guys. You know, bears. A skinny little thing like you, well ..." He let the words trail. "Sorry," he added.

I tried not to let my disappointment show. "It's no big deal," I said, hoping I sounded more convincing to David than I did to myself. "As long as this doesn't hurt my friendship with you guys." I hadn't lived in Indianapolis all that long, and David and Company were pretty much my entire circle of friends.

"No way." David gave me a sly grin. "The offer for the blow job still stands. Might take your mind off other things."

"Maybe later," I said, meaning it. It would, in a way, make David a substitute for the brother I couldn't have, but if he was willing. Well, I figured it wouldn't hurt to keep my options open.

Eventually, the boys tired of throwing the Frisbee around, but then someone decided to get a volleyball game going, and the twins and Brian went to see if they could get involved. Terry came back to our picnic area, not wanting to participate. "These wrists," he said, flailing his bony arms in front of him, "just aren't made for volleyball."

I didn't want to be stuck alone with Terry, and as Robert was still off jawing with his cronies I excused myself, saying that I wanted to stretch my legs. I wandered off.

I'm not sure if I consciously headed in the direction of the woods or not. Either way, I was soon walking along a path under a canopy of trees. The breeze stirs the branches, making a soft moan in the air. I made my way carefully, watching not only for snakes but for guys who were out in the foliage looking for a quickie. I hadn't walked too far before a sound caused me to stop. Off the path to my left, I could see a couple going at it. I couldn't see the kneeling guy very well due to the trees and bushes in between us, but his standing partner was definitely in view. He looked as if he were slamming his cock into the other guy's face with fury. By the sounds of his grunts I assumed they were nearly finished. I walked on.

Several minutes later, I began to be mildly disappointed in Robert's "sex woods." I'd only seen one couple so far and even then not very clearly. I had expected to see gays hanging off the trees like monkeys, waiting for a trick to walk by, so they could pounce.

"Hey."

The voice startled me. I hadn't seen the guy, but he was standing just a few yards away, next to a tree. He had probably been slightly behind it when I'd approached and had just emerged. He was about my age, maybe a year or two younger. It was hard to tell as he had a round, boyish face, and his light colored skin was dotted with freckles. His light brown hair was closely shaved down to just a stubble. He was wearing only a pair of baggy gray shorts and tennis shoes with short white socks. His bare chest and shoulders showed even more freckles. The shorts were shoved down to reveal his swollen cock, which he stroked slowly.

"Hey," I said back.

"Want to suck this?" he asked. His voice had a faint drawl, common to the more countrified areas of Indiana. He wagged his cock invitingly.

I obviously wasn't going to get anything from Mike, so why the hell not?

"Sure," I answered. "Yeah."

He nodded at me. "Come here."

I left the path and followed him behind a clump of trees. He stopped and turned to me. With a half-smile he said, "Get down on your knees and suck my cock."

By his manner and words, I pegged him as a closet case, a redneck country boy who didn't consider it "gay" as long as he was the one being sucked. That was fine by me. No names, no exchange of numbers – just a quick blow job in the bushes. If he wanted to come over all masterful to soothe his ego, that was okay. Actually, I found it very sexy.

I sank to my knees, grateful that I'd worn the jeans. At least I wouldn't have to show back up at the picnic site with dirt on my knees. The pants could be brushed. The guy grabbed me by the hair with just a hint of roughness and pushed my lips toward his rod.

"Suck that fucking cock," he commanded.

I tried to start off slowly, but he wasn't having any of that. As soon as I had the head of his prick between my lips, he gripped me on either side of the head and began to thrust. His dick wasn't the biggest I'd ever had in my mouth, but it wasn't small either. I fought my gag reflex and allowed him to pound his meat into me.

"Yeah, that's it, fag. Swallow that fucking cock."

My own dick was aching, so I quickly undid my jeans to release it. I started stroking my own rod, and he continued to invade my mouth with his. Part of my brain protested that he could be potentially dangerous. I didn't, after all, know anything about him. He could beat the crap out of me after he came, but somehow I didn't think he would. And, after all, as Robert had said, there were dozens of guys nearby. All it would take to get them running would be a yell.

"You like sucking that dick, don't you, fag?"

Truth be told, I did. I moaned to let him know. This seemed to excite him even more for he began to slam his cock between my lips even faster. I could feel him tensing. I was ready to shoot myself, and I wondered which of us would come first.

He did. With a series of grunts, he shot his load into my mouth. I swallowed the thick juice as best I could and let the remainder slide down my chin. I pumped my own cock harder and shot just as he was pulling his dick out of my mouth.

To my surprise, he helped me back to my feet. He smiled a crooked smile and said, "You've got my cum on your face."

"It'll wipe off," I said. Those were our last words together. He grinned again and pulled his shorts up before walking back off into the woods. I used my shirt to wipe my chin and retraced my steps back to the path.

Back at the picnic site, things seemed to have wound down. The volleyball game had worn out the boys, and Terry was getting bored, so we started to pack up our things and called it a day. As David and I put the picnic hamper into the trunk of Robert's car, he examined my face. "You look happy," he said.

"I suppose I am," I replied.

After all, there are worse ways of getting over rejection.

WALKING THAT WILD SIDE
By Stephen Osborne

Two years, my friends insisted, was way too long a period of mourning. The rational part of me knew that they were right. The truth was, though, I was scared shitless over the thought of dating again. I knew myself too well. I knew that the first person I had sex with after my long abstinence would suffer by comparison. How could he not? He wouldn't be Greg. That much was sure. How could he match up to my late lover, who knew every inch of my body and who could drive me to distraction with the tiniest nibble of my earlobe?

My first date should be disposable. Someone to whom I wouldn't form an attachment. Someone who would be just a sex object, a warm body to bring me to climax. Someone very different from Greg.

I had no idea where I was going to find such a guy.

Bars weren't my thing. I knew that from my time B.G. (before Greg). Shy around strangers, I could never bring myself to go up and chat with anyone, and if anyone tried to start a conversation with me, I tended to clam up like a monk who'd just taken his vows. Usually, I ended up sitting at the bar, nursing a drink or two, before finally giving up and slinking home.

My friends offered to come with me, but I knew that wouldn't help the situation. With them around, I would have a crutch. I wanted to be alone so that (if I could muster up the courage) I'd be forced to talk to strangers. If I didn't, I'd end up feeling like a twit as usual sitting there by myself.

That was the plan, anyway.

The bar I went to was called Oliver's. I chose it because it had a reputation for being a meat market. Glass House was more of a dance club and Portman Street Bar was more of a darts and pool table kind of place. Oliver's was, to put it mildly, skanky. Dimly lit, Oliver's clientele usually weren't looking for a long-term relationship. They came in horny and looking for sex. If their blood wasn't pumping when they walked in the door, it certainly was when they watched the porn films being shown on the television screens above the bar. Leather, boots, cigars, mustaches, S&M, bondage – all of these were associated with Oliver's, and more.

I knew the place would be packed on the weekend, and I wasn't sure I was ready for darkened rooms full of furtive glances, so I went on a Thursday night. Busy, but not overly so. I barely looked around as I made my way to the bar. My heart was beating a Samba beat as I ordered a gin and tonic and found a spot to sit. I knew as soon as I sat down that this was going to be a bust. It didn't feel right. I was too nervous. I couldn't even look around to see if anyone interested me. Looking up at the TV screens didn't help. The film was showing some guy in a cage sucking off his master with a desperation that made me feel slightly ill.

Maybe I wasn't ready after all.

I drank my gin and tonic and then made my way to the restroom. There were maybe twenty-five or so people in the two large rooms that made up Oliver's, and so far, I hadn't looked one of them in the face, with the exception of the shirtless bear of a bartender. Giving up, I decided I'd pee and then slink out the door and try again some other night.

The men's room in Oliver's was just as dimly lit as the rest of the place. There was one stall, seemingly occupied, and three urinals lined up uncomfortably close to each other. Luckily no one was using any of them at the moment, so I didn't have to bump elbows in order to piss.

I was midway through when I heard the door to the toilet stall open. A moment later someone came up beside me. A quick glance showed me he was fairly young (although in the light it was hard to tell) and not bad looking. A little on the rough side, maybe, with his close cut hair and tattoo on his neck, but not bad. He squeezed in next to me and unzipped his fly, making sure his shoulder nudged mine.

I bit my lip. Normally I'm a shy pisser and prefer to urinate with no one within several feet, but this was a special occasion after all. I was wanting to find some anonymous sex. I forced myself not to budge and kept contact with his shoulder. He didn't even pretend to be peeing. He took his dick out, but his gaze went right to my groin. "Nice dick," he grunted.

"Thanks," I said. I was done pissing and didn't know what I was supposed to do now. Did I stow my dick back in my pants? Did I reach over to take hold of his? Did I fall to my knees and scream to the heavens for him to take me? I hesitated.

He nudged me again. "Want to fuck me?" he asked.

I turned my head to look at him more carefully. He was definitely on the rough side, and the tattoo on his neck was some phrase that seemed to include the name Johnny, but it was too dark to make out the other words. He had nice eyes, though. "That could be fun," I replied.

He didn't answer or bother to zip his fly back up. He simply took me by the elbow and began to guide me over to the toilet stall. He swung the door open to reveal the filthiest, most disgusting toilet I'd ever seen. Piss coated the floor and most of the toilet itself, mixing with shit stains and God knew what else. I put my brakes on.

"Here?" I asked. "We're supposed to fuck here?"

He pulled me against him and tried to kiss my mouth. I twisted so that he only got a cheek. "Don't you want to fuck?" he whispered.

"I want to fuck. I just want to live through it," I told him.

He reached down with his right hand and tried to stroke my cock. My hips seemed to fly back on their own accord, and he only managed a quick feel. "It'll be fun," he insisted. He was trying to sound sexy, but the cigarette breath mixed with the beer burbs was ruining the illusion.

I backed away, putting my dick safely back in my pants. "I think I'll pass, thanks."

He said something, but I didn't catch what it was. I was heading for the exit and made it to the parking lot in record time. Oliver's was, as advertised, skanky. Unfortunately, I wasn't.

Once in my car, however, I mentally slapped myself. *Maybe a quick fuck in a filthy restroom was just what I needed. The guy had been kind of hot in that redneck sort of way. Maybe I should go back inside and see if he was still hovering around the urinals. Maybe I should ...*

A thought struck me. What better place for an anonymous tryst than a bath house? Indianapolis had two that I knew of, one that was a mere few blocks away. I knew that, technically, they weren't bath houses any longer but "clubs" that supplied men with workout rooms, a pool, sauna, steam room and whatever. Gone were the days of orgy rooms and fucking on the pool deck. Nowadays, the sex was confined to the private rooms and the steam room, as my more adventurous friends informed me. I'd never dared to venture inside.

I started the engine and headed west.

There was a tiny parking lot next to Lee Street Club. I pulled in, sure that everyone I knew in the city was watching me. It took several minutes to work up the courage to walk to the front entrance and open the door.

I don't know what I was expecting, but inside I found a drab foyer. Opposite was the door leading to the club itself. Along one wall was a window showing the tiny room beyond, containing an attendant at a cash register. A board on the wall showed the rates. The guy looked bored. "Can I help you?" he asked, his tone indicating that he really didn't care if you could or not.

"Yes," I answered, willing my voice not to crack. "I've not actually been here before, and I'm not sure what the procedure is."

"First you need to buy a membership, and then you need to decide whether you want a room for the night or just rent a locker."

A room sounded like too much of an investment since I wasn't sure that I wouldn't chicken out and flee the premises before an hour was up. I went with renting a locker. The cashier took my money and handed me a key and a towel. He then pressed a button to release the lock on the inner door. "Right through there," he told me.

I went through, feeling like Alice going through the looking glass. Inside was indeed a different world.

Men were everywhere, or so it seemed to me. Walking around with nothing but a towel around their waists. Leering men. Smiling men. Thin men. Fat men. Old men. Young men. Furry men. Smooth men. Twinks, construction-worker types – they were all there. Off to my left, I could see a workout room, and the men inside, struggling with weights and exercise machines, actually had on gym clothes. Their towels were nearby, though, ready to mop their sweaty brows. One young man was fully clothed, but he seemed to be an employee. He was busy wiping off the benches lining the walls with a cloth. I also saw someone wandering the halls wearing some sort of Japanese kimono, looking like some deranged reject from *Madame Butterfly*. He paused when he walked by me. I studiously avoided looking directly at him.

He finally moved on, and I breathed deeply. I briefly closed my eyes and forced myself to calm down. After all, what was I worried about? Most of these guys were here for the same reason – to have sex! I didn't know them and they didn't know me and that was fine.

Tonight, just tonight, I was going to be a slut.

Cruising for Bad Boys

Being a virgin at the baths (so to speak), I had to watch the other guys to know what the protocols were. There were pegs in the steam room/sauna area, and I wondered if one was supposed to enter these rooms naked. After observing a few others, though, I figured out the pegs were only for guys getting into the hot tub (a bubbling cauldron which was, at the moment, empty). I was thankful for this because I really didn't want to enter the steam room stark naked. I had decided to be a slut, but I still wanted to leave room for a little revelation and mystery.

Towel firmly in place, I opened the door to the steam room. A hiss and a blast of heat greeted me. I walked forward, letting the door close behind me. I couldn't see anything at first, but once my eyes had adjusted, I saw a medium-sized room full of nooks and crannies with plenty of benches. It wasn't easy to make out anything with the billows of steam rising up, but soon I could see shadowy figures. Some were standing against the walls, obviously to get a good look at whatever was passing their way while others were lounging on the benches. On one small bench, I spotted an older guy who seemed to have a package on his lap. The steam cleared for a moment, and I realized that what I had mistaken for a package was instead a young twink huddled between the man's legs, his head bobbing up and down furiously in the older man's crotch. *Way to go, older guy*, I thought. While twinks weren't really my thing, I hoped I found something that would strike my fancy.

The trouble was it was really hard to make out faces in the mists. You could see general shapes and sizes, but to really get the details as to nice eyes, a good firm jaw, or a well-placed tattoo on the upper arm, I could see that I was going to have to get closer to one of these shadowy blobs.

I moved further into the room. I could hear water dripping and the hiss of the steam mixing with slurps from blow jobs or other such activities. Following a slight bend in the wall, I nearly walked right into a rather muscular black gentleman slamming his cock hard into the ass of a moaning blond boy. The black guy smiled at me without pausing in his fucking. "How you doing?" he asked in a low tone.

"Good," I said, trying not to sound embarrassed. It was the first time I'd ever conversed with someone in the act of fucking another guy. It seemed a bit odd to me, as if I were dividing his attention when he should be concentrating on other matters.

I was about to move on and leave them to it when the black guy placed a hand on my chest. He stroked me tenderly. "You're a pretty boy," he said, giving my nipple a little tweak. "I like pretty boys."

I wasn't sure how pretty I was, but I was certain of how hot he was. Tall and finely-muscled, he had a shaved head and a great smile. The blond guy, hunched over and using the wall for support, looked back to see with whom his friend was talking. By the ecstasy in his eyes, I could see that he was really enjoying the ass-plowing he was receiving. I envied him. The blond guy grinned at me as well. He looked like a college student or a fresh-faced farm boy. "You can join us, if you like."

The black guy's smiled widened. He put his arm around my shoulder and pulled me closer. "You sure as shit can." His attentions to me had slowed down his thrusts into the other guy's ass. Blondie looked around again as if to say *come on, what's the holdup?*

The black guy gave him a few slow feeds from his big cock without taking his arm off me. "You boys want to come back to my room. I'll let you both have a taste of this dick."

Blondie grunted as the black guy pulled his cock out. "Sounds good to me."

I wasn't about to argue. I wanted to be a slut, but it would be more in my style to be slutty in a less public place. My two new friends picked up their towels, and without any further word, we headed out of the steam room.

As we navigated down the hall, the black guy nodded briefly at me. "Name's Ty," he said.

"Stephen."

Blondie, walking slightly behind me, put a friendly hand on my ass and gave it a squeeze. "I'm Jeff."

The "rooms" were really just partitioned off areas with a bed and a little nightstand. The walls didn't even go all the way up to the ceiling. Getting to Ty's room, he motioned for us to go inside. When he shut the flimsy door behind him, I noticed a placard fixed to the back of it that read, "No more than two people are to occupy a room at any time. Failure to comply with this rule may lead to expulsion from the club." Ty didn't seem worried by it, so I didn't say anything.

The space was tiny and so was the bed, and I was just beginning to wonder how we were going to manage when Ty spun me around and planted his lips firmly onto my mouth. I opened my mouth and let his big snake of a tongue invade me. I felt Jeff tug at the towel wrapped around me and off it came, exposing my hard-on. Ty pressed against me, and I felt his stiffened prick rub against my abdomen. God, he was hot. Then I felt Jeff embrace me from behind, his cock pressing against my ass crack. It was almost more body contact than I could take. I felt ready to explode.

Ty broke off the kiss. "So what you boys want to do? How do you want it?"

Jeff was nuzzling the back of my neck, making me gasp. His hand reached around to my crotch, and he started to stroke me gently. "I want to fuck that sweet ass of his," he said in a hushed tone.

My hand wandered across Ty's abdomen and finally down to his huge dick. I really wanted to see what that monster felt like in my butt, but I didn't feel like arguing. Ty grinned. "You boys get onto the bed."

We complied. It wasn't a large bed, but we managed. I got down on all fours, facing the foot of the bed. Jeff got behind me. I looked around to see him take a condom wrapper and a bottle of lube off the decrepit nightstand. Once he was sheathed, he lubed both his cock and my ass. I groaned as he placed the head of his dick against my hole.

Ty rubbed my shoulders as Jeff entered me. Luckily, he took it fairly slow. Ty's massage helped me relax somewhat. I looked at him as he stood over us at the end of the bed. "You like the feel of that cock inside you?" he asked.

I nodded, unable to speak.

"It's so fucking tight," Jeff whispered as he began to piston his hips into me.

Ty shuffled a little, bringing his crotch right up near my face. His strong hands moved from my shoulders to my cheeks. He lifted my face a little. "You want to suck my cock while he fucks you?"

Oh, yeah.

Soon that monster dick was in my mouth. I had to really open up my throat to keep from gagging, but somehow I managed. It took the three of us a moment or so before we got the rhythm down, but before long, Jeff's thrusts were throwing my face onto Ty's dick. I'd always wondered what it would be like to be taken from both ends at once. Now I knew. It was fantastic.

Ty came first. He grunted loudly before pulling out. He pumped his dick a few times and then aimed so that the juice would cover my face. I loved it.

Jeff began pounding harder and harder until I thought that one of us would surely break. With a loud cry, he fell onto my back, and I felt his cock throb inside me as he came. His skin felt like a mass of sweat against me. I reached down to my own aching dick and quickly got myself off. I wanted to come before Jeff pulled his sweet dick out of my ass and while Ty's juice was still dripping off my chin.

There wasn't a lot of talk afterwards. Ty suddenly claimed to be "shagged out" and wanted to rest a bit. Taking the hint, Jeff and I quickly grabbed our towels and went back out into the hall. Jeff patted me on the back as Ty closed the door behind us. "Thanks for the fuck," he said with a sly smile.

"Anytime," I replied with a smile, although I knew I'd never see him or Ty ever again.

I was smiling as I walked down the hall to the locker room. I could have stayed longer, since I had an eight-hour rental on the locker, but it wasn't necessary. Sure, I could have made my way back to the steam room or found someone else to have quick, anonymous sex with, but I didn't need to. I'd accomplished what I'd come for. I'd managed to put the past behind me. I could look to the future.

I was back!

CAR SERVICE
By Owen Keehnen

That was it! I needed to get back into shape. I used to run five miles almost every day for upwards of two years. I'd never felt better. I stopped a few years ago after being sidelined with some nasty shin splints and IT band issues. Too many miles running in shit shoes on pavement. I'd learned my lesson. This time, I was only going to run on the jogging path or at the gym on the treadmill. This time, I was going to get decent running shoes.

Hopping into the car, I made a left and headed to The Sports Authority a few blocks uptown. Rather than deal with the street parking headaches, I turned into the connected parking garage. It was one of those zigzagging concrete catacombs with the low ceilings and ultra dim lighting. I found an available spot without much of a problem. When I pushed through the Level-Two parking garage door into the hallway, the brightness was a bit disconcerting. A flight of concrete stairs led down from the garage to the entrance of the store.

The air conditioning hit me with a blast. I made my way through the golf, camping, and weight training equipment to the running gear and shoes. Finding the right pair of running shoes can be a bit daunting, but it was worth the effort. I'd made bad decisions before. A bargain wasn't always a bargain, especially when it came to shoes. I wasn't going to injure myself again just to save a few bucks.

The best way to decide on running shoes is to simply try them on. The first pair looked slick but were too tight at the arch. That minor irritation would mean serious pain. No thanks! The second pair was too constricting. That was no good. The third pair seemed fine, or at least better than the first two. I tried standing, bouncing on my weight, leaning onto my toes and then heels, and walking. I assumed a sprinter's pose to see if they were flexible at the toe. If the shoes didn't have the right amount of give it was a no sale.

I raised my head in preparation for the blast from an imaginary starting gun. Breathing deeply, I opened my eyes and found myself with a clear view up the leg gap of a pair of running shorts and into a very well packed jock. I froze. Sometimes, even the promise of a glimpse of cock can take my breath away, especially when it's unexpected and with a pouch that promising. It was clear that a rod of impressive girth was tucked inside that cotton cock sock. Nice. Very nice. My saliva was getting thick. Despite the air conditioning, it suddenly felt a little hot in there.

Looking up, I swallowed uncomfortably. I'd only been staring for what seemed like a moment. Apparently, it was long enough to be caught in the act. The lean and handsome owner of that impressive package was staring right back at me and wearing an overly confident smirk that said, "Yeah, you know you want it." He was cocky all right.

Before I could recover from the embarrassment of being crotch clocked, an attractive redhead came down the aisle and gave him a kiss. "Bill, I'm going to take the kids across the street to some of the other stores. They need to get some things for school. I'm not sure how long we'll be. We'll just meet you at the car."

"Sounds good." Bill had a deep and melodious voice.

Damn those metrosexuals! I felt like a predatory gay but figured there was no harm done. Bill would just have to take my drooling as a compliment. I shrugged off the whole incident as a moment of misplaced lust and chose another pair of shoes. This pair felt great. Good support, comfort, bounce, flexible but firm. I was sure I'd found the pair. When I turned to do a little more walking, I noticed Bill had one leg raised onto the bench and was tying a pair of shoes. He'd rearranged the merchandise. Now the impressive head of his cock and a bit of the shaft was peaking around the elastic side band of his jockstrap. Damn that was fine.

"I'm looking for a perfect fit," he said. The first words he spoke to me sounded like bad porn movie dialogue, but the grin that followed looked great with his square jaw.

I looked up into his eyes and smiled. I knelt and tried my sprinter's pose and figured what the hell, as long as I was down there. Whew! What a view! Nice fucking slab. The head had a rosy mushroom cap. I was dead-on about the girth. That pale beauty was soft and very full and looked to be getting fuller by the minute. As I stared, more of it was twitching and edging into view. Somebody liked the attention.

I coughed and took a look either way. The tease was nice, but now what? It wasn't exactly this guy's ego that I felt like stroking. This was all hot as fuck, but already complicated. Ninety percent of the time I would give my left nut to be dropped into a scenario like this, yet all I really wanted was a decent pair of running shoes. At least that's what I told myself.

There's some baggage here. I don't do married guys, not anymore. I'd done plenty in the past and even broke a cardinal rule by getting seriously involved with one. He broke my heart. That fuck-over experience made me feel like shit. Fooling with married guys is just asking for trouble. It was a sure way to up my blood pressure twenty points, knock my self-esteem down a few notches, and send me running to the refrigerator all at the same time. No thanks.

With a shrug, I turned my back on Bill and headed to the checkout. I had to get out of here before I did something really stupid, or at least something I would regret. When the clerk handed me my change, I grabbed the shoes and climbed the stairs back to my car. It took a second for my eyes to adjust to the grayness of the parking garage. I heard a scrape. Turning, I saw Bill leaning against one of the cement pillars. He looked right at me and smiled before reaching down to grope his basket. What a cocky bastard! Unfortunately, that was just the sort of ballsy shit guaranteed to get my cock throbbing. He cupped his crotch. There was no mistaking his meaning.

Sure, I'd made big pronouncements about married men, but every inch of his tasty six-foot frame was standing in front of me asking for it. My resolution faded, and all I could remember was the sight of that cock. He offered a mischievous grin. I wasn't sure what I should do. Let me rephrase that. I knew what I should do. Unfortunately, I also knew what I was going to do. My brain kept telling me to "Keep walking," but my thought center had shifted to about three feet south of there. Instead, I smiled and said something inane like, "Uh, hey." I needn't have bothered.

Bill didn't need much encouragement. Married guys are mostly ballsy as fuck when they want to play. Bill was no exception. He took one hand and pinned the root of his thick meat inside his shorts and began stroking the lengthening bulge with the other.

"What's up?"

He looked down at his stroking hand. "I think you know."

I swore I wouldn't do this. Married guys are fucked. It's all about them. I could be anybody. Yeah, but I was this lucky somebody. The voice of reason once again clicked off the moment I opened my mouth. "Listen, umm, we can go back to my place. That is after you call your wife or something."

Bill shook his head and kept running his hand up and down the length of his shaft. "Nah, I don't feel like talking to her. Why leave? Let's just do it here."

"Here? But we might get caught."

"I know, but that sort of adds to the suspense don't you think? You've got a sweet mouth. Come on," he winked with a look down at his stroking hand.

This guy was crazy and cocky and so fucking my type. Reaching out he grabbed me by the belt buckle. After some playful jostling back and forth he pulled me close and planted a solid kiss on my mouth. It was a strong unrepentant kiss that promised a lot. Breaking apart, he smiled and moved in again. This time our tongues went to work and our hands began to explore. Shit. This was crazy. Anybody could walk in here. They might even have security cameras.

I closed my eyes and went with it. I vowed this was positively the last time I would do it with a married guy.

With a hand still on my buckle, Bill spun me around, so my back was against the passenger door of the sedan. He kissed me again with a bit more tenderness. During this bit of spit swapping, he managed to open the back door of the car. In a moment, he shoved me inside.

I fell backwards across the seat. This guy was voracious. He was on top of me. His mouth was everywhere. He was kissing my face, my lips, my chin, probing my ears with his tongue. His stubble scratched in a way that sent my libido into overdrive. Oh yeah. His every move felt untamed and absolutely perfect.

Grabbing my hands, Bill forced my arms overhead. Holding them there he kissed me stronger than before. I could tell he liked a little rough play, and I was in no position to argue. All I could manage was a moan. There's nothing like being pinned in the backseat of a car.

Bill began to kiss down the curve of my neck. He started to suck, but I used my torso to push him away. There was no way he was giving me a hickey. I was his for the time being. He didn't need to brand me. Bill smiled and planted another fierce kiss on my lips before his mouth trailed down. He began to undo the buttons of my shirt with his teeth. It felt incredible. This guy was on fire. I was combustible in his arsonist hands. Once he latched onto my nipples and began to lick and suck and give little bites, I was right there with him. I didn't care where the fuck we were or if we were being broadcast coast to coast on *America's*

Raunchiest Home Videos. All that mattered was what we were doing.

He let go of my hands and yanked down his running shorts and jock in a single motion. Oh yeah. All resistance melted with this guy in charge. He had me rock hard. I was having the same effect on him. His cock was pressed against my thigh and leaving a nice little trail of pre-cum on the peach fuzz there. I involuntarily licked my lips when I saw that wonderful piece of meat in all its liberated glory. Bill knew what I wanted. He also knew I wanted it forcibly delivered. Without hesitation, he knelt on my arms, pinning them to my sides. Yeah, take charge motherfucker. Give it to your bitch boy. He began to rub his cock across my lips. I was given only the slightest taste. He was teasing me. We both knew it was only a matter of time. My mouth lunged for the prize a couple times before Bill offered his shit-eating grin and fed me that juicy reward. Rocking his hips, Bill was soon shoving his cut slab of straight cock in and out of my mouth. I was coughing and gagging and in fucking use-me heaven all at once. Give it to me. I don't care. Fucking choke me with that thick pussy pulverizing cock. We were both out of control. He was getting awfully excited. His breathing was forced. His cock was thickening. The head was growing more pronounced, and by now I could taste the pre-jizz. I was afraid that any minute my hip-bucking stud was going to coat my throat with a full sticky load. That was what I had in mind, too – eventually. Right now there were some other things I had in mind.

Managing to slip his throbbing cock from my lips, I slid down on the seat and went to work on Bill's hefty balls. Nice fucking nuggets. I inhaled deeply. He'd been wearing that jock a while. His sac had that tangy smell that drives me wild. I put my nose right up in them. Mmmmm. Nothing like a sweaty pair of nuts to push me over the edge. These babies were prime, nice full low hangers. He even shaved his sac.

Bill was jacking his meat now. I could hear it gliding through his fist and feel the leap of his nuts as he stroked. It drove him wild when I rolled my tongue over them and then hummed against that saliva soaked nutsac. I took each in my mouth for a nice suck, but I was anxious to blaze on to some of Bill's other tasty treasures. Bending lower I began to lick and kiss the patch of skin south of his scrotum. I gave several playful bites around the area before making a little sucking trail up to his puckered anus.

When my tongue flicked over his fuck hole, he let out a deep moan. Oh yeah, fucking give up your pretty hole straight man. By the sound of it, Bill liked having his butt eaten. Well, it was his lucky day because I was hungry for some hot anus. In no time, Bill was thrashing; reaching back, he parted his cheeks to feed me his musty hole with forceful downward thrusts. He started rocking his hips and riding my tongue. I was in heaven exploring one of the sweetest buttholes I'd ever had the pleasure of eating. I couldn't hold my excitement much longer. There was nothing better than jacking off with prime man butt on my face, suffocating me. I loved driving my mouth deeper and deeper into that delicious canal.

Following a shout of "Whew, fuck yeah, eat my hole," Bill showed admirable restraint and slid off my tongue. Eating ass is my forte. Not many men have the strength to get off that pleasure serpent when it starts going to work. Bill had some exploration of his own in mind. Wasting no time, he flipped me over. To my astonishment, he started making little licking circles on the furry globes of my ass, gradually nearing the crack. He pulled my asscheeks wide. His tongue was on my hole. Mercy! Yeah, Mr. Hetero, go for it. You're there – now do it right. Some married guys are just full of hidden talents. Maybe he did the same thing with his wife? Maybe he'd eaten the asses of dozens of guys? Who the fuck cared? None of that mattered. All I knew was his tongue felt fucking fantastic.

After a good couple minutes of loosening my fuckhole, Bill spit onto his hand and rubbed saliva around the glistening knob of his tool. I was ready. My hole was primed. I was relieved when Bill pulled a condom from his wallet. It was nice not to have to go there and have that conversation. If Bill was going to do shit like this on the down-low. at least he was taking some precautions in keeping his pecker clean.

Tearing the wrapper with his teeth, he gave me a wink, "You never know."

Rolling the rubber down that rigid piece of meat, he put another glob of spit in his hand and jacked the latex sheath until the opaque surface glistened. His coated cock bobbed at a ninety-degree angle in front of him as he began to feed one then another twisting finger to my hungry ass. I was beyond ready. My hole was voracious. I wanted this guy so fucking badly that I couldn't stand it. We both moaned as he slipped his thick meat beyond the muscled ring. By the moan that rose from deep in his throat, I knew he'd come damn close to finding his perfect fit. He rotated his hips to be sure his cock was hitting all the right places. It felt fantastic. We both knew there was no way we were holding back once things got going.

He pressed on, and in a moment that gorgeous piece of meat was all the way inside. It took my breath away. The thick ones always do. By the time he began to increase the pace of his thrusts, I had my bearings. I was meeting his every move and ready to take every bit of what he could give. It felt incredible, but also a bit awkward in the backseat. Grabbing me by the leg he flipped me onto my back. Much better. I could bend my knees. He knelt between my legs and thrust forward by rising from his thighs. Bulls-eye. Optimal penetration achieved. Once we got into a rhythm, Bill began to enter my pulsating hole with greater force. Deep and hard and fast. Yeah. Fuck. So fucking good. Oh yeah. That thick slab was driving home again and again. He was taking me there, and I was determined to give him a ride he wouldn't soon forget and drain his cock with my tight hole. I looked up at the ceiling of that sedan. I was right there and yet a million miles away. A furious fuck transports me to another world.

He grabbed my hair and yanked my head forward to kiss him deeply before plowing into my ass with a series of quick jabs that hit my prostate dead on. Wham. Wham. Wham. Hot damn man. By this point, my cock was flush to my belly and drooling a cock lube lake into my navel. His thrusts started to slow and deepen. Nothing was too deep for me. I was ready for it. I could have taken his fucking forearm by that point.

I was in ecstasy. I didn't know what the hell I was saying or if it was even a language. I was delirious. In no time, he was nailing me so forcefully and dead on that my head was banging against the arm rest. Fucking split my skull, I don't give a shit. I'd gladly suffer more for this ass pounding. I needed it bad.

In a minute, I felt his legs begin to tighten and twitch. Sweat was dripping on me from his hair and his chest, and the car was starting to smell a little funky. This was all so fucking hot. I reached back and felt his tight ass as it clamped and sent his juicy dick home again and again. My cock began to swell. He was getting ready to get his nut.

With a deep guttural growl, Bill cried, "Shit, fuck, shit." He froze for a moment and then began to shake. I could feel the spasms of his explosion.

"Oh yeah," I felt the pulse of him pumping out a big load and filling the condom with spunk. When the last tremor ended, he collapsed upon me. With our sweaty stomachs pressed together, I lifted my legs and thrust just a bit. My rod was so damn sensitive. I was on the edge and primed to shoot. With one more move, I felt my cock dump a massive load into slick union of our bellies. "Fuck!" My hands clenched along with my jaw. "Shit! Ahhhh. Yes!" Rubbing it in the sweat and spooge pool almost got me to shoot a second time.

We both lay panting for another minute. That was so intense. It was hard to even remember my name. Everything slowly came back to me. My breathing started to return to normal. I just kept thinking this is crazy. Bill was the first to actually break the silence. He told me to be careful not to get any jizz on the seats.

I pulled on my clothes. Bill raised his running shorts and jock from around his ankles. With a wink he opened the car door. I rolled my eyes when I saw I'd dropped my shoe box on the cement outside. Bill reached out the door and grabbed my hand. He held it for a lingering moment. I could really fall for this guy, but as I said, married guys are always trouble. Bill was the last thing my blood pressure needed. The memory would have to suffice. Anything more would be too complicated. "I should get going. Besides, we wouldn't want your wife to catch us."

Bill let go of my hand. "Why would she catch us?"

"Well, I mean if she comes back to the car."

Bill got out of the back seat. Closing the door, he looked at me with that shit-eating grin. "No worries, this isn't my car."

I watched him walk away with that cocky strut. My mouth was still open. He may have been great sex and all, but there was no mistake that he was trouble. Bill wasn't kidding when he said he liked to take chances.

8 BEAUTIFUL BOYS 8 – THE FOLLIES REVISITED
By Jamie Freeman

The room is dark when I first enter it.

It is dark and familiar even though it has been fifteen years since I first came here and perhaps a decade since my last visit. This place will never change. The Follies will live on, year after year, each season featuring a new crop of twinks who tread the boards with reckless abandon. Each evening the more seasoned members of the company will drink vending machine coffee and read newspapers in the lobby between scenes.

I played here at the Follies most Saturdays while I was enrolled in an expensive university in Northwest DC, learning to become a Foreign Service officer. I ducked my straight friends and became a regular at the matinees here. The theater became a playground, or perhaps more accurately, a laboratory for my sexual awakening, providing me an unending stream of unattached bodies with which to define the stats for my personal ad.

It was here that I got the first blow job of my adult life, in one of the filthy theater seats only a few feet from where I am standing now. I lean with my back against the wall and look down at the rows of theater seats thinking that perhaps in this seat, or that one in the next row up, I had sat in my Levi's and that black UCLA sweatshirt, trembling with fear as a man sat in the seat next to me. I remember the feel of his hand on my knee, then my thigh, then the feel of his fingers unzipping my pants. He was black with a handsome profile and a sweet smell, like stewed cinnamon or nutmeg. I remember his hands descending into my pants, my hips moving to allow him to pull my pants down and my dick out. I remember the feel of his hand, coaxing me to erection and then, unexpectedly, expectedly, his soft, warm mouth descending on me, that feeling of softness and envelopment. His hand stroked me, and his mouth caressed me with practiced skill. I was transported, back to childhood experiments, backyard antics then yanked forward into the vision of the huge writhing professionals fucking on the giant screen in front of me, into the depths of my crotch, into the deep throat of this kneeling man, into a world beyond childhood. And, I came, and he sucked and sucked, like he was afraid of losing even one drop. And, it was over. I lay back exhausted. He thanked me quietly and left in search of another cock. I tucked myself back in, regained my strength and my composure and eventually made my way to the exit, not realizing until I was on the Metro, staring distractedly at a beautiful blond boy in khakis and a white oxford, that I had a streak of dried, glistening come on the front of my sweatshirt.

Now, as I let my eyes adjust, the well-remembered smell of poppers and sweat and rot and sex assaults my senses. The room is warm, almost humid today. The spectators are a mix of older men dressed in business drag, post-clones in the jeans and T-shirt combo, Capitol Hill wonks in immaculate white oxfords and khakis, and twinks in shorts and T-shirts.

As I stand here in the semi-darkness, I feel a vague sense of physical connection to the shabby glory of the place. I look up at the peeling wallpaper and dark fittings, and I know that, although I will forget the men, I will not forget the Follies. This place has a solidity in my memories that assures it of immortality. The feel of the Follies is one that I can summon at will, like a well-remembered physical sensation, the feel of my fingers curled around the doorknob of my childhood bedroom or the feel of a favorite faded sweatshirt against my arm.

It has changed over the years, the old film projector removed, the back stairs and projection room converted into a warren of tiny cubicles and an upstairs room with barred

156

windows. Men walk back and forth through the labyrinth, restless, caged, emerging on the far side of the room, walking down the far aisle and disappearing into a long hallway that runs, if it too has not changed, behind the screen.

I remember a man giving me a blow job back in that hallway of cubicles, and I try to recall anything about him. I have the sense that he was older than I, a little overweight, perhaps. I recall white cotton as if he was wearing a white oxford, though there is no clarity to the memory. This man who sucked me off so eagerly was just one in a long string of men on their knees, as anonymous as blades of grass in the lawn of the house where I lived at the time. And, to him, I suspect that I, too, was merely one in an endless parade of boys dispensing their charms onto the soft expanse of his tongue, another pair of rounded buttocks to be groped, another choking sensation to erase the dull, dry residue of career, family, debt and home-ownership. We shared a moment that afternoon, reading from the same script for a while, coming together for our separate purposes, and although I now have only the vaguest recollections of the scene, it seemed important at the time, a pivotal moment somehow. There was something about it I thought I would remember always, but it is gone, washed away in a sea of other blowjobs, other bit-players.

Today, nearly fifteen years later, I look around the room. There are so many older men, many long past the age of retirement. I make my way through a group of men who stand around the entrance to the passage at the back of the room, mock nonchalance cracking as I pass between them.

Their heads follow me, fresh meat.

I glance into the cubicles, climb the steep wooden steps to the old projection room and watch disinterestedly for a moment as a fat man gives a thin older man a blow job, the flickering movie barely visible through the barred window above the kneeling man's head.

I stumble back down the stairs in the semi-darkness and make my way across to the far side of the theater, nothing peaking my interest. When I emerge back into the theater and make my way across the back aisle in the direction of the door that I came in, there is a disturbance behind me.

I move aside, and a cute blond man in matching yellow soccer shirt and shorts passes by me, grabbing the sleeve of my T-shirt and whispering "C'mon." I look at him in the flickering light from the screen, and seeing something attractive there, I follow him out across the lobby into a warren of connecting rooms, through another series of doorways and into the restroom. Behind the restroom door is an empty shower stall, the knobs long removed, the pipes closed over, an opaque shower door still intact, closing off the little cubicle from the world. He pulls me inside and kneels in front of me, hands already on my crotch by the time I have closed the door.

I am not hard, but within moments, I can feel the blood rushing to my crotch as his hands and his mouth assault me.

"Wait," he says, jumping up and pulling his shorts down and over his white sneakers, flinging them onto the filthy tile floor of the shower stall. "Do you like my diaper?" he asks grinning.

"Sure," I say, more curious than surprised.

"Yeah, baby, you're so hot. I just love hot guys to see me in my diaper. Yeah." He kneels back down, one hand rubbing his boner through the front of the diaper, one holding my cock in his frothing throat.

"Let me see your dick," I say, leaning back against the wall of the shower stall and looking down across my chest, my stomach at his tight white diaper.

He pulls his dick out and strokes it a couple of times. It is small, thin but well-shaped, not too thick, but not tapered to nothing like many I have seen. He himself is short, lean, compact. He reminds me of my ex, Robert, but not as beautiful, not as sculpted. I remember Robert, muscular and nearly naked in his diaper at Halloween last year and smile.

"You like it?" he asks. "You like my thick cock sticking out of my diaper?"

"Yeah, yeah, I do," I whisper, though in truth, the diaper does nothing but distract me and obstruct my view of his dick.

He returns to my dick, his throat opening to take it all in.

"I'm gonna shoot my load," he announces, too soon. "I'm gonna shoot my load all over my diaper."

I look down at him in silence, wondering where this all came from, how he became this particular person playing this particular role, in this particular place. Too many steps to contemplate, I suspect.

"You ready?" he asks.

"Uh, not yet," I say, somewhat surprised as I see him shudder.

"Yeah baby," he moans. "Look at me coming in my diaper. Yeah, oh yeah."

"You came?" I ask, trying not to sound incredulous, watching as his erection fades within the confines of the diaper.

"Yeah, I did. Sorry 'bout that." He leans back on his heels and reaches for his discarded shorts. "Maybe next time we can both come."

"Yeah," I agree, slipping my half-erect dick back in my shorts and watching puzzled as this little sprite of a man jumps up and flits out of the shower stall ahead of me.

I follow diaper-boy out into the lobby and duck back into the theater.

I wander in and out of doors, past old men in shirts and ties with cuff links and tie tacks; past an overwhelmingly ugly, but jovial overweight man who laughs and says, "Hey, didya notice we're the only ones here under seventy?" in a tone that implies that we have enough in common to spark a rousing physical encounter. I smile and walk away from him.

I brush away a dozen wandering hands, rows of questioning eyes, a score of whispered promises and pleas. "I'd love to get that knob in my mouth." "Just let me have a piece of that and ..." "If that thing gets hard, come find me, 'cause I'd love to suck on that for a while." "Hey, hey, you, come over here, come here."

A young man in a white shirt, dark tie and scared eyes wanders in, poses for a while, sneaking clandestine looks at me. I wonder if he sees in me a compatriot in this land of geriatric, overweight, homely, marginalized men, this world of darkness and age. He is a beacon to these men, many of whom doubtless see themselves in his visage. They see themselves as they were before the wrinkles, and the liver spots and the sage of encroaching old age took them firmly in hand. His crisp white shirt and immaculate hair seem out of place here, ivory tower meets sewer tunnel.

We fail to connect although our eyes dance a slow, furtive waltz. I reach out with my eyes above the chaos of his flustered appraisal of the room; he looks at me with immobilized hunger and bolts, disappearing out the front door, unfulfilled.

I wander out of the theater and make my way into a smaller room off the lobby where terraced seating faces a sextet of cubicles and a large television playing Hungarian porn. The step-like seating is covered with rough indoor-outdoor carpeting, for cleaning purposes, I suppose. I picture a bored man in flip-flops and shorts with a green garden hose spraying away the accumulated coded residue of a hundred million genetic dead ends.

Or perhaps the carpet is never cleaned, I think, noting the dark, ballooning stains and the thick smell of proteins, reminding me of chewed graham crackers. I also smell amyl nitrate, cigar smoke, sweat, shit, urine – all the primal smells that I have come to associate with the underground meeting places of my tribe, the smells below the dance floor, behind the curtains, in the bedrooms and bathrooms and basements of the world.

I climb up on the platform and watch the video for a moment. A black cassocked priest is talking to a peasant boy while a knight stands listening outside the door. Their mouths move with unfamiliar cadences, and garrulous voices speaking heavily accented English have been dubbed onto the soundtrack.

A man walks into the room from the darkened hallway under the television, looks up at me, starts to walk past me, then stops, interested. I have seen him before, in the dark cubicles, in the theater, alone each time, interested eyes peering out from a Germanic face. He is short like the diaper boy, like Robert, and handsome, blond, in his forties, tight chest, flat stomach, strong legs. When I first spotted him, I thought his T-shirt said "American" across the front, but upon closer inspection, I realize that is says "Banana Republic." He holds a Diet Coke can in his right hand, heavy gold link bracelet accentuating thick, muscular wrists and well-formed hands.

He looks up at me then flicks his eyes in the direction of the cubicles.

I raise a speculative eyebrow.

He grins.

I remain stoic for some reason, nervously immobile.

He walks over to one of the cubicles, leaves the door standing conspicuously open.

I feel a response in my pants, my stomach, the back of my throat.

I follow him.

He smiles when he sees me, evoking a nervous grin from me.

I turn to lock the door; he turns to set down his drink.

He wraps his arms around me, running his fingers up inside my shirt, kissing the side of my neck, my earlobes. He pulls back a fraction, and I expect him to kiss me, but instead he whispers, "Can I suck your dick?"

I nod, and he drops to a crouch, his fingers nimbly reaching for my zipper.

He has my soft dick out in his hands, massaging it, licking the tip and nuzzling my balls.

I look to my right and realize that the cubicle wall is incomplete and a figure in the next cubicle stands watching us in the darkness. A small television monitor above my head splashes enough light into the cubicle to make me feel spotlighted and to prevent me from seeing clearly into the darkness beyond.

The blond man between my legs has finally hit upon a rhythm, speed, and texture that sends goose pimples marching out across my thighs. I groan and lean back against the wall. He turns me so that he can sit on the low bench across from the television, his hands digging into my hips.

"Oh, yeah," I whisper, looking down into his pretty blue eyes, his lips pursed around my shaft. I smile and see the softening around his eyes, which, were his mouth not full, would have relaxed across his face in the form of a smile.

He pulls back, and I stroke myself for a moment, his saliva slick and warm against my skin.

"Are you gonna give me some of that hot cum?" he asks, grinning.

"Pretty soon," I inform him, touching the side of his head ever so gently with my left hand.

Well-trained, he responds to the slightest touch of my hand and returns to the rhythm that threatens to engulf me.

"Yeah, oh yeah," I breathe.

He speeds his efforts, fingers playing along the base of my dick.

"Oh, wait, wait, I'm gonna come," I say, touching his head with both hands, but he does not relent. Instead he redoubles his efforts, and a wave of sensation hits me. I feel the first floodgate opening, a precursor, like a clicking that resonates up from my balls. Then the flood reaches the tip of my dick and spurts out into his mouth. He moans with what seems in my weakened state to be contentment, then holds my hands so that I cannot withdraw myself and sucks me dry, tongue and cheeks moving, drinking deeply.

I let out a groan and a sigh, then a laugh as the sensations turn from the heat of explosion to the warmth of aftershocks that flow like waves and almost always seem to carry my laughter.

"Did you like that?" He comes up for air, finally.

"Yes," I sigh, still leaning back against the back wall of the cubicle.

He stands and begins to arrange himself.

"I haven't seen you here before," he says.

"I haven't been here in a long time," I reply.

"I'm Jack, by the way," he says, putting out a hand in what seems a disconcertingly formal gesture considering.

"Jamie," I reply, taking his hand, noting the manicured fingernails.

"Well, I hope I see you again, Jamie," he says, brushing past me to leave the cubicle.

"Yes, definitely," I say, smiling again.

He grins and disappears into the anteroom, and I walk back into the theater, watching a knight deep throat a peasant boy. I lean back against the carpeted step behind me and draw my knees up in front of me. I wrap my arms around my legs and rest my chin on my knees, gazing past the boys on the television and remembering my Follies.

A LARGE FULL MEAL
By Xan West

For B

Knives get to me like nothing else. I'm one of those tops that likes to start with a knife and a wall, and go from there. To trap my prey, cornering him with my body and my blade, until the wall is at his back, and he is stuck facing my bulk and my knife. Because knives get me hard, instantly. There is this electric metal taste that seeps into my mouth, as adrenaline starts pumping in tune to the movements of the knife in my hand. We play that adrenaline together, and I find myself soaking up the steely scent of it, sliding my tongue along skin to taste it, licking up metallic sweat.

So, it is not surprising that he got to me, and I came face-to-face with the fiercest animal need I have ever experienced. Objectively, in hindsight, it's not surprising. But, damn did it catch me by surprise.

A few months earlier, I had caught his eye at a sex club, but we both were busy at the time. I grinned when I saw him in the hallway at the queer conference that morning, telling him that I hoped I would see him at my workshop. I saw him again later in the day, sitting up front in my workshop, holding my gaze as I spoke, a wicked smile on his face. That evening, I was roaming the halls when I spotted him again. He was giving an impromptu lesson on cruising gay men to a couple of eager young transfags.

"It's all about the body language," he explained. "See, in gay men's community, touch is a primary mode of communication. Say I think that guy is cute."

He raised his brows at me as I was walking slowly past him. I turned slightly to catch his eye and cocked my head, pausing, eyeing his ass.

"So, I'd body up to him from behind, see?"

And he did, slowly. I could feel his breath on my skin.

"And, then I'd wait," he said.

I moved back slightly, completing the contact. He wrapped his arms around my waist, settling in behind me, resting his chin on my shoulder. Even from behind, I could tell his bulk was mostly muscle.

"See how I waited for him to complete the contact before I wrapped my arms around him? It's all about the subtle signals. Now I bet if I trailed my hand along his arm and tilted my head, he'd follow me. We wouldn't need to say a word."

He was right. I followed him into the single stall all gender bathroom and locked the door.

I play hard. It is the only way to play. And, I had a live one that night. A fellow top who by the grace of the gods had decided I was worthy. His strength was glorious, his power immense, and I was playing with someone who absolutely could take me physically if he chose. Our play was premised on his continual consent. There is nothing hotter than a faggot who owns his desires, especially desires that rarely get fulfilled.

It began with touch. His body against mine. My hands reaching around him and gripping the back of his neck. I was reading his response, his eyes. That's when I knew he wanted to be under me.

I pinned him to the wall with weight and leverage, and I focused on pounding and reaching into his skin to find the man underneath. This man with a wicked sense of humor, a twisted intelligent brain, and this incredible level of psychic and physical strength. I kept driving my body into his, grabbing him. I was determined to find him. With firm hands, with pounding fists, with skin grasping his. I wanted to learn him, know his body, devour him. He was no snack. He was a large full meal. All that strength and power, all that delicious desire. And, the most jolting green eyes that just opened to me as if it were effortless.

I can play, and it's about fear. Or about helplessness, or exposure, or shame. This was none of that. This was about hunger and faggotry. About wrapping my body around him, slamming it into him, grabbing for him under his skin. It was raw and hard, this incredible gift that still awes me.

I was ravenous for him. I could feel the hunger building; it kept driving me forward, crashing into him, with thighs and fists and gut. As we played, and more skin got exposed, my hunger deepened. And then, as I was sitting on him and punching his thighs, he bit himself to hold back a scream, driving his body up until he was sitting, his eyes holding mine. Those stabbing green eyes. Eager and hungry. Opening. Full of pain. Offering. I could smell the blood in his mouth. I could almost taste copper in the back of my throat. My hunger leapt to a new level.

I needed to slow things down a notch, ease off, or I would gorge myself, out of control. Sadism sometimes works like that for me. It is a beast inside me, usually caged, and this was tempting food in front of me. I was holding the leash on my beast tightly, but it was a battle.

This was an entirely different sort of meal in front of me, and it roused a different sort of hunger. So, it was time to back off just a bit, without letting this go.

My hands were searching his body for something to hold on to. And, then they found his knife.

If he was anything like me, he was rarely found without his boots or his knife. That's what it is to move around the world as a visibly queer person, especially for us visible non-gender-normative queer folks. You carry your power in your stance, your walk, the way you hold your head. You wear your tools, prepared to fight for your life if you need to. And, to fuck exactly how you love to. Life is too short for us. We seize opportunities as they come.

If I wanted to use his knife on him, I needed to pay it the respect it deserved. I touched it gently and asked permission. And, received it. This was a very nice knife. Sharp. Large for a carrying knife, just this side of legal size. Well made. With that delicious snapping sound upon opening. I let him know I found it so. Another way to show respect, to honor the man I was playing with.

A knife would help me slow down. A knife would require precision and very minute movement. A knife would demand the kind of deliberate intent that would gear my higher brain up, and give me what I needed to rein in this feral appetite.

I began exploring his skin with it. Savoring the stillness it brought. Sliding it along his flesh, I held my face close, so I could watch for minuscule shifts and smell his skin. I concentrated all of my attention on the flesh under the knife, learning him in this new way. I moved it up to his throat, his cheek, his lips.

That's when he did it. I had paused with the knife barely touching his lip, still. First, he opened his mouth and tongued his way up the blade. Then he lifted his head slightly, opened further, and gradually sucked it in, leaving his mouth open, so I could see it inch its way into him, sinking slowly until he had taken it all. I groaned and had to concentrate all my focus on keeping the knife still.

If I close my eyes, I can still see it. That wide soft tongue stroking the blade. That mouth reaching for it, opening to it, taking it in eagerly, making every centimeter count. I could almost come right now just from thinking about him devouring his own knife.

At the time, it short circuited my brain. All I could think about was slamming my cock into his mouth. Everything that had been focused on sadism was suddenly focused on sex. It was like a switch had been flipped in my head. I growled in his ear and that delectable dirty mouth growled back, telling me how much he wanted me to use him, to take what I needed from him. I was consumed by impatience. And, he could see it in my eyes. It made him smile in a completely new way.

I know I did other things to him before I fucked him. I have a memory of holding the knife against his eyeball, which is one of my favorite things to do with a knife. I have a memory of bending him over the sink and driving my upper thigh and knee into his ass and crotch in a way that was really just about a pounding hard fuck. I remember my hand in his mouth, his tongue driving me up the wall with need.

I started coming back when he was massaging my hand and wrist. His strong hands gripping me, stroking my skin, pulsating along my muscles. It felt like this exquisite handjob. His mouth lit up with a wicked grin when I told him so, and he exaggerated the movements as he held my eyes. I was jolted to clarity for just a second in that moment: My hand was my cock. My cock was in charge. And, all it wanted was to be inside him. Then, I disappeared into need again.

It is mostly a blur. Because my head did not clear until I was driving into him, giving him the hardest most relentless fuck I could. Opening him up for my pleasure. Taking everything he offered.

I can feel his thighs gripping me. I can see his face as I slam into him with my hand. I can smell sex on his skin, even now.

I was devoured by my own need. So filled with impatience that the idea of waiting five minutes while I strapped on my cock just did not make any sense at all. I wanted inside him, instantly. Once I was there, it was like riding a bronco, my muscles spasming, his thighs holding onto me, standing up to get more leverage so that I could pound him deeper.

I was reaching into him with all my might and all the while his mouth was spewing some of the hottest smut I have ever heard. Every word made my cock pulse until it felt like I was slamming my hand and my cock into him all at once. As if I had found him with all of my need. And, that thought was what made me come, as he growled and his thighs locked onto me with all their incredible strength. He milked me that way, groaning as he came, holding me in exactly the spot that we both needed me to be.

Afterward, I continued to reach for him, to hold him to me. And, we stayed wrapped around each other for a long time, neither wanting to move.

Later, much later, I had my patience back. And, I took out my cock, strapped it to my hips, and got it ready for his mouth.

"You've been asking for this," I said.

My brain had finally started functioning, and I was not just a twisting ball of hunger. I could string words together again.

"You are just the kind of cocksucker I need."

I reached for the back of his neck again, holding his eyes.

"You want this, don't you? Your filthy faggot mouth is craving my cock. Isn't that right?"

"You know it is," he growled.

I held him there, one hand clamping his face, one on the back of his neck. Letting his hunger build. I could feel it surge as I watched his eyes. He knew what I wanted to hear.

"Please," he whispered.

I tilted my head, met his gaze and raised my brow, indicating I had not heard.

"Please," he growled, louder.

The most erotic word in the world.

"Are you going to finish that sentence? Please, what?"

He clenched his jaw. And then he eyed my cock.

"Please fuck my mouth with your cock," he said.

I smiled. "Just what I wanted to hear."

I opened his mouth with my thumb, grazing his lips as I moved my hand down to stroke my cock. I put steady pressure on the back of his head as I pushed his mouth toward me.

And then, I was inside him. That aching pleasure of his wet mouth opening under me. I inched into him, gauging him, and began to thrust. One hand controlling his neck, the other clenched in his thick hair, I dictated exactly how much he would take, and at what pace. I was going to wring every possible ounce of pleasure out of that dirty mouth of his.

"Open for me. Yes. That's exactly it. I'm going to take what I need from you, faggot. Use your hole until I'm through. This raunchy mouth of yours will give me exactly what I need. And, I will take it all. I'm going to use all of you. Nothing will be wasted, don't you worry."

I rammed into his hole, my hands twisting his hair, moving him exactly the way I wanted, making full use of him.

"You asked for this. You invited me to make use of you. To take what I needed from you. And I need a lot. You have a lot to take, faggot. A lot to use. And I will grab for everything I need. I'm not holding back now. I will take it all."

I pulled out and gripped his gaze with mine. I watched the hunger consume his face. I knew he was a skilled cocksucker. I had seen him suck off his own knife. I had already experienced his mouth on my hand. But, this was not about his skill, not at that moment. This was about taking everything he had, making complete use of him in exactly the way that I chose.

I shoved into him, as deep as I could go, gripping the sides of his face. I was determined to use every inch of his hole. I could see his eyes widen as he gagged on my cock, and I didn't stop driving into his throat. His eyes were magnificent, and I soaked up the sight of him struggling to accommodate all of my cock.

"That's right, faggot. You feel so damn good around my cock. I am going to use every fucking inch of your mouth."

I slid back a bit, and shifted, grinding my dick into the side of his mouth.

"Use that tongue of yours. That's it. You made some promises with that tongue, and you are going to deliver on every one of them. You look so damn good with my cock inside you faggot. Taking it all down, knowing it's exactly what you ache for. You love it when I take what I need from you. You love that you have so much for me to take."

I started to thrust faster, the look in his eyes as I spoke to him spurring me on.

"You want to take it all, don't you? You don't want to miss an iota of it. That's it. Take me down. You know this is exactly what you have been asking for. Getting precisely what's coming to you faggot. I'm not going to spare you at all."

I started ramming into him with all my strength as I felt myself getting ready to spurt.

"Take it. Don't stop there. Take it all. You invited me to use your hole, to take what I need. And, I am. This is exactly what I need, your hole to use. It is a lusciously salacious mouth you have, and just perfect for my cock. Yes. Take it down. All of it."

I held his head still as I slammed my cock into him, spurting into his hole.

"Take it. Don't waste a drop. Yes. That's it. I'm going to use all of you. Take exactly what I need from you. Yes. Swallow it all."

I met his gaze as I slowly pulled out of his mouth, his tongue following me as far as it could.

"Damn. Your mouth is deliciously filthy. I enjoyed using it, faggot."

I pulled him toward me and clasped him in the strongest hug I could manage. His arms reached around to grip me tight.

"Thank you," I said gruffly into his ear as I held him.

It sounds like an old queer joke. What happens when you get two transmasculine faggot tops alone in a bathroom? A very wild ride. One I will never forget.

MY FATHER'S SEMEN – A Novella
By Mykola Dementiuk

One

Don't ever tell anybody anything! Absolutely goddamn right! The only reason I was in New York is because I talked too much in Cincinnati. Well, maybe not talked too much but certainly trusted too much. And, I had to get out because of jerk off dream I showed my asshole social worker, Ralph. It didn't matter that I wrote down the dream more than a year ago for this other social worker, Susan, who told me that since I found it difficult and embarrassing to talk about my masturbatory fantasies, maybe if I wrote them down it would be easier to talk about them later.

I did and felt like a dirty old man gaping at *Hustler* or *Screw* because the more I wrote the more I'd jerk off – well, at first because as new images began appearing in my fantasies, new scenarios and new contortions of legs around me, sudden twisting and glimpses of tits and pussy, cocks and pubic hairs, I had to stop jerking off and write down those new images or else I'd forget them as soon as I wiped the scum off my hand and belly. So I spent a lot of time jerking off, then stopping just to write them down, until I was sure I gave myself a good case of aching blue balls until my coming was nothing but a weak ejaculation of frustration, disgust, shame and anger.

This guy Joey I knew had once told me that if you want someone to fall in love with you all you had to do was jerk off to images of them, and they'd certainly notice you because it was just like a real dream when you're sleeping, Joey said, and when you tell someone you had a dream about them they always look at you as if trying to recollect a forgotten dream they had about you. But, if it's true someone is dreaming of you when you're having a dream about them, does that mean when you're jerking-off and picturing someone they're about to have an ejaculation on an image of you as well? That's what had gotten me into therapy in the first place: fantasies of people. Fantasies you can control, real people you can't because what if real people are using you as a fantasy as well?

I often fantasized about Susan, and when she left the therapy center to continue some schooling about six months later, I wasn't even jerking off as much anymore, though I continued to bring her all kinds of sex fantasies – I even think she got a kick from reading my dirty fantasies, stories she called them.

When she left the center, I was assigned to this creepy other social worker, Ralph, who knew from my file that I wrote erotic fantasies for Susan and wanted me to continue writing them for him. I hated the idea of having a man therapist and told him, and refused to write him anything that might be construed as a sexual fantasy. For Ralph? No way!

He had some strange ideas about trust, as if trust is so easily transferred from one social worker to another. Well, it doesn't; even though from Susan I learned that trust is the basis of all relationships – I used to like that phrase, she had used it at the end of our first session – the only thing I got from Ralph was just the opposite; trust is the basis of all betrayal.

Fuck, if I had known any of this back than I never would have shown Ralph that old fantasy about the little girl raped and murdered and stuffed into a trash can outside of Riverfront Stadium. I had never shown it to Susan, but it really happened, almost a year ago. Well, the cops caught the little girl's killer, arresting her mother's live-in boyfriend who had left behind clues a mile long, or so they said.

At the same time I was having daily sessions with Ralph, I also had to meet with Mrs. Gillette, who was an almost-social worker; she was the high school guidance counselor I had to see before they kicked me out for chronic truancy, which meant I was headed for reform school. I hadn't been to school in almost three months in my junior year, and they had suspended me anyway and were probably waiting after Christmas when they could expel me for good and not feel bad about what they doing. I had just turned sixteen, right after Thanksgiving, so I wasn't legally old enough to drop out of school on my own – dumb Ohio has these worthless laws. I suppose Mrs. Gillette was their last recourse at keeping me in school, I had run away a few times. I wonder if they really knew how she kept boys in line and staying in school?

Good thing was Mrs. Gillette didn't talk much about my truancy or what was I doing in all the free time I had but simply wanted to know if I was as good a carpenter as I had proved myself to be in last year's shop class. Carpentry my ass! But, the bitch was wearing low cut blouses right after I began and even one day came to let me in her house in a skirt and a black Wonderbra to make it seem as if I had interrupted her as she was getting dressed. But by then, I had proved myself as worthless in carpentry as I had been in mending little motors in shop class. Where did these people get their ideas about me? And the certificates Mrs. Gillette had up on her wall, as did Ralph had on his, what did that prove? That they were potential qualified police informants or they knew how to look respectable?

You'll do well, Mrs. Gillette simply said, smirking at me as I stared bug-eyed at the low-cut bra holding her tits. And, I started coming to Mrs. Gillette's house after school every Wednesday and Friday, but soon I was dropping by every day. Besides acting like a carpenter, I was doing other things as well. A wall needed plastering and painting, the windows had to be washed and cleaned, the Christmas tree had to be set up, and wouldn't it be nice if I could pick up the laundry and do the grocery shopping? It wasn't long before I became Mrs. Gillette's servant. But, that was the way of becoming a family member, wasn't it? I had never asked if there was a Mr. Gillette (she had a ten-year-old daughter), divorced or separated I didn't know, but it was a good feeling whenever I'd go there, one that I looked forward to.

But, it was awkward when Mrs. Gillette started kissing me. I always turned red-faced from that because I felt my hard-on spring up as if in surprise, which it wasn't, I was expecting that from her nearness. At first, it was on the cheek when I'd leave for the day, then on the lips as I'd arrive the next day, until we would greet each other in our arms as our tongues were probing and flitting each other before she broke off giggling and wiping her lipstick off my face.

And, I suppose that's when I started getting into trouble, when I started imagining not only kissing Mrs. Gillette but fucking her as well. Because isn't that where all this hugging and kissing was going and isn't that what she wanted from her jack-of-all-trades, a good old fashioned man-sized fucking?

One Thursday afternoon, when Mrs. Gillette had a few drinks and was feeling mellow – too mellow, I was certain – she was in the kitchen when I stepped into her daughter's room going in for a measuring ruler that her daughter had borrowed some days ago. The little girl's clothes were on the bed and chair, but what caught my eye was a lavender-colored T-shirt that the cops said the killer/rapist had ripped off the little girl.

I fingered the soft T-shirt then pawed it about – it felt lush and very soft on my face. I lowered it and caressed my hard dick, breathing in and out, when I saw Mrs. Gillette staring open-mouthed at me from the doorway.

I knew it was over, and I shamefacedly left her house, undecided what to do. Fortunately, she didn't call the cops, but there was no guarantee that she wouldn't later. I just packed what little I needed, and without a word to my grandmother was shrugging off Cincinnati. It was two days before Christmas.

Two

My father lived in New York, ever since I was little, and I haven't seen him six or seven years. Every Christmas, I'd get a card from him with a check for a hundred dollars – which I immediately cashed – I suppose it was his way of saying, "Don't bother me until next Christmas!" My mom I never heard from; grandmother told me she was in San Francisco with her lesbian lover. Oh, I said, and shrugged. Grandmother knew a lot more but didn't say much.

The station was packed with people coming and going, but I had to take a non-descript seat and keep out of trouble. Wasn't too long ago – about year – that I got picked up in the Greyhound men's room, doing nothing, just standing there, but the cops hauled me in anyway.

Cincinnati has no claim to fame, besides Steve McQueen in *Cincinnati Kid* which took place in New Orleans, and Loni Anderson in *WKRP in Cincinnati*, a TV show meant more to show off Loni's tits than her acting ability. And, one time the city was known as Porkapolis, before they changed the name to Cincinnati, in honor of some local Indian chief lord, hell, do you think people like to call their home a sty? Fuck off, Cincinnati, or should I say, Oink! Oink!

I only knew three things about New York. It was big, my father lived there, and whatever Joey told me about it. He had been there about a year ago; having spent a week there, also running away from the therapy clinic his parents put him in because he was gay. His parents were rich enough to send a bounty hunter after him, and he nabbed Joey right in the back of the NYC bus station, on his knees, and sucking cock in between two cars. Getting caught in the act was bad enough, but before he nabbed Joey, the bounty hunter snapped a Polaroid of Joey sucking cock, which he used to blackmail Joey into giving him blow jobs all the way back home to Cincinnati, or else he'd give the photos to Joey's mom.

Which he did anyway; an envelope full of photos of Joey, kneeling before men, bending over to a standing man, sometimes sucking off one guy while jerking off two others. And, of course Joey's mom never asked why he hadn't brought Joey home the first day he spotted him but took an entire week to amass twenty rolls of pornographic photos of her son or why there was a receipt among his bills for the Motel 6 outside of Cincinnati.

She paid him 25 thousand dollars to bring me home, so he could fuck me right on her doorstep! Joey told me. No wonder he said it took him six weeks to track down Sheila (our friend) in Reno; he had her in a motel for a month, the bastard!

But, my grandmother wasn't as rich as Joey's parents were, so I knew no bounty hunter or parent would come looking for me; but Ralph? Who knew how the social worker would rat me off to his respectable pig friends? Who knew what kind of all-points-bulletin would be issued on me? Warning! Child Molester on the loose! Beware of dreamy-eyes loners writing poetry! That's him, he's the one! Smell the little girl all over him! So that's why I was headed to New York, instead of Chicago, which I had tried three times before.

And, since that night and day I sat on the Greyhound bus playing out my memories of Mrs. Gillette kissing me. I had never kissed a girl, and Mrs. Gillette was the first woman I kissed and liked it. There were guys I had let kiss me, mostly faggot guys I'd meet and go off with them for some dollars, but with Mrs. Gillette I felt I wasn't doing anything wrong, until the last moment, at least.

I had no idea where I was going to stay once I got there; I had already dished out $63 from my father's Christmas present and had about thirty bucks to live on. But, I wasn't worried, I had seen all the movies, gazed in the books and magazines, and somehow knew I could survive on the streets of New York, or at least try doing it.

The bus station in New York is immense, and it's called the Port Authority Building; it says so right in the front. And, it stretches for three blocks, in the 40s from 8th to 9th Avenues, and is, I guess, almost five stories high. You could probably fit all the people of Cincinnati inside and still have room for the nearby city of Paducah, too.

When my friend Joey ran away to New York two years ago, he told me that for the first two days he didn't leave the building but survived on food that people threw away as they rushed to catch buses taking them out of town. But, this time the cops were everywhere, and I'm sure that that even Joey, with all his smudged biker tattoos, would quickly be spotted as a loiterer and troublemaker.

There were even more people on the street outside entering the station. It's as if everyone was leaving just as I arrived. But, this was rush hour, and nothing like the morning or afternoon drives in Cincinnati. I pushed my way out of the station.

Three

Just as Joey had told me, 42nd Street was lined with movie theaters on both sides, but each theater was boarded up and shut, and the marquis, rather than showing off some future attractions, had some strange markings and readings which seemed like ominous end-of-the-world-is-coming: Life in not a rehearsal. This is not the end. I walked on, not knowing what any of them meant.

Joey had told me he had survived in all-night porno theaters, where he said he made money letting guys do him. The bad thing was when he made what he thought was enough to leave, some black guys ripped him off in the bathrooms or lobby or even right in the seats. Forty-second Street was very dangerous, even though it looked pretty tame now. The street looked like one of those Hollywood stage sets, when the actors and directors all went home for the night, leaving the people to hurry after them.

I kept walking down 42nd, not knowing which was to turn off on, up or down 7th Avenue, so I crossed over and quickly found myself on Broadway, where a few steps across, I read the strange sounding Hotalings, an out-of-town newspaper store. Unfortunately, they wanted $1.25 for a Cincinnati paper, which they kept behind the counter.

Try the library, the store clerk suggested. Then shrugged and added, "They're probably closed for Christmas."

Still, I asked, "Where is it?"

"Look for lions in the street," he smirked, but I didn't understand.

I continued on 42nd Street until I came to 5th Avenue. Of course, the lions that guarded the building were another symbol of New York, as much as were the Statue of Liberty and the Empire State Building. They always showed them in some movie or TV show, either with birds sitting on them or Christmas wreaths around their necks, which is just what they were wearing now and sitting like sentinels to keep the ignorant and stupid out. That's the kind of library I'd be proud of entering, not that prison-looking piece of shit in Cincinnati that practically had no books published before 1985, as if literature began with Tom Clancy, reached its shining hour with Stephen King, and was slowly mellowing out with Anne Rice. Oh, God! Pathetic!

It was Susan who got me to admit I liked poetry, and brought me two paperback books by Allen Ginsburg Howl and Kaddish. Man, were they weird! But I loved them, reading each one and reading them again and hoping she had other books let me read. Before that, I liked songs by Led Zeppelin, Metallica, even Meatloaf, but since I couldn't play any instrument except air guitar, I couldn't really compose much music and quickly forgot what gibberish I did compose.

I had a NYC map, actually a NY Subway map I had ripped out of a NYC phone book in the Cincinnati library. It was in my knapsack, but I didn't care about the rest of the city, the boroughs, but only Manhattan because it was easily laid out in a grid, and most of the avenues and streets were numbered in sequence, and it would be impossible to get lost as uptown meant high numbers and downtown meant the low-numbered streets. Easy, no? Well, it wasn't really all that simple, but I felt good about where I was going, downtown, as if I'd been there lots of times.

It's funny to walk in a strange city and feel that you fit right in, well, I didn't feel different I felt I belonged here. Looking at the Empire State Building was beautiful and immense! It surged up to the sky, its top lit by red and white lights for Christmas that even shone over the clouds and mist fogging the high building. As I kept walking, I kept turning around to look at the tower above me, like a beacon landmark that even if I got lost would be my direction back home.

Four

The streets eventually cleared of that mad crowd of people rushing somewhere with packages and on the streets in the 20s; I sometimes walked for an entire block without anyone passing me by.

On 26th Street, I saw the dark bundles of trees and came upon a park, which was probably my destination all along. Another beautiful tower hung over the park, a clock tower also festooned in bright red and white and green colors of Christmas, and I entered the park as easily as I was entering the gay cruising parks of Cincinnati. And, it was just as easy and obvious as I had expected.

Just like at home, I'm certain it was the same in New York that people who go into parks at night only go there because they're up to something or other. I went in because I was horny.

Cruising for Bad Boys

With me getting tired and getting horny are the same thing; I sometimes think one leads to the other. The longer I stay up without any sleep, the harder my dick gets, and the more I jerk off. I once went without any sleep for four days and must have jerked off at least 200 times before I collapsed with exhaustion, but still holding my dick as I fell asleep. So, by the time I entered the park, after that long fifteen-hour bus ride to NY, my cock was itching for a good jerk off session. Plus I needed a place to stay.

My eyes quickly got used to the darkness of the curving lanes of the small park. The park was only a few blocks long and only one block wide, but even as I entered I could make out the images of an unmistakable shadow of someone standing against a fence by a tree, or sitting on a bench, or two figures going together, probably after discussing a price and where best to go and do the act.

I stopped, took off my knapsack and dropped it on the ground. I leaned against a fence and propped up my leg against a lower railing of the fence. I felt pretty good, happy I was in NY, and even more happy that I had gotten out of Cincinnati. They'd never find me here; no one even knew I left. But, I was sure the quack social worker Ralph would tell the police I disappeared, probably to Chicago again. And, I was grateful the weather wasn't too cold, not like they sometimes showed of a frozen New York. I only had my Cincinnati Bengal's jacket, but even back home it was already too cold to comfortably wear.

I looked up at the pretty tower; a little after 8:00 p.m. I wanted to take out my notebook and write something about being in NY and standing below a clock tower. I thought of Susan; I missed her a lot. Not only did she show me that poetry didn't have to rhyme, but that I could write it, too, without embarrassment.

I must have been looking up at the clock tower and dreaming about Susan when I next looked and saw one of those muted shadows inching closer in my direction. My prick immediately grew hard, but I could hardly make out his features in the park's darkness, but he was short and fat and most likely balding, with a slash of hair above his ears that circled his head like a laurel crown, much like creepy Ralph.

I always wondered about Ralph, whether he was gay or not. That would have been some betrayal on Susan's part, wouldn't it? When she told me she'd be leaving the counseling center, I asked that her replacement be another woman. She said she couldn't do that and her last day there, told me that Ralph would take over and help me. I said, "Yeah, sure," to myself and shook her hand and left.

I looked at the Ralph-looking guy inching nearer and shifted off the rail and raised my other leg up behind me, sitting on the top rail of the fence and dangling my free leg, as the Ralph-looking guy stood and watched.

There is always a kind of wariness in the approach of a pick-up; a kind of edginess and uncertain fear. With all the bullshit of the openness of the gay movement, people are still afraid of coming together. Or, maybe that's what makes the coming together so interesting, that first wariness of approaching or being approached by someone. It's really nothing but a dance, that one side has to show off to the other, just like animals on those Nature shows on public television. I once even got a hard-on looking on TV at one bird dancing and showing his feathers to another bird that pretended she wasn't impressed until the first bird pounced on her and fucked her like crazy. Well, it's no different with people, whether some guys tried to impress some girl in a bar, or an office, or on the street; his entire showiness is no different: to fuck her.

And, just as I knew this Ralph-bird would, he slowly walked past me up the lane, though keeping his eyes glued to my crotch and licking his lips, first the lower lip, then the upper. I regret I wasn't wearing tighter pants, wishing I could show off some cock-bulge, but my baggy jeans were the only ones I had.

Ralph walked past me, then paused and leaned against the fence across from me. I smiled, but as he stood leaning against the fence in an unlit part of the path, I couldn't see if he smiled back, but I certainly saw his arm and fingers gesturing I come closer to him.

I looked up and down the path, then pushed myself off the fence, picked up my bag and went to Ralph.

He was even uglier and bloated than I first imagined, his face sprinkled with a sheen of sweat that even in the dimness of the dark path gleamed like so much obscenity. But, I suppose girls feel it all the time when they walk down the street, and I, too, hated it when someone looked at me in that rape-desperate, sex-lust kind of way that only wanted my body, as if anybody would do, but since mine was available, might as well have it, too. It's as if my walking down the street and looking as I did was simply for him to get his kicks off me, as if I exist only for your pleasure and sickness.

Ralph's hand went to my crotch and squeezed. I gushed in air, pretending I was as horny as he and quickly raised an erection from his groping, to which I suddenly ejaculated onto his hand feeling my hard dick melting against my pants. Hell, I had been horny ever since I walked into the park. But, even with the ejaculation ripping apart my body, I remained still, as if nothing was happening, simply scratching my face as if I had an itch in an attempt to hide and dispel the contortions trying to get out.

I learned a long time ago that in these park and street pick-ups no one wants to see your pleasure; the entire point of anyone's approach is to get pleasure from you and never mind your getting any pleasure from them. The few times I unknowingly allowed my ejaculations to sweep visibly over me in shudders and contortions, I was simply dropped as the sexual partner walked away in disgust. It seemed that my pleasure and satisfaction was an insult to them. And, maybe it was. No one enters a dark park looking for mutual sharing or pleasing togetherness; it's all a matter of selfish anonymity and objectification. Like a john looking for an anonymous prostitute some gay asshole prowling the park, or in movie balconies, is only looking for a whore to please himself with. Men who just bought themselves a hooker don't expect her to show pleasure of any kind, besides her usual sham groaning and sighing, so why should it be different when some man attaches himself to me? Because it's probably the anonymous coldness of being a stranger, a stranger clinging to you, that arouses a man with a prostitute more than any kind of warmth or physical pleasure of being with you. I was very good at not showing my feelings and emotions, and Susan, notwithstanding, but why should I show a stranger how I felt?

The Ralph-gay-guy looked up and down the path, and seeing it was deserted, put his arms around my waist and pulled me to him. His hands went under my jacket and up my back and we were face to face. He smelled of heavy aftershave, and I was repulsed by his avid sweaty face. I slightly pulled back, but separated my legs in an attempt for him not to think I was disgusted with him. I looked down and put one foot on the bottom railing of the fence. I raised my arms and put them on his shoulders, then raised my other foot and stood up, my legs wrapped around him like a girl for fucking. He was panting and gushing very heavily, clutching my back tighter to him.

I started riding him, lowering and raising myself, in a dry hump mimic of the real thing. Even through my loose baggy pants, I could feel his erection breached in his own pants, and I knew he wasn't far from an ejaculation.

He began kissing my neck; I knew he was aiming for my mouth and face, but I was able to raise myself up on the fence too high for his lips to reach my mouth. I hate it when men kiss me. Because it's not a kiss they lash onto me, but a desperate biting and sucking as if not only trying to eat me and swallow me, but to devour my life and soul for their fleeting lusts. Each kisser always leaves me with red bite marks and brown suck marks as identity scars that signify I am theirs, or was, for a brief insignificant lusting moment.

And, of course, in between the sucking kisses, there were the usual clichés of, "Ooo, baby!" "Ooo, honey!" "Ooo, sweetie!" and the stupid questions of "You like it?" "Is Daddy good for you, baby?" and one he got stuck on and kept repeating like a dirge, "What am I doing to you?" I kept reciting in monosyllables, "Nice!" and "Doing good," but I knew that's not the answer he wanted as his questions seemed get sterner and harsher, "What am I doing to you?"

I refused to say it; I didn't want him to hear that he was fucking me, and I didn't want to chant, "Fuck me! Fuck me! Fuck me!" Because it was obvious that if we were naked his cock would be riding up my ass, and I would have to pretend to be screaming "Harder, you bastard! Harder, oooh!" But with all the disgust his kissing brought upon me, and my own stifled half-hearted ejaculation, I suddenly didn't want to give him any more pleasure. I suddenly dropped my feet off the fence rail and slid down his body, pushing myself off him at the same time.

"No!" he squealed, gripping my crotch with one hand and reaching out for me with the other. "No!" he yelped, squeezing the outline of his dick in his pants, and I knew he was coming.

It was funny to watch him twisting and contorting, and I only felt a vague curiosity at how long he would be out of control.

I smirked, and at that moment he looked at me, and his own face, skewered in that pleasurable contortion of pain and release, surged with bitter hate at my smirking. I picked up my bag and slung it on my shoulders.

"You mother-fucker!" he grimaced, then doubled over at his ejaculation.

"Faggot!" I simply said, and walked away from him.

"Fucking bastard! You fucking creep!"

Five

Tall buildings skirted around the park, and as I walked, I began to like the comfortable anonymity I felt myself to be in. But, all of NY was huge, and you were like a tiny speck lost in the mystery.

On 23rd Street, a tilted-like building rose up from the island on which it stood, in the center of the avenue. Damn! I couldn't remember its name, shit! Seen pictures countless times.

I looked down Broadway, took a few steps and looked down 5th Avenue. The avenue seemed broader and livelier, as if there were some people on it, but I only saw a few rushing by, and I took a step back and looked down the smaller Broadway, seeming to weave its way down in the darkness.

On 22nd Street, I decided to turn and walk a short block to where I could be back on 5th Avenue. Now when I think of it, why wasn't I bit more wary and alert? I saw the two guys coming but didn't pay them any mind, seeing them separate on each side of me to give me room to pass, or so I thought, and it happened as suddenly as it usually does. An arm went around my neck as the guy before me held a knife before my stomach. *Fuck*, I thought, *I'm being mugged!*

I felt the guy holding my neck search my back pockets as the guy before me pawed inside my jacket and shirt looking for other pockets. He pulled out the $30 and the few singles I had in my breast jacket pocket and demanded where the rest of my money was. I mumbled I don't have any, hoping they didn't see my lie and make me take off my boots to reveal my last 20 dollar bill I had in my sock – I had saved that from a time had hustled in Cincinnati. The guy behind me grabbed my knapsack and tossed it to the guy in front, who ripped it open and upturned my few clothes and notebook folder. He rifled through my clothes, then kicked them, scattering them apart and under a parked car.

"He ain't got shit!" the guy behind me said, slightly easing his hold on my neck.

"Mother-fucker!" the guy next to me cursed, kicking my notebook and scattering the papers and my poems down the sidewalk.

I knew they'd let me go, and I sighed, and that sigh suddenly enraged the guy in front of me, and he swung at me and hit the side of my face, and hard, too. I saw lights and stars and sagged against the guy holding me, who let go, and I struck a parked car, tasting blood in my mouth. The side of my face hurt, and my eyes welled in tears. For a moment, I caught my breath and saw the two guys cursing and laughing and walking away.

I spat out blood and picked up a T-shirt and wiped my face. Good thing there was little blood. As quickly as I could, thinking they might come back, I gathered a few poems and clothes, bending under a car to retrieve the rest, then hurrying away to get out of there. But, a few blocks away, I realized I was walking uptown, the streets getting higher and higher. I looked at the park across the way of a large avenue then turned and walked down a darkened street.

My paranoia was alert and cumbersome, turning about every few steps I took, but not one person was in sight. Boy, nine o'clock during Christmas week and nothing! I walked past what looked like an empty huge parking lot; I was sure that in the day it was filled with cars and trucks. I made my way across it.

Against the other end of the lot were the backyards of buildings, also tall and reaching upwards, and I walked near them until I found one fence that was falling down. I looked around, no one, and stepped in through the fence. I was in back of a building; I took a few more steps, the street was no longer visible from where I stood. I leaned against the building and slumped downwards. Amazing what tension I had been under, but now I felt relief coming over me. I freed myself of my knapsack and lowered my head, hoping the night wasn't too cold for me.

I don't know what awoke me, the clatter of a garbage truck on the street, the light snow falling on my face, or some dream that instantly vanished at my awakening. But, it was still dark and I didn't know how long I had slept, a few minutes or a few hours. The fire escapes above me had kept most of the snow from me, but little mounds had gathered in the center of the crevice from the buildings on either side of where I had slept, and it was a lot colder than before.

I touched my face, a large bump was on the side, and it felt twice as large as it did before. Another truck clattered down the street, and I heard shouts of people shouting and laughing at each other. It was probably near dawn, and I knew I wouldn't sleep anymore.

I sat up, my body sore and aching, as if I had been beaten all over, instead of the side of my face. I wanted to take the twenty dollar bill out of my boots but then didn't. What if I saw the two guys again? Would I recognize them? Would they recognize me? How many people did they rob and beat in the night?

I crawled out of my crevice and stepped into the parking lot. I walked to the street and saw the sky in the east was dawning with a grayness streaking in between the thick clouds above. I went to a parked car and looked in a mirror. I suddenly snapped to attention, looking around me for the two guys I imagined were close by. Everything was now scary, and I had to be alert. I scooped a handful of snow, actually ice, from off a car, and suddenly jumped back. The car alarm went off at my touch and wailed in a police siren mimic. I walked away, gently wiping my sore face, the coldness felt bitter and stinging but refreshing and easing. I gazed in the mirror of another car, slightly bending over without touching the car. There were no distinguishing marks that I'd been punched, just my usual morning tiredness.

I crossed 5th Avenue. The clock tower read 5:15 a.m. I had fallen asleep around midnight, so at least I got about five hours of sleep. Damn, I didn't want to be seen crawling out of the crevice in daylight. If the people who ran the parking lot saw me coming out they'd seal up the hole in the fence I went in.

Once more, I started walking along to the park. A few people could be seen now, holding cups of coffee and walking briskly. A Christmas tree stood in the center of the big lawn, and its lights shone brightly in the gloomy snow-misted morning. The snow was letting up, but also it was very cold.

Other figures were entering the park, also carrying coolers with their lunch, hurrying to work, talking, laughing, each carrying a folded newspaper under one arm as if that was a part of their working uniform. I wished I had a job to go to; I wondered what kind of job I'd have? Probably some bullshit job.

I walked out of the park and headed to 5th Avenue. From my mental image I had of the avenue, I knew it would run into Washington Square Park and Greenwich Village, where my father had his antique store. Though my father never put his return address on his Christmas cards, to me it was easy to find it in my grandmother's papers. He had a shop in the Village and an apartment upstairs from the shop. Most likely my appearance would be unwelcome in either place. Still, this was the first year my father had actually penned something in his card besides his printed name. "Merry Christmas, Dad, I love you," he wrote, and my grandmother was very pleased by that. Never had he written that he loves me. "He's trying," said my grandmother. Would he try enough to reach out to me?

It being a Saturday morning, besides the workers I saw in the park, there weren't that many people on the streets, and as I walked down 5th Avenue, my steps were the first ones to crack through the crisp iciness of the fresh snowfall.

On 17th Street, as I had seen a truck do on 19th Street and 20th, and probably doing down the avenue, was making stops at each deli and restaurant and taking delivery bags into the cafes, if they were open, or attaching a bag to the gated front. At most of the open stops, the driver made two or three trips back and forth from his truck carrying large bags of rolls and flat boxes of pastries. Though I knew it wasn't happening, I imagined I could smell the lush scent of fresh baked bread, the stunning warmness of baked crullers and donuts and Danishes. My mouth quickly watered.

From a block away, I could see the driver jump out of his truck and tote a large paper sack, attaching it to a fence covering the closed restaurant, then jump back into his truck to make other deliveries along the way. I slowed my pace, watching the truck slant its way across the avenue, make another stop, then continue for about two blocks then I saw him make a turn and disappear from the avenue.

I looked behind me; it was the same as before: not a person in sight, and only a few cars on the slippery avenue. I slowly walked against the buildings and shuttered shops and reached the paper sack dangling from the café/deli. The top of the sack was twisted shut and laced with a hook-like wire, which sealed the sack and let it dangle from the front gate. I pulled a pen out of my jacket and stabbed the bag, immediately piercing the paper, though careful not to rip it too greedily and spill out the rolls and breadstuffs.

I only wanted one roll, well, maybe two, and I was hungry for a mouthful would've done; I hadn't eaten in almost thirty hours, but even when I had gone without food for two or three days, I still didn't have that much to eat to recover. A bite or two, and I felt myself coming to.

I looked around me at the empty street and made a hole deep enough to insert my hand a feel a roll, looking around me. I pulled it out and immediately took a bite. It was delicious! I took another bite, clutching the roll with my teeth, and pulled out another roll, sticking it in pocket. I almost retrieved another roll but instead lifted the bag off the fence and spun it round to conceal the ripped hole, hanging it back on the fence.

I quickly walked down the avenue, which I'm glad I did, at that moment a police car slowly passed me with the driver cops looking after me in the rear view mirror. Boy if I had been seen eating the rolls before the store, they'd have certainly stopped and arrested me. I didn't have any ID and how fast they'd arrest me as a runway I didn't have to ask.

On 14th Street, I finally saw the famous Washington Square Park Arch. I crossed the avenue, getting a clearer view of the arch from the middle of the avenue, the overcast graying morning outlining the Arch in crisp clarity against the buildings around it. A large lit Christmas tree stood in the center of the Arch, and I hesitated before I turned right on 12th Street. I was on the street where my father lived, but the numbers were very low, and he was at the 400s.

The quiet walking and the roll I had stolen revived me a bit, but now that my hunger was appeased, I felt sleepier than ever. I heard laughter behind me, and I turned to see a group of people coming out of a building, the three men dressed in suits and loosened ties, and the three women in open fur coats exposing their bare legs under very short skirts. *Must have been an all night party*, I thought. And one of the men looked at me intently, probably wondering what I was doing at the early hour, and I almost thought it was the Ralph-guy from the previous night, his fat red balding head almost like a replica of one who tried to kiss me last night. But, the eyeglasses that framed his face were like an attempt to mimic an intellectual, and I smirked, thinking of Ralph who had been mimicking the same.

"What a fake!" A woman next to him said who was clutching drunkenly to him and giggling, and I knew his look was one of lustful craving, and I'm certain I could've had him except for the woman he was with. That's happened lots of times, a look, a gaze, and off I go after a man attracted to me, or at least the opportunities of my hard dick.

The bunch of them walked right into the street, ignoring the scattered traffic, and the men raised their arms and began screaming for taxies that weren't even there. It's funny how rich people expect and demand immediately whatever they wanted, like a taxi, even if one is not in sight. A few of the couples strode out into 5th Avenue and started hailing non-existent taxis, but the man who had stared at me clutched his date and started leading her drunkenly down 5th Avenue. The woman slipped a few times in the snowy ice, but the man clutching her to him turned a corner and disappeared. The other couples didn't even seem to notice that they had gone. But even in that fleeting moment of looking after them in the distance, I could see the man's free hand groping the drunken woman's breasts. But, what had the man seen in me that made him look so long in recognition? I'll never know. I walked down 12th Street.

On 6th Avenue, I saw another clock tower standing a few blocks away. It was now five minutes after six, and I was tired but continued on 12th Street. Snow wasn't that bad, now that daylight was coming, and I passed a few people on their morning walks for papers and other goods, all bundled up and staring right through me.

Then I saw it: Mata Hari, Art Deco Antiques, my father's shop. I stood and looked at it, biting my lower lip. He was cozy and warm sleeping snuggled into a warm bed upstairs never knowing his son was damp and cold on the street below. I looked at the shuttered windows of the three story building and wondered which was his. The shop was enclosed by a gate, but I could make out its smallness and antique decorated window display. A lamp with a colored-glass shade stood in one corner of the window, an old radio stood in the middle, and a tall elegant female mannequin dressed in a long gown and holding gloves stood at the other end.

I never understood what people saw in these old things; it would make sense if they had been alive when these objects were used, but some of them were fifty or a hundred years old. In Mrs. Gillette's house, one room was devoted to just such a display: a Biedermeyer sofa reclined next to a Tiffany lamp, which stood atop a little table, which I'm sure had a name to it, too. To me, they looked like simple old couches, lamps and tables. I immediately hated my father's shop. If Mrs. Gillette was a bitch because she possessed such expensive objects and always suspected everyone for trying to steal them, what was my father like for supplying those objects? Would he accuse me of robbing from him, too?

I glanced at a handwritten sign in the doorway: "Special Xmas hours: open Xmas eve 9 to 9," and underneath that a gold leaf etched sign in the glass: "Mitch Lescoux, prop.," and underneath that, "Josh Rankling, asst." I frowned; my father was such a fake. Josh Rankling was the name, along with his, that appeared this year on his Christmas card, but every year the name that came with his was a different one. I sneered in disgust. I wondered how much he had to dish out each year for a new gold sign to be etched in his window; he probably had more money than my grandmother suspected.

I crossed the street and looked up at the small building. It was nestled in between two large tenements and looked very old compared to most of the other buildings on the street. That's what my father would do, live in the oldest building there was. I wondered which room he and Josh slept in; no matter how many times I got picked up and went to bed, I never ended up staying the night with some stranger. The idea of waking up next to some stubble-faced asshole was always repulsive, and I always fled in the morning, disgusted and hating myself for having spent the night with a stranger. I know I always did it for money, being nothing but a whore, and afterwards it would be some time before I tried going with a guy again, yet I always did.

I turned away from my father's building and felt much as I did those Cincinnati mornings when I walked out of some stranger's arms and bed: disgusted, hating myself, hating the world for what I had become – a male whore. Still, didn't I resent the strangers name below my father's? Did I want to lie underneath my father as well?

I walked back along the small street my father's shop was on. Wouldn't it be best to show up after the shop was open? Would he see that as an intrusion into his business? Would there be so many shoppers so early in the morning that my appearance would destroy my father's mood for the rest of the day? Still, wasn't I reading too much into his handwritten Love, Dad message? Who knew why he had written that? Maybe guilt, maybe a sense of his own mortality, maybe a way of atoning for all the years of his ignoring me? Who the hell knew?

I walked on, and pretty soon spotted the same clock tower I had seen moments ago on another street. It was red and stone colored, something so amazing in the tall sameness of the surrounding buildings that it seemed out of place and contrary, an oddity that would certainly be replaced by the architectural conformity of the city. It seemed that it should be in my father's shop for display or careful purchase. It rose up from a triangular block of its own, to what seemed to be a garden at the rear of the building, and when I walked all the way around, I found the short main stairway – gated as much as the entrances to other buildings – was a public library that would open at 11:00 a.m. but close at 3:00 p.m. for Christmas Eve.

And, just as I had seen in other doorways and against buildings, a clump of blankets with obviously a person sleeping underneath, and bundles of much used shopping bags, and sometimes even shopping carts, was pushed as close to the building as could be. Back home in Cincinnati, I had seen pictures on television of all the homeless people in New York, but they were presented the problem as in one or two city blocks. Yet, here they were everywhere. Outside of the bus station, along the streets and avenues, here and there on the streets to my father's house, on the steps of this library, and most probably on every street I was bound to walk.

It reminded me of an old couple that appeared not far from the social worker therapy center when I first started going to see Susan. They were probably my grandmother's age, in their 70s, and each day they sat in the doorway of a vacant store that once held a travel agency, the vacant-eyed deteriorating couple a stark contrast to the vacation posters still hanging in the closed store window of other couples, younger, skinnier, fit and tanned in bathing suits and romping through the surf and sands on Cancun, or Hawaii, of Tahiti. It was as if the homeless couple mimicked another poster which would read "Hey, folks, don't be like these old farts sitting in this doorway; be like these beautiful young people in the sun in these posters!"

I never knew why these old people appeared in the first place; neither Susan nor Ralph ever said anything about them. Did they lose their home to a fire or their inability to pay the rent or fight off a co-op conversion? They just appeared in late summer and just as suddenly disappeared in early winter. I like to think some family member or some shelter took them in, though the reality was most likely they froze or starved to death.

By the time I made it back to 5th Avenue, a light but cold drizzle had started and the crisp frozen snow on the sidewalks quickly turned into slush, which instantly soaked through socks and boots. I wished I knew where to go to get out of the rain, but so early in the morning the record stores and book stores were locked and gated up, even though more and more people started appearing on the streets.

I walked around the Washington Square Arch – even the Christmas tree was locked up behind a fence – and continued to the tall buildings surrounding the park. New York University read the carved notation, a V for a U, I figure. Was there some memory or association in my head with the name? I thought of Susan trying to understand (that's the term she used Trying to understand) why I was planning to stay out of high school in my second year no matter what happened.

"Why?" I had asked, "To get into college?"

"To finish something you started," she said.

I knew that for her to be a counselor she definitely had to have a college degree, but why did she assume that what was right for her was the same for me? I always wanted to ask her that but didn't. Why did people always assume that if their lives were going good I should be like them? What crap! Ralph even hinted that his life was an example of a contented life; he was married, had two kids, and a job that he liked, so nothing was wrong. Or was there? If I analyzed Ralph, I was certain I'd find a hell of a lot of faults in him. Susan, too. And, Mrs. Gillette most of all. Real assholes, the entire bunch!

Six

I walked in the slush, the rain a fine chilly mist that made the day seem bitterly cold. The rain had soaked through my Bengal's jacket, and I felt my arms and shoulders shivering from the cold. Man, I hadda get warm! And fast, too!

A few blocks away from the college buildings, I saw a man struggling with the heavy locks of a metal gate he was trying to open.

"Mother fucker!" he mumbled, then reached for a bottle and downed a drink. Two gift-wrapped bottles were under each arm, and he went back to forcing the locks to open. Must have been frozen with the cold outside, I thought. I again looked at the man, a red and white fake fur Santa Claus hat roosted on his head. I smirked.

"Same shit all the time!" he said, and took a step back and kicked the lock and gate. "Goddamned piece of shit!"

It didn't do much good, and once more he started fumbling with the locks.

"Fucking garbage!"

He suddenly saw me and turned. His eyes were glassy wet, and his face was unshaven and haggard, but the stench of alcohol hung heavily in the air around him.

"Hey," he mumbled. "Can you give me a hand, buddy?" "Hold this." And, he conspiratorially winked but warned, "No sneaking a drink, ok? He stood weaving and went back to the locks."

I slung my backpack on one shoulder and took the two boxes of liquor, the open box seemingly a lot lighter than the closed one; it was obvious he had been nipping from it and soon would begin on the closed one just as well.

"Piece of shit!" he repeated to the stubborn iced-over locks. "I shouldn't even go in. Serve 'em fucking right if I didn't clean their fucking pig-sty! Let 'em come in and find it like they left it. What am I a fucking animal, cleaning up their dirt?"

He suddenly succeeded in freeing one lock, shoved it in his coat pocket, and just as easily freed another one. He winked at me, and his face had that familiar look I knew so well, his eyes going down my pants, and I wondered if my lips looked as wet and rapid as did his?

"Go on," he winked. "Take a drink if you want; my other jobs left me presents, not like this cheap piece of shit company."

He uplifted the barrier and started freeing the doors, and I reached in one of the liquor boxes and lifted out the bottle. Only a quarter or so of the gin left, and he winked at me, took the bottle and drowned it. Yes, I wondered, why was gin always the preferred drink of those trying to make me? Is there a particular drink for every perversion? If faggots have gin, do whores drink bourbon? One time in Cincinnati a guy dressed me up as girl and made me sip blackberry brandy while he just had a beer. And, what does the S&M crowd drink, vodka? What about the guy that killed a little girl in Cincinnati? What does he drink, probably Shirley Temple's? Oh, what the hell do I know?

Without a care, Santa just tossed the empty bottle in the street outside, rolled down the gate behind us, and we were in.

He let out a deep sigh of relief and reached for the bottle I was holding, ripped it open and this time just took a sip and tiredly sat down in a row of seats. He looked at me glassy eyed, as if trying hard to remember who I was, then his cheeks puffed out and he belched. "Bouah! Bouah!" Again his eyes drooped, but I was glad to be in a warm place, if only for a short time.

I looked around. It was dark – just a Coca Cola sign shone brightly on one wall – and after his little gagging I didn't expect any real movement from him. But what did I think was going to happen? Well, maybe because the way he looked at me I felt I should play this out to the end. But that's always been my problem, thinking that the look of sexual desire and lust in the eyes of strangers could be more than just a look of sex, but also a longing for love. Sometimes I've always felt I should never disappoint someone hungry for me, as if their hunger for sex should be appeased and rewarded by my giving of myself to them – and how easily I have given myself to others. But what sexual satisfaction or sharing would I get from the drunken Santa whose need for a bed was to sleep it off and not screw me in?

Santa let out a few more retches, but they were mostly dry heaves. I moved to another table. My feet were wet, my shoulders also were wet, and the hood of my jacket was sodden and did nothing to keep the snow off my head. Santa slowly got up and shuffled behind the counter. Then he stopped, staring at me as if unable to recall who I was or what I was doing there, but the sight of his liquor bottle brought back some kind of recollection as he sheepishly grinned, wiped his mouth, and said, "Shit, I shouldn't have drunk it so fast."

I grinned and snorted, but said nothing, as he looked at me.

But, I was glad to be in the store where it was incredibly warm; and the fragrant smell of pizza dough, cheese and sauce – even though they weren't being baked at the moment – hung aromatically in the air like a welcome treat from the bitter slush and cold outside. I took off my wet jacket and set it on a stool backrest, thinking, maybe I could stay here? Maybe he'd give me a job in the shop?

"Is this your store?" I asked.

Santa didn't look at me, but rubbed his face and sat back down next to his bottle of booze, and started fumbling the package trying to rip it open. He did, and brought the bottle out. Suddenly, I changed my mind about being here, the smell of alcohol and vomit was quickly over-powering the sweet smell of sauces and pizza dough.

Again I asked him if the store was his.

"Wha ...?" he slurred, looking at me. "What ...?"

I sighed; I was familiar with this time-lag, the almost slow-motion response of drunks, being told lots of times to jerk someone off when I just did, and them not understanding why it was taking them so long to ejaculate. Drunks don't know that their sexual strength goes with each drink they have.

"Are you the pizza guy?" I asked.

He contemptuously snorted and lifted the bottle. It was a brown colored liquor, and I knew if he started mixing it atop the clear gin there'd be real trouble.

"Nah," he said, "I just come in every morning and clean the place up."

He held the bottle and looked at it, then pushed himself up from the stool and went behind the counter and retrieved a bottle of beer from the store refrigerator. He cracked the top off and took a deep swallow, letting out a sigh of satisfaction. I don't know how people can drink beer after drinking gin then setting off to drink whiskey. He took another swallow, then reached into the refrigerator and pulled out another bottle of beer, then returned to the table and held out the beer bottle to me. I opened it and took a small swallow. I never liked the taste of beer, and since I was tired and hungry, the taste repulsed me even more.

"What happened to the side of your face?" he asked, slowly sipping his beer.

I looked more closely at a wall mirror and saw the left side of my face was huge, puffed up and bruised looking, where the mugger had stuck me.

"I got mugged," I simply said, but I noticed he wasn't paying me any attention, nodding out again until he jerked up again.

"Wha…wha…?"

"Good beer," I simply said, raising the bottle and pretending to move it into my mouth.

He did the same, took a sip, then set the bottle down on the table and sleepily looked at me. This was it, I knew it; the whole point of me being here with him. He moved so his legs were open and smiled. There was no choice. I got down to my knees and smiled back at him. Slowly, I tried pulling his pants down under his ass and down his thighs. The rancid stench of dried urine on his underwear surged into my nostrils, and I hoped I could get away with giving him a hand-job and didn't have to take his smelly cock in my mouth.

I sighed, but kept smiling, and lifted the limp penis and gently began stroking it back and forth, doubtful I could raise his drunken cock to erection. Then I heard the snore and looked up. His arms were crossed over his chest, his pants were down his legs, the Santa hat rakishly roosting on his head, and he was asleep.

I held onto the cock, gently pulsed it in my hand because if I let it go and made a movement he'd instantly stir awake. Being drunk and plastered as he was there'd be no trouble in keeping him that way; as long as I kept quiet.

I examined the cock I was holding. Limp, but just as cock-looking as any I've seen. What was the fascination some people had for detailed examination of a cock, or a cunt? I didn't understand those incredible close-ups of a wet cunt or scummy cock in porno videos and magazines; bodies aroused me, not detached orifices or severed photos of something entering them. Entire body photos turned me on, especially photos of women with men, as I've always imagined myself to be the woman under the man, but whenever I looked at page after page of cocks and cunts I grew quickly disappointed.

I gently let go of the limp dick, settling it to fall down to the loose droopy balls between Santa's open legs. I had been gently holding the soft penis for almost five minutes, and I was certain Santa was in a deep sleep, probably dreaming of erections and liquor bottles and spotless pizza shops. This one certainly wouldn't be cleaned up, I smirked.

I reached into Santa's coat pocket in a side chair and gently pulled out his ring of keys, careful not to jiggle too much. It took almost five minutes inserting the various keys into locks until I hit upon the correct one; the lock snapped open. I was about to go out, but then I went to the refrigerator where he had gotten the beer and looked at the food. My mouth quickly grew wet and I wiped my lips. But I settled on a two-pound package of ricotta cheese and two bottles of orange juice. I stuck that in my knapsack and put my damp jacket back on. Santa was still snoring, his exposed dick hanging limply, and I shrugged, recapped the bottle he was drinking from, and took that in my knapsack. Suddenly, I felt sorry for Santa; he probably would lose his job for sleeping half-naked in the pizza shop and not cleaning up the place. What a Christmas surprise he would be? I snorted, and went out, frowning that it was still raining and snowing.

I scooped up a handful of slushy snow off a parked car and washed my hands and fingers of the uriney smell. Again, I felt sorry for the drunken Santa, but then said, "Oh fuck him! Christmas is a time of revelation, lots of things come out in the open. I'm sure that Santa was a good cleaner, after all, he had the keys to the place, but after this he'd be left keyless out in the cold … like me."

Seven

I walked on. More and more people were filling the streets, either rushing to last minute work or carrying shopping bags of wrapped presents. Sooner or later, I'd have to head back to my father's place. But why? He didn't know I was in New York. What did I expect from him? A Christmas greeting? A firm handclasp? Some kind of hope that his Christmas card's message of Love, Dad was for real? But where did I get the idea that he would welcome me like some prodigal son who had strayed and gone away?

I had wandered up a few streets and on a quiet 15th Street, I stopped in a doorway. The single building took up one side of the street while another building took up the other side. I leaned back on the door, and it instantly gave way to a large delivery dock with a shuttered gate drawn over what was probably another locked gate.

Probably closed for the holidays, I thought, and let the door close after me. It was as cold in here as it was outside, but at least I was out of the dripping rain and slush, my breathing even misting heavier than on the street outside. Only a little grey daylight came in from the cloudy day, and it would probably be pitch black by nightfall, and I certainly wasn't going to be here then.

Then I was grabbed from the rear. A guy was on me before I could think of running and getting away.

"Don't move!" I heard a voice say.

It was obvious that whoever it was certainly was accustomed more to the darkness than I was, and it was also obvious he wasn't the only one in the place. On the platform, which I assumed was a loading dock, shapes and bundles were rising from the floor, coughing, spitting, that it was also obvious that the voice behind me had awoken them.

A figure quickly leaped off the platform and approached as a hand behind me grabbed my shoulder strap and pulled the

205

knapsack off. The approaching figure suddenly punched me in the chest and pushed me against a wall, grabbing my knapsack before the other figure could get at it and quickly un-zipper the pack open.

"Well, well, well," the guy said, pulling out the liquor bottle. "It's sure gonna be a Merry Christmas today!" He turned and lifted the bottle over his head, showing it to other shadows on the platform who cackled and coughed and laughed, and called out, "Bring her over, Stanley! We could use a new whore!"

Stanley quickly ripped open the colorful package, reaching in for the bottle and opened it, and took a deep swallow of the liquor. Instantly, he shook his body as he gagged and doubled over, than spat out a heavy sigh of exhaustion as if taking the drink was some kind of triumph or accomplishment. He recapped the bottle and put it back in the box. "Not bad," he said, "for whiskey."

He again went through my knapsack, pulling out the cheese, the bottles or orange juice, my notebooks and all my T-shirts and my one extra pair of jeans. And by now, the three other figures had climbed off the platform and shuffled over to us. Two of them were clad in piles of shirts and jackets, while the third, who timidly stood between them, wore a huge overcoat with tattered nylons and mismatched shoes; her longish hair was dirty and matted, with the brown roots almost half-way to where they met the blonde intruders. And, the lack of makeup and the stubble on his chin made it was obvious she was a man, one of those New York transvestites I'd heard about.

Behind me, I again felt the hand go over my body, rifling my pockets and finding a few scraps of paper, like the Burger King Coupons I got in Cincinnati. Disgusted with the meagerness of my knapsack, Stanley threw the bag down and stepped away. He was just like the other homeless guys there, piles of shirts and jackets on him, unwashed, putrid smelling, a bum. When did it become politically correct to label shiftless unwashed thugs, hooligans and alcoholics as homeless unfortunates instead of calling them what they were – bums?

I started picking up my shirts and putting them back in my knapsack, thinking I'd get out of there, when Stanley turned and growled, "Where do you think you're going?" He glared at me. "I need a whore to keep me warm, honey."

Stanley grabbed the front of my jacket and pulled me to the loading dock. Tattered pieces of cardboard boxes stood around the dock, and the two other bums crawled into one box and worked their way under a blanket; the bum in a long overcoat also snuggled down between them. Stanley made me crawl feet first into the box and crawled in after me. It was like crawling into a bum's underwear, smelly, stagnant, oppressive, and when he lay down on top and started kissing me, I almost vomited in his face from his stench.

He rolled off a few times, pawing between my legs – I refused to get hard, imaging it was social worker Ralph molesting me – and pulled down his two pants and began jerking off his limp dick.

Suddenly, he crawled out of the box, growling I stay in, and pulled up his two pairs of pants. He removed the bottle of whiskey, gagged at his drink, and roused the other bums, all the while searching for other clothes he had nearby.

"Get up, you losers!" he roared. "We're gonna have a wedding!"

The first one out of the blankets was the sorry-looking transvestite. I suppose if she had a bath with perfumes she wouldn't look so bad. She looked so frail but then saw what Stanley was holding and surged toward him in a rage, her eyes wide, her mouth open in disbelief.

"No, you promised!" she hissed. "You said it'd be mine!"

Stanley looked her up and down, then spat in disgust. "Fuck you!" he said. "You're a disgusting skank! Take a look at yourself in a mirror, you slut!"

The transvestite sorrowfully said to him, "But, you promised."

Stanley grabbed the front of her coat, twisting whatever tits she may have had, and squelched, "You promised! You promised!" he mimicked. "If you don't shut your mouth, I promise you won't have one!" He flung her across the dock and she fell against the other bums, catching her balance but running into the cardboard box and flinging herself into it. I could hear her sobbing.

But shit, I didn't know what was going on with these bums, and more than that, I had no idea how to get out of the loading dock. Maybe the company that was here shut down, and this loading dock was now the home of the bums. As my eyes had gotten more and more used to the darkness, I began to see that the place was even more dirty and filthier than I first imagined. The blankets under which the transvestite dirty blonde sobbed seemed to be tattered and frayed to something that was brought here weeks or months ago. Stanley's cardboard box, into which he had pushed me and where he couldn't get an erection, seemed to have lain pressed against the wall for weeks. I began to suspect that this building was actually vacant, and the loading dock hadn't been used in months if not years. These street people and bums had quickly taken over to enforce their squatter's rights. The loading dock was theirs, and that's all there was to it. Still, how come they hadn't risen up above the loading dock? I suspect that the massive gate at one end of the wall kept them from exploring any further.

Stanley undid the parcel he was holding and pulled out a white satiny and frilly long dress. For a moment, I thought it was an actual wedding dress, but it was too short, looking more like a little girl's Holy Communion outfit than a young woman's marriage gown. From a plastic bag, Stanley sniffed at what looked like white nylons – certainly not meant for a little girl to wear, but maybe it was. I couldn't even imagine where a bum like Stanley could get a hold of the girlie clothes.

Stanley ordered I get out of the box than said, "Get dressed."

I hesitated, looking from the clean white dress to filthy and vile Stanley.

"No way," I said. "You're sick!"

Amazing how fast a bum like Stanley moved, but he was on me in an instant, holding my jaw until I could feel my teeth snapping into bits, or at least that's what I thought.

"Get undressed, mother fucker!" he ordered. "And, that means now!" I could feel his putrid breath was over my face – pickles, sardines, pizza, who the hell knew what he ate? "Kappish?!" He flung me aside and tossed the white dress at me. "Get dressed, whore!"

I looked at them staring at me, the two other open-mouthed bums with Stanley and the wet-eyed blonde transvestite then took off my jacket and began unbuttoning my shirt, sliding it down my arms and raised the T-shirt over my head. Stanley sat down on a blanket, but another bum came to me and began to feel my flat chest, kneading my breasts like they were fulsome breasts until Stanley jumped up and pushed him away.

"Get the fuck off my woman!" he hissed. "She's mine!"

I remained still, forcing myself to stay unresponsive to Stanley's hands, but I also knew I was getting aroused by the feeling of myself being treated like a woman. Just the thought gets me horny; it's what I always imagined myself to be, a girl, a slut, a skank on my knees and taking it from all sides; in those alleys and rooms and cars in Cincinnati; to that Ralph-guy in the park last night, and that Santa this morning, men were after me like they should be. After all, I was their little girl-whore.

I smiled at Stanley and lowered my pants, my stiff penis sticking out before me. I could see Stanley's mouth fall open. I lowered my head, like a shy little girl, and removed my pants. I guess I could explain my attraction to men as acting and being like a girl to them; if I didn't feel myself as such, the horror and disgust of homosexuality would have been unbearable. That's why I always took on another persona, a girl's persona that would please any man that wanted relations with me.

Stanley stared at my penis jerking and pulsing in the chilly air, and started slowly jerking me off, but my eyes and thoughts were on Blondie, the wet-eyed sad transvestite under the blankets. I was aroused by her even more than by scabby Stanley.

"What the fuck?!" I heard a bum say. "Look at her ass. All pimples, bet you she has AIDS."

"Yup," said another bum. "AIDS for sure."

I could just imagine I heard three bum's cocks drop forlornly down. Never did the scare of a disease have such an effect as did AIDS. I been hearing about it in Cincinnati, and here I was New York City, and the scare was as prevalent as the sickness was real.

Stanley let go of my dick and spun me around; I almost fell over from my pants around my ankles.

"AIDS!" he said. "The fuck'n whore has AIDS!" He pushed me away from him and was mumbling to himself. "I was gonna marry you," he sadly said. "You were gonna be my wife," he whispered, and fell back against a wall, pressing the white dress he was holding to his face.

One of the bums watching Stanley, snatched up the liquor bottle Stanley had ignored and moved to Blondie, who jumped out of her blanket and came and stood next to me. The bum shrugged, then took the bottle and tried taking a sip when Stanley was on him. I started getting dressed.

"You have AIDS?" Blondie asked.

I shrugged. "Who knows?" I looked at her. "I've always had pimples on my ass. I know they look disgusting," I said, turning red. "There's nothing I can do about them."

She snorted and smirked. "Sure scared them."

I smiled back, and I continued dressing while looking at her. I wanted to hold and caress her, no matter how man-like she looked in her clothes and no matter how shabby and smelly she was. I took a step toward her, and she came into my arms. For a long time we stood like that, holding each other, gently swaying, my erection in my pants nudging the stiffness under her overcoat and under her skirt or dress, until we both spasmed in ourselves, clutching and holding to each other as if our mutual ejaculations completed the shared loneliness of our desperation.

I took a step back, drawing her with me, and slid down the wall, as she settled with me, cuddling in my lap and clutching her legs under mine. We kissed a few times, and I asked, "How do you feel?"

She beamed at me and smiled, "I feel beautiful," she said.

It was as if we had actual intercourse with each other, yet this was so much better. I'm sure she felt the same, as her intercourses must have been rougher and uglier than mine ever were, taking more men in a single night then I had in a week.

When we broke from our kissing, and she settled her face against my cheek, we both saw Stanley looking at us. There was contempt and disgust in his eyes. He suddenly flung the white dress across the loading dock. I looked at him, then went and picked it up and crammed it into my knapsack.

"Fucking queers!" he cursed. "I shoulda killed you when I had the chance!" He kicked at the items before him, looked desperately around him, and leaped to the other bum who was again holding the liquor bottle of his lips. Stanley surged at the bottle, spraying it from the bum's lips, and kicked him.

"Mother fucker!" Stanley yelled and began to stomp on the bum, who scrambled out of the way, dragging the blanket with him, but Stanley kicked him a final time, and the bum went down and stayed down, his head covered by the blanket.

Stanley spat at him, dragged the blanket off his fallen body, spat again, and lay down, covering himself with all the blankets. Blondie and I simply sat huddled together, neither of us taking an interest in the downed bum.

"What are you doing here?" I asked.

She sighed and looked sadly at me. "I got nowhere to go," she said and put her head on my chest.

"Don't they have shelters in New York?" I asked.

She snorted and looked up at me, her eyes curious but at the same time sneering.

"Where you from?" she asked.

"Ohio," I answered. "Cincinnati. Just got in last night."

"Wow!" she said, looking at me. "Last night, eh?"

I nodded my head.

"I wish I had just arrived," she said, "then I'd get the fuck outta here."

"Don't they have any shelters for homeless people?"

She snorted. "We spent a week in one, one time, and we had to leave. My sister got raped the first night we were there. She was just a kid."

"You were with your parents?"

She looked sadly at me. "That's my dad," she said.

I looked at Stanley, holding the whiskey bottle but having somewhat fallen asleep.

"Your father?" I sadly asked, looking at Stanley. "Didn't you call the cops?"

She snorted again. "There were these security guards. Who the hell was gonna believe us? They threw us out, in about a week."

I looked at her. "Where's your mom?" I asked.

She shrugged. "When we lost out home to a fire, Mom stopped taking her medicine and was very depressed and lay in bed all day. After a while, she didn't even cry anymore." Blondie was thoughtful then said, "She was depressed all her life. Only about a year before the fire did she seem happy and interested in things, and even stood up to my father who was more and more drunk." She sighed. "But that was the medicine. When she stopped taking that, she was depressed as when I was a kid."

"So what happened to her?"

"When they threw us out of the shelter, she was so depressed, my aunt took her in; she didn't want her sleeping in hallways and park benches."

"She didn't take you?"

Again she snorted. "Said I was a guy and I had to stay with my father." Blondie raised her head off my chest and looked at the blanket clump under which Stanley, her father, lay. "My aunt said she was gonna take care of my mother and kid sister and I had to watch over my dad until the family could get together again. That was almost two Christmases ago."

My eyes narrowed sadly that the bum in the corner was her father and she was his son. Who had decided to dress her up as a female whore and have her trick on the streets? And, how come she had remained loyal to someone who had no concern or caring for her? What was it? Family values that she tried to preserve? This family that sticks together stays together even if it was a slow stroll toward perversion and death.

We looked at each other then Blondie said, "You'd better get out of here. When they get up, they'll blame you for something and beat you up."

We gazed at each other. I bit my lower lip. "Come with me," I said. "You don't have to live like this."

She frowned. "How else can I live? Even looking as bad as I do, I can make a few dollars every night. You'd be surprised how many guys wanna blow-job from someone who looks homeless, even if it's a guy dressed up as a girl, like me."

"Ain't you afraid you'll get hurt you when they find you're really a guy?"

She shrugged. "One look at me, well ... shit happens," she thoughtfully said, lowering her eyes. I was sure she had been found out a few times.

We were silent, and I held her, gently stroking her bundled arm.

"There's a place we can stay," I said, "on 25th Street, off an alley, by the park nearby."

She sat up. "No," she snapped. "I'm not going anywhere. This is fine here."

She pushed herself up off my lap and shrugged. "You better get outta here. And, I mean it."

I wanted to ask if she was at the end of the line but didn't. I got up off the ground.

"Please come with me," I said. "I think I can get some money. My father owns a store in the Village. I'm sure he'll give me something more for Christmas. Please ..."

She stared at me. "Your dad's probably no better than mine; that's why you're on the streets, just like me."

She turned away and went to the blankets close to where her father was asleep with his whiskey bottle. I sighed, looked at the comatose figure on the floor then picked up my knapsack. My clothes had been scattered between the mattresses that lay on the ground. I picked them up and walked across the loading dock. Maybe she was right; it's best to get out of here. I looked back at Blondie, but she was facing the other way. I opened the door and went back out.

Eight

The snow had gotten heavier, but the street was quiet and unpopulated, and the sidewalks remained as undisturbed and untrodden; a sheen of white lay everywhere. I walked slowly, confused and disappointed by what had just happened. Blondie's voice telling me not to take less than a dollar remained echoing in my skull. Is that what's going to happen to me?

When I got to the big street I again saw the clock tower, 1:35 p.m. it said. Had I really been that long with Blondie and her father? It was barely 7:00 a.m. when I first met Santa; about 8:00 when I left him. About 8:30 when I wandered into the loading dock, so I had spent about six hours with them. Damn, what a way to kill the morning!?

Though the snow was falling thickly and steadily, I was surprised at the amount of people on the big street trudging through the snow carrying bags and bags of last minute presents, though probably cursing themselves for having waited so long. Radio speakers in store fronts blared Christmas Carols, and the disk jockeys kept bawling, "It's a White Christmas! It's a White Christmas!" after every song and announcement.

Was it snowing in Cincinnati? Was my grandmother worried about where I'd be spending the night? I had spent lots of nights out but never on Christmas. Or, had that social worker scum Ralph sicked the cops on me, certain I was up to no good? Oh, fuck him!

Nine

It wasn't long before I was again on that big street going to my father's house and shop. The gate in front of his shop was gone, the lamps were lit in the window, and even from the distance, I could see people entering and leaving his shop. But would he be glad to see me? Or disappointed? And, I couldn't just show up out of the blue, especially if my grandmother called and told him I was missing again.

I walked toward his house and looked at it from across the street. A tree stood in front of the house, the snow packed thickly on its barren white branches, but even through the fog of falling snow, I could see someone moving in the lit second story window.

I crossed the street, took a deep breath, feeling very afraid, and pushed the buzzer. I stared at the side of the gate, certain I was being observed from the window above, and then heard the crackle of a voice in the intercom.

"Yes?" it squawked.

"My name is Billy!" I yelled, louder than necessary, smirking to myself as I imagined the listener at the other end jumping back from the jarring shouts. "I'm looking for my father, David Lescoux!" I felt weird about saying his made up name. My own name is Leshko; but Dad had to Frenchify it – after all, this was Greenwich Village, where people were supposed to be hip.

There was a pause of silence, as I'm sure the voice was taking in what I said. Maybe I should've gone into the shop and looked to see if my father was there; maybe he had people working for him and didn't have to be there all the time. Maybe the squawky voice was now getting my father from another room. Hell, what did I really know about him?

"I'm coming down," the voice finally said, and I cursed, thinking I'd have been let in immediately if I were welcome. My face turned red, and I squirmed under my wet coat, remembering a doorway in Cincinnati, where I'd have to wait for gay Vinnie to come down because the intercom worked, but the front door buzzer was broken, and it took Vinnie forever to come to the front door. I'd wait patiently, huddled in the doorway, looking up each end of the street, not wanting to be seen because Vinnie lived a block from school, and I knew that many of the kids walked past his building on their way to and from school – I had done so myself when I was a kid – and sure enough, coming up the street, and certain to spot me lurking in Vinnie's doorway, were Petey and Mikey, two not-so-good friends of mine. It's as if the three of us were on that street intentionally to meet up with each other because from down the street we each made eye-contact with each other, and Petey and Mikey immediately turned to look at each other then back at me, their faces in smirking grins. They knew what I was doing in Vinnie's doorway. The door opened, and Vinnie let me in, I entered hearing loud laughter after me. I still remember the scorn which they called me back in school, "Billy the Fag," "Billy the Filly," "Silly Billy," and finally, "Billy the cocksucking faggot just like his queer dad!" But that was a year ago, and I still feel ashamed.

I heard the clatter of locks opening, and the door swung inside. Through the gate I looked at a goateed and bald man, studs in his ear lobes, black T-shirt, his arms tattooed, his jeans tight with cowboy boots on his feet. We looked at each other up and down; he smiled, I smiled back. It was an unmistakable look, the kind I'd gotten in Cincinnati and a few times in Chicago and now in New York.

Suddenly, I heard a buzz at the gate, and I pushed it open. The man stood aside and let me in.

"Oooh, get out of that coat!" he grimaced. "You'll freeze!" He shook all over.

I wanted to smile at his voice, real classic faggot-like and lisping. I dropped my knapsack and got out of my sodden jacket.

"Does your father know you were coming?" he asked. "He didn't tell me anything. By the way, I'm Josh."

I stamped my boots on the carpeted floor and rubbed my upper arms. My long sleeved shirt was also wet, as I'm certain was my T-shirt and underwear. If I had to walk another hour I'd probably have frozen to death.

"Is Dad in the shop?" I asked. The words sounded funny on my lips as I had never uttered them, simply calling him now what he had written on his Christmas card, as Dad; my grandmother always threatening me to be polite.

He nodded his head. "Oh, gee, he didn't say you were coming for Christmas!"

For all his tough macho image, he was pretty effeminate, not really talking, but gushing, as if each word and sentence were an affirmation of how much he was enjoying life and the moment he was in. People like that make me nauseous.

"Nope," I shook my head. "He doesn't know. It's a surprise."

The man looked at me, his eyes wide, his mouth open, then clapped his hands together like a little kid, and spun around in a dance, squealing, "A surprise! A surprise! David loves surprises!"

I smiled, almost caught up in his glee, but I felt sad. How would I know what my father liked? I'd only seen pictures of him over the years, pictures he had sent only to my grandmother.

"But first," the fairy said, "you must get out of those wet clothes. Gee, you'll catch the death of you. We wouldn't want that to happen, now would we?"

He again looked me up and down, and it was the look I'd been getting from guys out on the streets ever since I arrived in New York; was the entire city gay? And was it so obvious what I really was, too, an image of my father?

"I suppose you've got dry clothes in your bag?" he asked.

I shrugged; besides the dress and an undie package Blondie had handed me as I left the dock I didn't have anything else to wear; but I didn't care, if I could get out of these wet ones that would be great.

Josh led me upstairs to an open floor that covered the length and width of the building, the large loft room divided only by partitions, which made the room into a sleeping area, a work space, and a lounge type of area with exercise equipment, barbells, and two stationary bikes. Dad must have looked very he-man macho type, I thought. Just the little I saw of downstairs, I was surprised by the expensive lavishment of my father's house. Did selling old furniture make all the money he had?

"The bathroom's in here," Josh said, pointing to a small doorway next to a window facing the rear snowy courtyard of the building.

"Thanks," I merely mumbled and opened the bathroom door. I think I blinked in surprise, as the small cubicle-like-door opened into another large room with not only a bath and shower in one corner of the room, but also a hot tub and sauna at the other end. Beautiful white soft and immaculate looking towels hung around the room, all in reach of wherever the bather or sauna user may be in the room, and it looked like something out of a display store catalog, a picture showing off something that didn't really exist out of a house designer's imagination. But, here it certainly did.

I slid open the shower door, turned on the water, testing it for warmth, than quickly and greedily took my wet clothes off. A mass of switches were on the wall next to the door, and I assumed they were for all sorts of lights and heating lamps that were on the ceiling, but I didn't touch any of them.

There was a knock on the door, and I heard Josh call, "Give me your wet clothes, I'll throw them in the dryer!" and the door opened.

I was caught totally unprepared and barely had time to grab a towel and cover myself. Josh had seen what his eyes were looking for, and he snatched up the wet clothes, and giggled, "My, my, you surely are your father's son, aren't you?" He hesitated, licking his lips, "Take your time, David won't get up till maybe seven or eight, it's only three."

We both looked at each other, both knowing we wouldn't even need all that time, and Josh left.

I wished I could sink and loll in the tub, soaking in the warmth of the water, but I washed quickly, unplugged the tub and let the shower water run to give myself a good rinsing. Who knew how long before I washed again, because I sort of knew that my unexpected arrival wouldn't be greeted with the giddy glee that cheered Josh. I doubted that Dad would be cheerful. I wrapped a towel around myself and stepped out of the bathroom.

The large loft room was empty, and I walked to the bed and sat down on the edge of it. The short bath made me sleepy and hungry, and I wished I had the cheese Stanley had taken from me. I lay back and sighed. I slept because when I jerked awake, Josh had undone my towel and was on his knees before my outspread legs, caressing my soft penis and smiling up at me. He pushed himself up from the floor, crawling on the bed beside me, and pulled me up with him, so we could lie fully on the bed. He was also undressed except for a pair of tiny leopard-spotted underwear that only held his cock and balls, like a man's g-string, worn more for teasing than for comfort. It would be crazy to go out into the snow with those under your pants – the chill and ice would get to you fast. He leaned over me, and we looked at each other, then our lips met and he plunged his tongue in my mouth and down my throat. I gagged, and Josh snapped his tongue out and giggled.

"Just like your father," he said, "can't take too much tonguing!"

I smiled, and Josh was on me again, kissing my lips then working his mouth down my neck to my chest and belly all the while gently kneading his stiffening penis. He knelt up, facing me, and slowly lowered his tiny panties. I marveled at the small length of his cock but which made up for it by his width and bulk – short in size but a very nice mouthful. I'm certain the silver cock-ring that glimmered between his pubic hairs had a lot to do with increasing the size of the cock; still, it was certainly impressive, and I doubted I'd be able to spread my cheeks so far apart enough to easily enter me. I foresaw pain, but pain was part of good sex, I thought.

My own cock was as stiff as it would get, and Josh again knelt between my legs and moved his small cock atop mine. The sensation was ecstatic, and I put my fingers at the base of my cock so as to stand it up to meet Josh's movements. It reminded me of a guy I'd meet in a lot filled with yellow school buses stored for the night who simply would hold my cock under his, and the two of us would simply sway into each other as if we were fucking the other until we got so good in reading the other's point of arousal that often we'd ejaculate onto our cocks simultaneously, which only heightened and intensified our arousal and excitement in each other. I met him almost every night in the lot, but one night when I got there early and was skirting my way around a bus, I saw another kid making his way onto the front of the bus. I saw the man wiping his cock with some tissues, and I suddenly understood the feeling of being a sloppy-second. I turned and walked away from the school buses.

I ejaculated, Josh gripping my cock, pulling the foreskin as far as it could go, bloating and exposing my cock-head so nothing would hinder the eruption, and he pulsed his fist around my cock to heighten the pleasure of release. I don't think I had ever had an ejaculation like that, clenching my eyes shut in pain, my body rocking on the bed, and as soon as Josh had gripped me, I actually saw stars exploding in my head.

When Josh finally let go of my dick, and I opened my eyes, I saw he, too, was in a frenzy of pleasure and pain, but his cock-ring cinched him tightly around the base of his cock and around his balls keeping him in a torrent of un-release of any kind. He kept snatching at the cock-ring, trying to find a grip hold and release some of the pressure, but the ring held him too tightly refusing to yield the desperation wracking his blue-colored cock. The only freedom he'd get was if his hard stiff cock loosened some of his stiffness.

I quickly spun around, kneeling on the bed, and put my mouth over his cock. I could hardly get my mouth around his cock when he exploded in a torrent of ejaculation, falling backwards off the bed and striking the floor in a spasm of rocking and coming.

I leapt off the bed and straddled him, Josh's dick coming and tapping my ass, my arms and body pressed to his in an attempt to appease the uncontrolled rocking of his own body. It was something most guys wouldn't do for me – touch and hold me when I shot out – as if in getting pleasure from the fact that they weren't giving me any, indifferently looking at my frenzy as if resenting the fact that I was deriving pleasure when the entire point of our tryst was for me to give them pleasure.

Josh finally lay still, breathing heavily, his fat bulky penis softening against my ass cheeks and thighs, until he slightly nudged me to climb off. I did so, and he immediately gripped the cock-ring and slid it under his balls and off his cock.

"God did that hurt!" he said. "But it was the best I ever had!"

He fell back on the carpeted floor, and I again straddled him and lay down atop him. Josh's hands and arms went around my back, and we kissed. I settled my head against his face, and we must have fallen asleep because when I next opened my eyes Josh was brutally pushing his body against mine and pushing me off.

"David, no!" I heard him say. "It's not like that, please!"

"I looked up and around me." My father stood in the doorway. He was a tall man, but I didn't know that. His hair was black and curly and went down his back almost to his shoulders, like on the *Blonde on Blonde* Bob Dylan album Joey in Cincinnati had hung the wall of his room. I knew Dad's hair was a fake; the photos in my Grandmother's album showed him with brownish straight and flat hair that in various photos receded further and further back atop and around his head. He was wearing blue jeans, a tan studded cowboy shirt, and a denim tie around his neck; I wondered if he had just taken off a leather jacket downstairs, and I'm sure he was wearing cowboy boots. For a moment, we looked at each other, my father's eyes straining at some kind of memory as if not being able to place me in the picture. Josh kept mumbling something about, "You don't understand, and I can explain," but my father kept looking at me.

"Get out!" he finally said. "Get dressed, and get out! Both of you!"

He turned, and I heard his boots thudding down the stairs. Josh had already put on his g-string and glared at me.

"You heard him," he snapped, his eyes a burning glow of venomous hatred, as if I was responsible for everything coming apart in his life. "Get out!" he shrieked, mimicking my father and ran after him.

I remained on the floor, looking after them, puzzled that my own father really didn't seem to recognize me. Over the years, I knew my grandmother had sent him photographs of herself with me standing by her: my first Holy Communion, one of my eighth grade graduation ceremony, and one of me alone behind the wheel of her car the day I got me driver's license. Dad never recognized me, or if he did, he didn't care. I don't know if I felt sad just very numb. But, whatever I was feeling, I knew I had destroyed whatever relationship my father had with Josh, and I knew that for him his relationship meant as little as did his relationship with all the other names on Christmas cards over the years. Why couldn't I stay out of things? Why did I always make a mess?

I heard my father's voice screaming from downstairs. Scattered phrases about working hard, and that it's Christmas time! And finally one shrieking yelp of "I know who he is! Am I blind?"

I was quiet and still; my father knew who I was and found me unworthy of even the slightest recognition! Just as I was alive because of him, so, too, was I a nuisance that had to be abandoned and discarded. Look what a mess I had just done! Aw, Christ! I was his son, but I was a mistake. I should not have been born, but since I was, I was simply tolerated and dumped on my grandmother. I sighed. My mother had it so much easier: she simply disappeared and the hell with the little shitting baby.

I heard my father shout, "Some Christmas present you give me!" but I shut the bathroom door behind me. I felt myself being in a cloud, as if I was sleepwalking, remembering taunts from schoolmates about my father, about my following in his footsteps, about my failures and worthlessness, that when I removed Blondie's dress from my knapsack I didn't know what I

223

was doing until I was straining to pull up the dress zipper on my back behind me.

I sighed; I was a faggot with a little white dress and ready for a fucking. Yet, it was an almost a perfect fit, a little too tight under the armpits but it hung evenly and was aligned on my body as if it had been measured for me. At the time, I blushed, and reached in the knapsack for Blondie's never worn pantyhose and slid them on my legs, tucking my cock and balls between my legs and stretching the hose tightly beneath them. The cock and balls stayed put. I strained into the shoes no one on the dock saw me gather up, a little worn out, but succeeded in plopping my feet into them, and tottered across the floor tiles to the medicine chest above the sink.

One thing I knew about faggots – and Dad was one – was that they always had some kind of girl's makeup in their bathroom chests, either a bottle of facial cream, or a tube of lipstick, or some kind of mascara and eyebrow pencils. Why? I guess to make themselves into that secret image they so want to be.

I was in luck, immediately spotting on an upper shelf a bottle of Cover Girl, a Maybelline eye-stick next to it, and three lipstick tubes of various tints and hues. Still, I wondered who wore the makeup in this house, the macho-looking Josh with his cock-ring or my father the fag with his fake shoulder length curls and twirls.

I picked up the Cover Girl and looked myself in the mirror. A dark swatch of baby down hairs covered my upper lip, and other dark swatches swooned down the sides of my face as if straining in a mimic of Elvis-like sideburns. I had never shaved before, but I knew I'd better do so before I put on the makeup; the strong lighting in the bathroom made my naïve-*ness* so apparent. But, I shrugged and scooped up whatever girly makeup I could find in the cabinet and tossed them in my knapsack.

I went to the door, slightly opened it and heard my father and Josh going at it downstairs. I shut the door and turned back to the medicine chest. Why did I so quickly ignore the package of cheap disposable razors and allow my eye to settle on a long oblong box knowing it contained an old fashioned straight razor and probably an antique from my father's antique shop, one he had set aside for his own personal use?

I opened the box and looked at the elegant brown mahogany handle of the blade. No way could the cheap yellow plastic handles of the disposable razors ever compare to the old-styled elegance and craftsmanship of the old blade. I flicked the blade open, as if I'd always held one, and it hovered easily in my fingers, ready to shave my-virgin face. I heard my father's voice.

"Hey, you!" he yelled, banging on the door. "Come out of there! I want you out of this house, now!"

I looked at myself in the mirror. I wished I had the makeup on. On another shelf, I suddenly spotted another lipstick tube. I picked it up and curiously looked at it in my hand. The plastic wrapper was still on around it, and it had never been used. I set it down and again fingered the razor blade. The door shook and rocked and again my father screamed something. I lifted the blade and swung it down on my left arm, instantly slashing my wrist, surprised at how easily and readily my arm fell as if severed from my body and hanging in a limp clutch as if about to fall totally from my body.

Dad surged in, and for a moment he was speechless, then he shrieked like a little girl. In a way it was funny, his squealing shriek not so much of horror and surprise, but one of hate, as I suppose a girl would cry out at the moment of losing her virginity to some unknown rapist. It was pleasure and fear and revulsion all at once, with also some kind of calculation of how to get out of this incident and how to explain it afterwards when there could be no explanation except cover up.

Josh burst in after Dad, and for a moment we stood looking at each other, my arm dropped into the sink and leaking my blood in spurts and spits. I was certain I had probably cut an artery, but I didn't quite understand what those little white severed cords were doing in my arm. I was puzzled, and suddenly my eyes widened in a sensation of total awareness and understanding. They were put in me like the strings of a puppet, so as to manipulate and hover me about like I was in a performance by a puppet circus, unable to take actions of my own but responding solely to the pullings and tuggings of a lunatic puppet master.

But, when had this insertion of my puppet strings taken place? I certainly hadn't volunteered they do this to me; or was it something done when I was a child or while I slept or still a newborn? Maybe that's why my mother left me because I wasn't a good performer? Maybe that's why my father left me because my performance had shamed him? Maybe that's why I was left with my grandmother, that she looked after and took care of the accident I was growing up to become? Whatever it was, it made perfect sense. They've been controlling and tugging my strings for my entire life! And, whatever stupidities I had gotten into was most likely my form of rebellion and rejection of those manipulations. No wonder I could never fit in; it wasn't me at all!

Josh also screamed, "What have you done?! What have you done?!"

I was pretty much bored with both of them, holding my arm over the sink, grabbing a towel off a wall hanger and wrapping it around my wrist. I was strangely pleased, not a drop of blood got on my white dress.

"We'll need an ambulance!" Josh gushed, going into a tirade of ambulances and hospitals, when my father interrupted him and asked, "Look at the way he's dressed! What will we tell the police? Oh, Jesus!"

"But, David," Josh hissed, "he's your son!"

And, suddenly Josh lowered his head as if suddenly remembering what had just occurred. My father looked at me in a sense of disgust and again my feelings of being a puppet came back.

"We'll get a taxi!" said Josh. "We'll take a taxi to the hospital!"

My father sneered at Josh's suggestion. "How will we get a taxi on Christmas Eve in the middle of a freak snow storm?!" He looked from me to Josh and sadly said, "Why did you let him in? Why didn't you call me in the shop?"

"I'm sorry," Josh whispered. "I thought you were expecting him."

They stood looking at each other, lost in their own feelings of betrayal and weakness. I glanced at the towel on my wrist; the blood had quickly soaked through. I knew I'd better get to a hospital.

"Can I have my coat?" I simply said.

They looked at me, but came apart to let me pass, as if I was wielding the razor blade and was coming at them.

"It's downstairs," said Josh.

I wobbled on my heels, tottering down the stairs, grabbed my knapsack and put one arm in my jacket. Josh ran after me reaching for his wallet. He shoved a twenty dollar bill at me and said, "Take a cab! Tell him Saint Vincent's! It's on 7th Avenue! The cabbie will know! It's only a few blocks away!"

Good, I could add his twenty to mine from Cincinnati, but still, I was curious as to why Josh was doing all the shouting, yet I looked at him as he was helping me with my jacket, which was dry and clean; Josh must have thrown it in the dryer. He must be a real nice guy, I thought and staggered outside.

I had walked past St. Vincent's a few times that morning as I wandered along Greenwich Avenue. Josh just closed the door behind me, and I never thought why Dad didn't come down the stairs.

Ten

They must have thought I was a girl, and I must have staggered in from being raped since the blood had be now covered the front of my dress in one long streak from my waist to my bottom hem. And, things were happening fast: when I slid down on the hospital gurney there must have been a dozen nurses hovering about me, my dress raised, then just as quickly they scattered as soon as they discovered my gender under my white hose. But, in between the various injections and questions – I told them my name was the social worker Ralph and gave them Dad's address; let them figure it out. I wanted to sleep, and for the first time since I got to New York, I felt I could sleep in some kind of safety and warmth, as if I belonged in this room no matter that the nurses who passed my gurney giggled or sneered to themselves as they looked at me.

I don't know how long I lay there, but when I opened my eyes, I was being wheeled across a long hall. I shut my eyes to keep my head from spinning and wheeling until finally stopped; I never even saw who had pushed me from the emergency room to this room. A doctor was looking at me over his glasses that hovered on the tip of his nose. I knew I shouldn't smile, but the way his glasses hung on his nose reminded me of the grade school principal I had in Cincinnati whose authority made the kids in school fear being sent to his office – all he did was feel me up while lecturing about God and Christ and Heaven; I didn't think he was that bad just a weird homo flaky.

Somehow my bleeding had stopped as I lay on the gurney. The doctor picked up my arm and looked at the wound. I also looked – a mass of red tissue surging from under the flesh, bloated, wet, the severed white cords still poking outside of the globulous muscle.

"What's that white stuff?" I asked.

The doctor put down my arm and looked over his glasses. "Tendons," he blandly said. "You severed your tendons." His lips seemed to tighten. "Fortunately, you only cut one. If you had cut twice, you'd walk around for the rest of your life with a claw for a hand." We looked at each other, and he raised his arm to his chest and contorted his fingers into a grotesque vulture-like claw. He raised the arm as if going for me. I turned my head away. "If you had cut all three tendons," he coldly said, "you may as well have cut the arm off and thrown it away." He shrugged and sat down on a stool next to my gurney. "Don't look," he told me, and I turned my head away and felt his poking about my hand and wrist.

And, just as time seemed to disappear in the emergency room, it, too, faded into an almost stillness of peace and quiet. Why is it that only around dull and apathetic strangers did I feel myself attaining some kind of comfort and acceptance? These people were only doing their jobs; they had no interest or concern as to my well-being beyond that of their experience as care-givers. I wondered if they were as seemingly compassionate or caring of others in their own lives. Was Mister Social Worker Ralph as coldly indifferent to his own children? Was Little Miss Social Worker Susan as caring to her own boyfriend? Or did people shed their work-persona-abilities the moment they left work, putting on different personas as they were putting on their jackets to go home? Maybe all of life was just that, role-playing, pretending, acting. Would Susan tolerate the stupidities of her boyfriend the way she tolerated mine? Would Ralph drag his own son to the police if he wrote a poem about a little girl being murdered? Would I have gotten dressed as a girl if my father had loved me as a son?

"OK," I heard the doctor say. I turned, looked at his eyes over his glasses; there was a faint smile on his lips, almost like a shrug. I looked at my wrist. It was bandaged up, the bandage on my arm and hand looking incredibly clean and immaculate. "All done," he said then turned away from me. "They're going to take you to Bellevue psychiatric; you did try and kill yourself, didn't you?" He rolled the gurney down the hall, and I was beginning to feel dizzy. "Rest," he said. "Don't think about anything."

He must have seen my face cringe in fear because who wouldn't cringe at the word psychiatric and the possibility of being committed when you're dressed up as a little girl?

"Someone will help you," he said, "so you don't have to try doing this again."

I shut my eyes as the gurney rolled again, the boot of the gurney hitting and pushing open various doors then we were outside as I was pushed into an ambulance. I shut my eyes, the two ambulance guys talking and laughing about a lady that they knew, and I must have slept because once more we were rolling down corridors again. A security guard – like they have in large stores and malls – stood before a large metal door at the end of the hallway while another guard peered through a wire-mesh window in the metal door.

"They'll take care of you," one ambulance driver said to me, and I was left alone with the guard.

All of a sudden I knew I had to get my wits together. This was big time, a psycho ward; no lunacy here or you'd get locked up for a long time. One guard opened the metal door and pushed me in to the other guard.

"Hey, nice dress," he said, and the two of them burst out laughing, as the huge door slammed behind me.

Whereas in St. Vincent's the attitude of professionalism was certain, here in Bellevue the attitude of paranoia was prevalent. Since you had been brought to the psychiatric ward, the suspicion of the attendants and security guards was nothing but an attitude of certainty that you were a psycho and deserved to be treated as such.

"Here's another skirt wearing one," said one guard to the other, "that makes four, don't it?"

"Who the fuck knows?" answered the other guard. "The night is still young, I guess."

Possibly at that point, I became incredibly lucid and aware that one mistake on my part would get me locked up for a long time with the other slashed wrist transvestites. Wrist slashing is a sort of rite-of-passage, a coming-of-age ceremony that initiates you into a world you were not born into, a world of exaggerated femininity and outrageous promiscuity. A slashed wrist is like a medal of honor, a purple heart on your chest that you have severed the link that would keep you in one gender when you raged and screamed to join and belong to another, leaving one gender, though still unable to be a second one, yet becoming a third, of male and female as one, together – a transvestite.

Of course, I was a long cry from even pretending to mimic femaleness, but already I felt the dress I was wearing, the makeup jar and lipstick tubes and mascara pencil I had in my coat pocket were and soon would be a vital part of my existence. If only I could get out of this sick psycho ward.

The metal doors clattered behind me, and I was told to climb off the gurney and take a seat in a large waiting room; I immediately noticed the seat legs were screwed to the ground and clutched by metal hasps to the wall. Childlike drawings were pasted about the wall, probably drawn by Art Therapy classes in the wards upstairs. If they knew I wrote poetry about murdered little girls, would I now scratch out drawings of their lifeless bodies as well?

At the other end of the waiting room, across from the guard's station, near the locked door, was a water fountain. I stood up.

"Sit down," a guard instantly snapped, putting down the newspaper he was looking at.

I remained standing.

"I wanna a drink of water," I said.

"Sit down!" he said again. His voice was firm, stern, unfeeling.

I sat down; the water fountain was close, and the more I stared at it, the more thirsty I felt, certain my mouth had never been drier or my lips more parched and blistered from the thirst. Still, I had to pretend everything was OK; I knew I had better not start getting argumentative as my reactions to the guard could be very decisive as to whether I was let go or dragged to the wards upstairs.

I slumped down in my chair, crossed my legs, daintily covered my knees with the dress, and stretched out an arm along the tops of chairs next to mine.

A gripping spasm tore through my left arm, as if I was viciously being pulled and tugged and gripped. I yelped in pain, the arm contorting back to my chest, my other right arm desperately gripping and holding the hurting one. Ever since I had been sewn up, I held my arm braced upwards along the metal side railings of the gurney, the doctor even positioning a sling to the bars to hold it upright should I doze off to sleep, but my sudden almost nonchalant jerk of stretching the arm up suddenly made it clear how brutally I had hurt myself.

I doubled over and rocked back and forth, the pain slowly easing as my arm remained in one steady position. I looked at the guard; he was looking at me, and I don't know what I must have looked like, but he scowled and coldly said, "Go ahead, get the water," and he settled back in his chair and smirked, "but there's no more cups."

I didn't care; I stood up and shuffled to the water fountain. It was one of the plastic-bottled refillable kinds, with two little red and blue spigots at the front, and I suddenly knew my dilemma. I would need two hands and arms to take a drink: one to push the spigot and the other to cup my hand and catch the water in my palm. How did the guard drink? I wondered but knew it best not to ask. Was this some kind of psychological problem, a test that was being taped by some hidden camera so that my sanity and competency could be studied and examined?

The guard was looking intently at me. A few paces from the water bottle a clear plastic garbage bag hung taped to a wall, bulging with a few discarded newspapers and masses of crushed discarded paper cups. I reached into the bag, rummaged for the least crushed cup, and leveled it under the blue water spigot. I pushed the spigot and the water swooshed into the cup and just as it appeared, cold and clear and inviting, so, too, it tasted on my lips as I drained the cup and refilled it one more time. The guard had been watching me all the while, and after three cupfuls, I again felt my thirst abating. I put the cup into the trash bag, leaving it uncrushed for the next psycho patient, winking at a camera as I returned to my seat. I was certain I had passed a secret test.

After I had drunk the water, I sat back down, knowing I had better not act crazy; though I wanted to talk to myself I knew that this time someone might be listening and paying attention. I kept quiet. It was so much like sitting outside of the principal's office when I was a kid, or sitting in the counseling center waiting for Susan or Ralph, or just waiting in my whole life. A lifetime of waiting for help, but did I ever believe any of them that they only wanted to help me? Each counselor shuffling me to another, my file growing, thickening, the writing undecipherable to the next healer, care-giver, duplicitous social worker.

I suddenly heard the guard's door clatter with that jail-like clanging that either clanged shut with your imprisonment or clanged open for your release. Two women came in through the door, both carrying clipboards and both pausing to look at me, the black woman entering the glass partitioned cubicle near the guard's station. The white woman picked up another piece of paper – it was the same paper I saw the doctor who had sewed me up had been writing on – a transcript of my conversation with him? – and she curiously peered over the paper and studied me a moment.

I wanted to smile, not because I wanted to seem friendly, but because the look was another constant in my ongoing reality of my life. Do they learn that in their schools, to look inquisitively at their patients as if assessing them in an instant without even having spoken to them? A look; not only for preconceived notions and judgments, but also one of those instant condemnations? Ralph always looked at me like that, as did Susan in the beginning before she seemed to have mellowed, and Mrs. Gillette's look only got more and more critical and outraged as I kept coming to her house and always somehow disappointing her. What did she want and expect anyway? Aw, hell, I could never win with people looking like that at me, and I knew that this time I could lose out mightily.

I lowered my head, staring at the bandage on my wrist. An oily looking brown smear seemed to be edging its way through the porous fabric where I was certain I had slashed my wrist. I tried moving my fingers but could only get them to slightly react – my hand a claw for the rest of my life, eh? Would it matter so much anyway?

I, at first, supposed that the woman was some kind of nurse, she wore a white robe, but unlike the other nurses who were completely in white, she wore regular clothes under the robe. Her name plate above her left chest was a complicated tangle of letters, mostly Zs and Ws that I didn't ever dare try and pronounce, and her bright blonde hair strangely bee-hived at the top of her head almost seemed like a mimic of a nurse's caplet she wasn't wearing. Still, her stern blue eyes belied any kindness and tenderness in her demeanor, and I supposed that if she wasn't a real nurse she was probably the warden of this place. I knew I had to be careful.

As the guard watched from his station, standing up when the woman first beckoned me, I walked across the waiting room and entered her cubicle office. I almost exploded in an Ah ha! of realization, as if I should have known it from the start, because I probably did, and what I saw on the far end of her desk, propped up against the wall, was the familiar bible of social workers, the blue book called *Casework*, which Susan also had in her office, as did Benedict Arnold Ralph, and probably sits on the desks and roosts in the minds of all social workers all over the world.

Once more I was sitting in the presence of a social worker; would I ever be rid of them? And once more, I had walked in like a lamb for his slaughter. I wondered if that wasn't another thing social workers kept in their desks, an axe at the ready to flail my bared neck and skull.

"Name and address," she said, and was as unfriendly and alien as if I had landed on Mars and was being interrogated by an envious green sister of the red planet.

She looked sternly at me and at the form before her as if confirming my identity with the form before her. Was the official looking paper able to reveal more about my identity than I could? She stared at me calculatingly, than asked, "Do you know where you are?"

I snorted then said, "In the hospital."

"Which one?"

I knew I had gone to St. Vincent's, but I didn't quite know where the ambulance had escorted me in the night, and I told her so. And, her eyes slightly softened, as if the awareness of my own experience and its memory disproved the question of my sanity. Still, I didn't crack a smile. And once more, she looked sternly at me, as if hesitating before she asked her vital question.

"Why are you dressed like that?" she asked.

I turned red and lowered my head, the front of my dress forever ruined by smears of my dark blood; yet if I could shed more blood and sprinkle it around the sides and back of the dress I could probably succeed in making the plain white fabric a mélange of polka dots.

"I was at a party," I lied.

The woman's looks again softened, and she eased back in her chair.

"Were you drinking at the party?"

I nodded. "Maybe too much?" I said, again lowering my head. How incredibly easy it was to lie to people! Just tell them what they want to hear, that's all; that way it's not really a lie since they expect it. And, sometimes it's not even wrong to lie, especially to social workers, since they have the power over your freedom, once you have fallen into their clutches and you must do everything to hold onto your dignity and self-preservation, which sometimes means you must lie.

"What happened at the party?" she asked.

"It was like a costume party," I answered. "And, I had too much wine."

"Do you take drugs?"

I looked at her. "Only pot."

"Were you drinking wine and smoking pot at the same time?"

"Uh huh," I nodded again.

She wrote a few sentences on the paper before her and put the pen down. A faint smile eased across her mouth, as if my lies were a confirmation of her diagnosis.

"And, what happened?"

We looked at each other. "I went to the bathroom," I said. "I wasn't feeling too good. I threw up. I looked at myself in the mirror. I looked ugly. There was a razor on the shelf. One of those razors that carpenters use to cut sheetrock. You know the kind, with the blade at one end and a handle at the other?"

"Yes, yes, I know," she said, and I knew I had her, as she wanted to hear my lie.

"There were a lot of gay people at the party," and I saw her tender smile and went on with my lie. "I wouldn't have gone, but there was this girl."

236

"Are you gay?" she asked.

I hesitated then said, "I've been with gays," my face flushing and embarrassing red as if I was ashamed and regretted my betrayal of my sexuality. But, lots of people think being gay is a choice; that we turn to another of our sex so as to fit in or have friends or being accepted by the crowd. I know it's true, and I'd often admit the same to Susan, knowing that option was being liked, as though I was trapped by circumstances around me and who I was with, that is, getting money from guys and also having my sexual needs satisfied. But, you have a free choice of changing, Susan always stressed. And, I suppose I did, but why do social workers always want you to change, and change in a way that they want you to change?

"Do you like being with men?" she asked.

"Not really," my face even a deeper red than before. I don't know how I was able to carry it off. I started believing my own lies.

"There was this girl," I suddenly blurted. "She was beautiful. She was dressed like a pirate, but all in red and green, like a Santa's helper. She was with another girl who was also dressed like a pirate, but a captain pirate, and I knew that the other girl was a lezzie." I blushed and looked at the lady, then went on. Told her the lez had very short hair, like a boy's, while the girl I liked had long hair and lots of makeup. And, her pants and shirt was real tight. The lez had loose pants. They saw me looking at them. "And the lezzie said, 'You're a fine wench and that you'd make a fine whore for their crew.' But I kept looking at the other girl who seemed guilty about something until the lezzie put her arm around the girl's shoulders, very possessive-like and controlling, as though the girl was hers. But the girl I liked started laughing. 'You look ridiculous!' she said, and the two started laughing. I went to the bathroom. Saw the razor. Slashed it across my wrist."

We were silent, looking at each other.

"Did you want to kill yourself?" she asked, looking at intently at me.

"No," I shook my head. "I was embarrassed. The girl was so pretty, and she was laughing at me. I was ashamed."

"Do you always have problems with girls?"

I smiled; she was setting herself up for this one.

"Only when dressed as a girl," I winked then turned red, and for the first time since the interview started she cracked a smile and snorted a laugh.

But, she asked, "Do you often dress as a girl?"

"It was a costume party," I said, "I don't know why they had it on Christmas Eve; maybe they missed Halloween or something."

The social worker or psychiatrist or whatever she was softened somewhat and looked relieved. I wondered if my strained attempt at humor eased her suspicions that I should be dispatched to the upstairs loony bin. Susan once told me that what would save me was my sense of humor; that given the time I could find and see the humor in every situation, which would lead me to forgiveness and peace. But, she didn't say anything about my humor as manipulation that could also save my life. To do that, I'd even lie to the beautiful Susan and the hell with trust being the basis of all relationships, when trust can also be the basis of all betrayals.

"Can you get home on your own?" she asked.

I looked at her. *Think, asshole, think!* I thought. The ambulance ride didn't seem all that long, and there were only a few turns. Damn, I should have paid more attention.

She looked up from her form. "You live in the Village?"

I knew my father's house was in Greenwich Village and nodded. "It's a short walk, not far at all."

She looked at me. "If you don't mind looking like that, she said, I'll give you a pass to leave, OK?"

I nodded reluctantly, but I was overjoyed.

You can sit in the waiting room and wait till it's daylight.

I weakly smiled. "No, I'll be fine. Thanks very much."

She stared at me, then said, "If we let you go, will you try and cut your wrist again?"

I shook my head, "No, ma'am, I just wanna get home and get some sleep."

The humor that I had stirred up was gone; her face was thoughtful, but no longer condemning or judgmental. An expression of serious concern brooded about her eyes, and she finally decisively bit a corner of her inside lip as if this allowed her to make a conclusive decision.

"We have a daily clinic," she said. "You can walk in any time, or you can call, and I want you to know if you ever feel like harming yourself that there are always people here willing and ready to talk to you."

I looked at her. "I'm not gonna do this again," I said. "I feel stupid about it already."

Her eyes opened wide, a flash of concern.

"Do you feel ashamed?"

"Just very tired," I answered.

Again she bit her lip then said, "When you feel better tomorrow or any time, come in and talk, OK?"

I nodded, maybe a little too eagerly, but I was bored and disgusted by her solicitude and concern. Come in and talk? I talked for almost three years if not my entire life in Cincinnati and if anyone of them ever got me again I'd certainly make sure I would kill myself then. Talk to these social working quacks and shrinks? Fathers, counselors, girls, friends, grandmothers, what did anyone of them know why I wanted to hurt myself? I certainly didn't, and I certainly had no faith in either of them helping me to understand the roots or basis of myself hatred. Oh, I recognized it now, the cowardice, the fear, the disgust, the confusion, the apathy. All I wanted now was to be out of here, back on the streets, away from the lot of these social workers and psycho do-gooders who in the blink of an eye can turn their compassion for your suffering into a jail sentence that can make you the loser forever. Survival and sanity had nothing to do with the truth. If there was any compassion in the world it must be for oneself. And, the vital thing if you must love, do not love too much.

She pushed back her chair and stood up. "I'll take you to the door," she said, "and tell the guard you can go."

I also stood up, bracing my arm against my chest and holding it up with my other hand. I followed her out of the office and back into the waiting room. Another patient sat in the room, his hair disheveled, his face looking stunned, but his eyes the most pleased and peaceful I'd ever seen. He smiled at me, and when I got to the guard's station, I overheard the guard telling another guard, "He drove a nail into his foot because Jesus told him to," then he trailed off at our approach, his face reddening from embarrassment.

"He can go," the woman said to the flustered guard and gestured at me. "Take care," she said, but her eyes were already looking at the friend of Jesus, her next patient, and I was already far from her thoughts. Would he lie to her as I had just done? Or, would he tell her the truth and would she be able to handle it? And, what was the truth he would relate, forgive them Father, for they know not what they do?

But I was once more my own, walking past the busy emergency room entrance: people sitting in chairs, others leaning against walls, and all waiting their turns for some kind of treatment, something to soothe them or calm them for a brief moment that someone was taking an interest and preserving their lives and sanity as if on Christmas Eve the only place to feel oneself cared for was a hospital emergency room. When no one wants you alive, here they will do everything to keep you living.

Too bad there was not a place such as this to keep you feeling loved.

Eleven

Outside the snow had stopped and a crisp sheen of ice covered the sidewalk that crackled beneath my heels. Christmas lights merrily twinkled in the windows above the street, and I was happy to discover that once more I was walking downtown. Back in the hospital, I had put my pants back on and covered the dress I still had on with my Cincinnati Bengal's jacket over that. My arm felt numb, and I was very tired. But where to go? I turned west on 23rd Street and once more found myself near the park that I had passed. What? Yesterday?

But, I knew my dress would deceive no one and that my ski cap would do little to alter the fact of my masculinity, but as I walked I saw the headlights of a car slowing to a crawl and inching to stop beside me.

A fat-faced man lowered his window and leered at me; once again the glassy and watery eyes unmistakably glistened with lust and passion, plus a victorious look at having won me over by the mere fact of having spotted me, as if coincidence was destiny and we were meant to meet. But did he know I wasn't a girl hooker? Or did it matter to him?

"Ain't you cold to be walking around like that?" he asked, as his car slowly moved with me up the street.

I shrugged. "A little," I said.

"You look like you could use a little warming up," he smiled, stopping and letting a side door open. "I know I could use some warmth," and he winked at me.

I barely smiled, but he saw it was a friendly face, and my hardening cock suddenly plopped out of the side of my panties and shot out in my jeans, luckily they prevented that from happening too much. I pretended to shiver, as if his suggestion was what I needed.

241

"Get in," he said. "I'll give you twenty bucks and that will warm you up, and give you a ride where you wanna go." He winked, and I could feel the warmth of his car wafting out his open window. I stood still for a second then shrugged and circled around the car to the passenger side. The warmth was soothing, and I relaxed in its comfort, as if I was home in bed under the covers on a rainy, snowy night, all safe and sound.

He turned up the radio, and a cowboy song blasted from the speakers, and he quickly changed the station to disco. From the radio, his hand went to my legs and up my dress and quickly found my hard dick.

For a moment, he tensed, as if surprised, and I was ready to bolt out of the car. Did he think I was really a girl? But his fingers remained circled around my erection, and he stroked it a few times then let go and cupped my balls and leered, "Feeling warmer?"

I moaned a sigh of contentment, nodding my head so girlishly, and he gripped the steering wheel, shifted gears, and started the car up 23rd Street turning down a deserted 25th Street. We rode about two blocks, and I glimpsed the cloud-like tree shapes above Madison Square Park, also glistening in frozen snow. Even in the cold, I saw two huddled and bundled up figures walking on the untrodden snow leaving their foot imprints behind them. I recognized the man who had felt me up on the day I had arrived from Cincinnati. Along side of him a huddled young looking kid, I guessed my age, walked slowly beside. I smiled and shrugged.

"Someone you know?" the driver asked, once more inching his free hand up my thigh. "Sit closer."

I inched closer to him and slightly opened my legs, the vision of my skirt rising and falling but covering my cock made me even harder.

"Ain't he a bit too young to be hustling?" I said, looking at the young kid with the old man.

The driver looked at them. "Aren't you?" he said, looking at me blushing. I ran my tongue around my lips and wished I was wearing lipstick.

The driver gripped my cock tighter then again his hand went up and down my thigh.

"But let's go here," he said, putting his car into motion once more. We passed the park, and he drove west – I could see the street signs. But in the car a warmth had settled on me as if I was home and safe in bed.

"Let's stop here," said the driver, coming to a stop in a quiet street. I saw row upon row of warehouses and shuttered gates on the street outside. In a window, a clock peered out, 2:30 a.m. I must have been walking at least a half hour or forty-five minutes before I met the feeler who had his arm up my dress, making his way past my pants and reaching for my penis. I moaned, and he saw the bandage on my wrist.

"What's that?" he asked.

I shrugged. "A cut. No big thing."

He looked at me then said, "Let's get in the back," opening his side door and getting out. I quickly did the same, grateful to jump into the warm back seat from the brutal cold and wind. We relaxed a bit breathing very hard, then he undid his pants, raised himself up and slid them down his legs to his knees. Immediately the car smelled like cock and balls, urine and pubic hairs, and I knew that clumps of hairs were stuck together around his crotch and thighs, the hairs plastered and held by dried scum, either his own or another's.

I've often wondered, when I went off with some guy, whether I was his first of the night or just one of many, often getting my curiosity speared by the shrugged comment that I wasn't as good as the last one was, or sometimes, that I was even better when I knew that even my best would pull them to leave and eventually find still others. Whether it be cruising along the river, prostituting for money, giving and getting hand-jobs in the parks, it would never lead to any kind of peace or acceptance. Anonymous sex leaves you as unknown to yourself as you never allow yourself to uncover the unknown about your partner. Is it really a search for love, all those garish prostitutes, the boys in tight T-shirts, girls in skimpy bras, the runaway children, the crack addicted kids, the petty thieves sleeping in hallways, huddled on rooftops, in back of trucks, in cardboard boxes? Or, are they there because they once knew where love once dwelt and existed but was never offered or given to them?

The driver put his arm around my shoulder, gripping my neck and pushing me to his crotch.

"C'mon, baby," he hissed, get to work, "you know the routine."

But my left arm was somehow twisted and contorted under my body as I tried to go down on him. I yelped and jumped back up, clutching my arm to my belly.

"What's with you?" he angrily asked. "When you're a fairy that's what you do: suck cock and bend over ... that's what you're good for, right?"

I whimpered. "But I had an accident; I hurt my arm."

He shrugged. "Just use your mouth," he said, suddenly frowning as he noticed the bandage peeping out of my jacket sleeve.

We looked at each other

"Let's change seats," he finally said, pulling me atop him, his rigid cock tweaking my thighs and back, and I offered to remain atop his lap, but he kept pulling me to his other side. I plopped down from his lap and immediately went down to his cock, filling my lips with its smelly putrid bulk, my left arm arched at the elbow down my side.

But, it wasn't a real sucking, simply an open-mouthed bouncing atop his cock and not a lavish tonguing, drooling, sucking like they show in porno theaters. As if we're all porno stars, aw Jesus! I wonder if girls are the only ones who really know how to suck cock: but I felt like I knew it, too.

I sighed, compressed my lips around his cock, gripping his cock-skin around my lips, and settled my head as far down as I could go. His response was instantaneous and fast: his torso buckled upwards and I gagged from the entire penis, but I held my lips tightly shut around his cock, his pubic hairs ticking under my nose, and readily swallowed his semen surging down my throat.

I knew I was good, looking up at him with my tender eyes, and his gentle pats and strokes on my head proved that I was. Most strangers who pick you up won't even offer a caress afterwards, they want as little to do with you as possible; but not him. I swallowed him whole, the semen almost like a nutritious treat appeasing my hunger since I haven't eating in almost two days.

His cock went soft in my mouth and finally dribbled out. I sat up, and he was immediately on my face, kissing and licking my lips and probing his tongue in my mouth as if greedily wanting to lap up his own semen. I let him, amazed that he did that, and with one hand reached under my dress and stroked my still hard penis.

My eruption was probably as immediate and powerful as was his own, and for the first time in my life, I actually saw tweaks of glimmering stars under my clenched eyelids, like a meteor shower exploding in my brain and body and existence that proved I was as good and sexy and beautiful as the rest of them – and I had done it to myself.

Sure, the night's disasters, the meeting with my father, his lover, my slashed wrist, the earlier conversation with Blondie and her own father straining into my ass, the conversation with the shrink in Bellevue had probably strained my consciousness to its limit, and only a sexual ejaculation could bring me back to my sense of awareness and self-control.

I had two days full of people in my life, and probably of all those people, only Blondie was of any value. Trust is the basis of all relationships, Susan used to say; well, maybe, but if that were true, you also had to discover that trust could also be the basis of all betrayal. Wasn't I in this city because I felt myself betrayed in Cincinnati? Wasn't I sucking a stranger's cock on Christmas morning because I had expected too much from my father, expected something he could never give me? Maybe, I wish I could tell Susan, "If you must trust, do not trust too much."

We broke from each other and fell exhausted back in the seat. He sat a moment then suddenly bolted upright and pulled up his pants, as if suddenly realizing how openly exposed we were in the car in the well-lit street. But, fortunately no one was looking, and I doubt if even a car passed us by on that cold Christmas morning.

He zipped up and opened the back door, stepping out of the car. I did the same and quickly rejoined him in the front seat. For a moment, he looked at me in some surprise, as if expecting me to stay outside.

"Five, wasn't it?" he angrily said. He looked around as if looking for a place he could go before anyone saw him.

"You said twenty," I quietly said.

"Twenty! But you didn't do anything!" he flared. "Where did you get the idea a measly blow job was worth twenty?"

"I didn't ask for it," I said, "you're the one who said twenty."

We looked at each other.

"Well, OK," he finally said, reaching in his back pocket and pulling out a wallet. I saw there were more than twenty dollars

"Well," he mumbled, "it's getting late."

"Can you gimme a ride? It's not that far," I meekly protested, then added, "Please?"

What would Susan say about that, adding two emotions, anger and pleading, to get what I wanted?

"Ok, where to?"

I felt very peaceful.

"Fifteenth Street," I said, "on 10th Avenue."

He looked at me. Then reached for his car radio and turned the dial away from disco and back to the country station that was playing before he met me.

"You'd better fix your lipstick," he said, "if you want to go there." He winked and we drove off.

I pulled out a tube of lipstick I had in my jacket and tried putting it on without looking into a mirror. He reached over for the sun visor and lowered it, so I could see. I smiled at him and looked at myself in the mirror. Blowjob mouth, I'd call someone who looked like me, the lipstick smudged heavily over my lips, like streaks of clouds staining the sides of my mouth. It was obvious I had just sucked a cock and was looking for more.

I did nothing to fix my mouth but applied another coat to my lips. The driver squeezed his cock in his pants as he looked at me.

"Is that where you usually hang out?" he asked. "I've never seen you there."

"You gotta keep looking," I simply said, pressing my lips together and looking in the mirror.

We drove some more, and he finally said, looking at the desolate streets, "There aren't many ... girls out tonight."

I looked around. "They probably got picked up real fast," I shrugged. "On Christmas Eve everybody wants you to spend a whole night with them."

How did I suddenly get so street-smart tough-talking, as if I could take care of myself? Maybe I suddenly knew something

Cruising for Bad Boys

incredible about myself and what I had to offer, and it would certainly go to the highest bidder.

"Is that what you want," he asked, "spend the night with someone?"

"Nope," I said, "I'm not into that lovey-dovey stuff," smacking my lips together a final time and flicking the sun visor closed.

He looked at me then contemptuously shook his head. "You're a real Wham-Bam-Thank-You-Ma'am whore, aren't you?"

"Hey!" I snapped. "Do I go around calling you names?"

We turned off 23rd Street and made our way down 10th Avenue. In the distance, I could see the dark building where I first met Blondie and the sick bums. A tall black transvestite stood on the corner, shivering in high heels, white nylons, garters and red panties fully exposed, with a white furry jacket atop her shoulders but doing little to protect her from the cold. Looked like a late summers get-up. As the driver's eyes went wide and we passed her by and he said, "Wherever you want to be dropped off?" It was obvious he wanted to get back to her before anyone else did.

"15th Street," I simply said, and it was only a block away.

He stopped the car, and I got out, not even offering a goodbye, as he said nothing to me but sped away turning the corner burning rubber as he sped to catch back up with the skimpily dressed transvestite.

I made my way down the street, shivering from the cold, and wondered if I would ever be able to stand on a street corner only in panties and nylons. Is that how Blondie did it?

I stepped into a crevice of a scaffold and made my way into the deserted warehouse loading dock. The smell of extinguished candles hung in the air, as if they were just blown out. I let my eyes settle in the darkness, so I could see clearer.

248

I made my way toward the shape where I knew Blondie had her sleeping niche – other body-bundles lay scattered about, but no one stirred. Blondie looked up at me. Had she just blown out the candle?

Next to her sleeping bag was my notebook. I smiled, but suddenly realized that I felt better about seeing Blondie than my notebook, though grateful she had rescued and saved my poetry. I reached into my pocket and pulled out the pink lipstick and dark eyebrow pencil.

Her eyes widened to see better, and she sat up and relit the small candle beside her. She held out her hand.

"Oh, you got them," she said.

She took the makeup from my hand, clutched them to her chest and held out a corner of her blanket for me to crawl in.

I did so; her arms went around me, like a father's around his son. We kissed, and I felt right at home, as if I had been searching for it for such a long, long time.

ABOUT THE AUTHORS

AMANDA YOUNG is a multi-published, erotic romance author. She tends to write whatever strikes her whimsy from hot manlove to creepy things that go bump in the night. For more information about Amanda, please visit her Website: www.AmandaYoung.org.

BARRY LOWE is an Australian writer whose short stories have appeared in *Hard Hats*, *Cargo*, gay-ebooks.com.au, *Mammoth Book of New Gay Erotica*, *Surfer Boys*, *Flesh and the Word*, *Best Date Ever*, *Boy Meets Boy*, *Out of the Gutter*, and others. He is also the author of *Atomic Blonde*, a biography of 1950s blonde bombshell Mamie Van Doren, published by McFarland. He co-wrote the screenplay, *Violet's Visit*, and his produced plays include *Homme Fatale: The Joey Stefano Story*, *Dutch Courage*, *The Extraordinary Annual General Meeting of the Size-Queen Club*, *The Death of Peter Pan*, *Seeing Things*, and *Rehearsing the Shower Scene from 'Psycho.'* Visit Barry at www.barrylowe.net.

CHRISTOPHER PIERCE is the author of the novel *Rogue:Slave* and the editor of the anthology *Men On The Edge: Dangerous Erotica*, both published by STARbooks Press. The sequel to *Rogue:Slave* is forthcoming. Visit Chris at www.christopherpierceerotica.com.

DAVID C. MULLER lives in Israel. His writing has appeared in numerous places: a fictional series called "Peachtree Passions" appeared in *David Atlanta Magazine* under the pen name "Day-Day Los Angeles" in 2003 and in 2006 many stories were published in English: "I Met God Once" in *Shevet: New Voices from Israel*, (published by the Bar Ilan University CW program); and "Renata's Three Statements" in *Jane Doe Buys A Challah*, (published by AngLit Press). In 2007, the story "The

Galilee" appeared in *Gay Travels in the Muslim World*, published by Hawthorn Press and another story entitled "The Beekeeper" appeared in *Love in a Lock-Up* published by STARbooks Press.

Traveling in Haiti, **DAVID HOLLY** developed a deep love for Haitian culture. However, his knowledge of the Haitian tongue is far from *Kreyòl natif natal*, and he can only hope that his usage is not too *estipid*. Find David Holly's complete bibliography at www.gaywriter.org.

DERRICK DELLA GIORGIA was born in Italy and currently lives between Manhattan and Rome. His "Courtesy of the Hotel" was published in the anthology *Island Boys*, Alyson Books.

JAMIE FREEMAN always dreamed of being in the Ziegfeld Follies but was born too late and with too little talent. He went to college in Washington, D.C., and eventually became a writer. The rest is history.

Published in dozens of gay erotic anthologies, **JAY STARRE** pumps out fiction from his home in Vancouver, Canada. He has written regularly for such hot magazines as *Torso*, *Mandate* and *Men*. His work can be found in titles like *Love in a Lock-Up*, *Don't Ask, Don't Tie Me Up*, *Unmasked: Erotic Tales of Gay Superheroes*, *Boys Will Be Boys – Their First Time*, and *Ride Me Cowboy*. His steamy gay novel *Erotic Tales of the Knights Templar* came out in late 2007. Look forward to his upcoming erotic book *Lusty Adventures of the Prince of Knossos* to be published by STARbooks Press in spring 2009.

MARTIN DELACROIX writes novels, novellas and short fiction. He lives on Florida's Gulf coast.

Though born in West Germany **MYKOLA DEMENTIUK** is Ukrainian and grew up in the United States. He is the author of *Times Queer*, *Vienna Dolorosa*, *Holy Communion*, and other writings. Over ten years ago, he suffered a stroke, while in the process of working on *My Father's Semen* and now writes with one finger on his left hand, but other things still work, and he is doing quite well.

OWEN KEEHNEN is the author of *Starz, More Starz,* and *Ultimate Starz,* a popular series of interview books with gay male porn stars, published by STARbooks Press. His fiction, nonfiction, and erotica have appeared in dozens of periodicals, newspapers, and anthologies worldwide. He resides in Chicago with his partner, Carl, and their dogs, Flannery and Fitz.

ROB ROSEN is the author of *Sparkle: The Queerest Book You'll Ever Love* and *Divas Las Vegas,* and has contributed, to date, to more than fifty anthologies, most notably for the STARbooks Press titles: *Ride Me Cowboy, Service With A Smile, Boys Caught in the Act, Unmasked II,* and *Pretty Boys and Roughnecks.* See him at www.therobrosen.com.

RYAN FIELD is a freelance writer who lives and works in both New Hope, PA, and Los Angeles. His work has appeared in many collections and anthologies, and he's now working on a four book series with Hollan Publishing and ravenousromance.com.

STEPHEN OSBORNE has had stories published in *Ride Me Cowboy, Unmasked, Boys Caught in the Act, Ultimate Gay Erotica 2008, Hard Hats, My First Time Volume 5, Best Gay Love Stories: Summer Flings, Frat Sex 2* and many other anthologies. He lives in Indianapolis with Nicademus the Neurotic Cat and Jadzia the Wonder Dog. He can be reached at www.myspace.com/StephenOsbornespage.

XAN WEST is the pseudonym of an NYC BDSM/sex educator and writer. Xan's work can be found in *Best SM Erotica Volume 2, Got A Minute?, Love at First Sting, Men on the Edge, Leathermen, Backdraft, Hurts So Good,* brotheroutsider.org, *Frenzy, SexTime,* and *Best Gay Erotica 2009.* Xan wants to hear from you and can be reached at Xan_West@yahoo.com.

ABOUT THE EDITOR

Mickey Erlach is a Senior Editor at STARbooks Press, and this is his third anthology. His other anthologies include *Boys Will Be Boys – Their First Time* and *Boys Caught in the Act*, and he has picked up his fare share of bad boys. His next anthology, *Pretty Boys and Roughnecks*, will be released in the next few months.